praise for SAINT IVY

"A truly memorable novel that makes the sometimes quiet and unasked questions of growing up and figuring yourself out feel big and bold and heart-shifting and profound. Part page-turning mystery, part emotional character study, I loved every poignant, intimate, and wise page. And I loved Ivy and her deeply relatable journey most of all."

—Corey Ann Haydu, author of *Eventown* and *One Jar of Magic*

"I loved this wise, warm, and utterly relatable story about kindness—a topic that feels especially timely. Once again, Laurie Morrison has created a complex, authentic character readers will eagerly embrace."

—Barbara Dee, author of *Maybe He Just Likes You* and *My Life in the Fish Tank*

"Morrison has crafted a beautifully triumphant story. It is layered, warm, and sweet, just like the perfectly imperfect Ivy herself."

—Carrie Firestone, author of *Dress Coded*

"Feelings, life, and people are allowed to be complicated in beautiful ways in this page-turner."

—*Kirkus Reviews*

"A keenly observed portrait of a girl who goes way overboard on a good thing."

—*Bulletin of the Center for Children's Books*

"Relatable realistic fiction . . . navigating friendships, boundaries, and identity, with appeal for fans of similarly themed stories such as Varian Johnson's *Twins*, Shannon Hale's *Real Friends*, and Celia C. Pérez's *Strange Birds*."

—*School Library Journal*

SAINT IVY

KIND AT ALL COSTS

Laurie Morrison

AMULET BOOKS • NEW YORK

**For everyone who
struggles to be as kind
to themselves as they
are to other people**

PUBLISHER'S NOTE: This is a work of fiction. Names, characters, places, and incidents are either the product of the author's imagination or used fictitiously, and any resemblance to actual persons, living or dead, business establishments, events, or locales is entirely coincidental.

Cataloging-in-Publication Data has been applied for and may be obtained from the Library of Congress.

Paperback ISBN 978-1-4197-4126-5

Text © 2021 Laurie Morrison
Book design by Marcie J. Lawrence

Printed and bound in U.S.A.
10 9 8 7 6 5 4 3 2 1

Amulet Books are available at special discounts when purchased in quantity for premiums and promotions as well as fundraising or educational use. Special editions can also be created to specification. For details, contact specialsales@abramsbooks.com or the address below.

Amulet Books® is a registered trademark of Harry N. Abrams, Inc.

ABRAMS The Art of Books
195 Broadway, New York, NY 10007
abramsbooks.com

CHAPTER ONE

The first anonymous email wasn't that big a deal. Not right away, at least.

Ivy was on the bus, heading home from school, when she saw it on her phone. The subject line said, "Thank you," and the sender came up as downby thebay5@mailme.com: no name. For a second she thought it was spam, but the preview text started with the words "Dear Saint Ivy."

Saint Ivy. That's what her best friend, Kyra, called her sometimes, and how would a random spammer know that? So she opened the email and read.

To: Ivy Campbell <ivy.campbell@lelandmagnet
.org>

From: <downbythebay5@mailme.com>
Subject: Thank you

Dear Saint Ivy,

Somebody really smart used to tell me that there should be two different kinds of thank-yous. A basic, throwaway kind for when somebody holds a door open or says bless you when we sneeze or something. And then a special version that tells a person, "What you just did for me *mattered*. It gave me hope when I didn't have any. It turned a really awful day into an almost-okay one." Because if we just mumble a quick *thanks* either way, people don't know when they've really made an impact, and that's a shame.

So, here goes. My day today was really awful, and you made it almost okay. It probably wasn't a big thing for you, what you did. But it was a big thing for me. So I want to let you know that. I want to say the special kind of thank-you.

From, your friendly anonymous
good-deed appreciator

Huh.

The bus turned left, rumbling past the used bookstore, the Italian restaurant Ivy's family used to love, and the CVS.

Was this a joke? It didn't *seem* like a joke.

If she really improved somebody's day this much, she was happy. But she was confused, too. Why did this person want to be anonymous? Who was it? She scanned the email again, searching for clues, but she came up empty.

Kyra was the one who started calling her Saint Ivy, but now some other kids said it, too, and anybody could have heard. And Ivy had done nice things for a lot of people that day.

Maybe the email was from Sydney DelMonte, a junior in high school who lived next door to Ivy's dad and had been crying on a bench outside the middle school that morning. Or Lila Britton, who'd borrowed Ivy's math textbook so she wouldn't get in trouble for forgetting hers for the third time in a week. Although . . . Lila wasn't exactly Ivy's number one fan. Or maybe Josh Miller, the boy Ivy's other best friend, Peyton—and pretty much everybody else—had a crush on. He'd been hobbling around on crutches after he hurt his knee so badly at soccer, and Ivy had picked up his things when they spilled out of his backpack and then carried his bag to his next class.

Actually, the email could have been from Peyton herself. She'd been extra quiet today, and extra appreciative when Ivy went with her to the music room and played along on the piano while she practiced her solo for chorus. But Ivy did stuff like that for Peyton all the time, and Peyton had already thanked her plenty. Plus, Peyton had told Kyra that "Saint Ivy" was kind of a strange nickname since Ivy was Jewish on her mom's side and Jewish people don't even *have* saints.

The bus pulled up to Ivy's stop, so she put her phone away and let the mystery go, mostly. Maybe she'd figure it out later, once she loosened up her mind and stopped actively wondering, the way she could sometimes remember a word in Spanish class as soon as she moved on to something else. For now, she and Nana had some pastries to bake.

Nana used to live in the suburbs just outside Philadelphia, but she'd moved into the city last year. Now she lived five blocks away from Ivy, down the hill in a one-bedroom rental on the twenty-first floor of a big apartment building.

Every Friday afternoon, Ivy went to Nana's after school. Today, Nana was waiting in the hallway, wearing an impressively bright pink apron that said *F.A.B.* in black cursive letters.

"Ta-da!" Nana said, doing a little twirl. "I got us aprons. Do you love them?"

"Um, wow!" Ivy replied. "They're—"

"I know!" Nana pointed at the letters one by one. "Friday Afternoon Baking. F.A.B. *Fab*-ulous, right?"

"Definitely fabulous," Ivy agreed.

Nana kissed her cheek. "I knew you'd love them."

She handed Ivy a matching apron in bright purple. It was stiff and scratchy and completely ridiculous, but Nana's whole face lit up when Ivy put it on.

"Now, don't just stand there," Nana said. "This hallway's sweltering and our time is limited."

Ivy wasn't sure if Nana meant "our time" in a literal sense, as in the two and a half hours before Ivy went home and Nana went to her neighbors' apartment for Shabbat dinner, or in a more philosophical sense, as in their time on this planet as mortal beings. It could have been either, because Nana said tons of super-morbid things. Mom said it was because she had too much time to think, now that she'd retired from her job as an elementary school principal.

In fact, the whole reason they'd started Friday afternoon baking lessons was because every time

Nana baked something delicious, she reminded Mom, Ivy, and Ivy's brother, Will, that she didn't "cook from a book," so after she died, all her recipes would go with her. Mom got sad and flustered every time she said it and Ivy didn't have anything else to do on Friday afternoons, so the whole thing was a win-win. A win-win-*win*, actually, because everyone got to eat a whole lot of truly outstanding desserts, too.

Nana led Ivy into the kitchen, where she'd lined up flour, sugar, salt, walnuts, and chocolate chips on the shiny-clean counter.

"It's a perfect day to make rugelach, don't you think?" she asked.

"Definitely," Ivy said, because rugelach was delicious—especially Nana's rugelach—so there couldn't be an *im*perfect day to make it.

Nana plucked the cold stuff out of the fridge, adding butter, cream cheese, and blackberry preserves to her ingredient parade, and Ivy turned to a fresh sheet of paper in her recipe notebook.

She wrote the word *rugelach* in her prettiest handwriting and copied down the facts Nana rattled off: how the word *rugelach* was Yiddish for "rolled things," and rugelach was an American version of an old Eastern European pastry called *kipfel*. Nana said the only real difference was that Jewish bakers in the U.S. had added cream cheese to the dough a couple generations back.

"Now. It's fine to change up the filling however you want, but the dough is just right as it is, you got that?" Nana said, pointing at Ivy with a bright pink fingernail that matched her apron—Nana believed in "signature colors," and bright pink was hers.

"Got it," Ivy replied.

"No substituting coconut oil or fat-free yogurt or any of that health-food stuff for these good fats. Rugelach isn't going to be healthy, and that's *why* it's good for you. You write that down, too."

That was kind of a knock on Ivy's dad and his partner, Leo, who had gone through a health-food kick recently when they swore by chia seeds and flaxseed meal and made some extremely disappointing cookie bars, but it wasn't a *mean* knock, because Nana loved Dad and Leo.

Ivy wrote, "No substitutions for fats!" and then they got to work. Ivy copied down measurements and ingredients, and they cut and dumped and sifted butter, cream cheese, flour, and sugar into the food processor. Then they pulsed it all together until a delicious-smelling dough formed.

"Almost like magic, huh?" Nana said as they put the dough in the freezer to chill.

And it *did* feel a little bit magical to see how much the ingredients changed one another when they came together to create something new.

They mixed up the blackberry-chocolate filling, and once the dough was cool enough, they flattened it out and sliced it into triangles with a pizza cutter. Then Ivy spread the gloppy filling across the top, as flat and even as she could.

"Oh, don't bother trying to make it too neat," Nana said. "It's all going to ooze out the edges and make a big, beautiful mess."

They formed all the pastries into crescents and baked batch after batch. Some ended up crooked, some stretched out skinny and turned brown on top, and all of them were sticky and crumbly and delicious.

They packed some up for Ivy to take home, and then they walked back out into the hallway together. As the elevator climbed up to the twenty-first floor, Nana cupped Ivy's cheeks in her soft, cool hands.

"You're such a sweet girl," she said. "I appreciate you doing this with me."

She'd gone so suddenly serious that Ivy braced herself for some extra-morbid reflections, but then she just kissed Ivy's forehead and said, "I'm here for you anytime. You know that? Anything you need, I'm around."

"Okay, thanks," Ivy said. "I know."

Nana sighed. "I worry about you with your big, soft heart. Your brother—he lets everything out. But that heart of yours is like a sponge."

The lights in the hallway buzzed, and it really *was* sweltering out here—ten degrees hotter than inside Nana's apartment, at least. The elevator doors slid open, and Ivy hugged Nana goodbye and stepped inside.

What did that even mean, that Ivy's heart was like a sponge? It was a *good* thing that Ivy cared about other people and tried to help them. Just ask down bythebay5@mailme.com! Having a kind heart—doing generous things and caring for other people—that was the thing that made Ivy special. It was the thing that made her *Ivy*.

She wasn't a genius like Kyra—that had become obvious once they'd started middle school. She wasn't an amazing singer like Peyton or a star athlete like Will. But she was kind. The kindest. She knew who she was and she liked herself, almost all the time.

There were a zillion new texts in the ongoing group chat with Kyra and Peyton, so Ivy didn't have time to focus on Nana's super-sentimental send-off after she got out of the elevator and walked outside.

She had to catch up on what they'd been saying without her and figure out something good to add, because she was a little bit afraid they might start a new chain without her next time if she didn't.

Later, she couldn't believe she hadn't realized why Nana had gone all serious like that. But it wouldn't have occurred to her in a million years that Mom would tell Nana what was happening before she told Ivy.

CHAPTER TWO

The next morning, Ivy woke to the sound of Dad's voice drifting up from the kitchen.

It was just Dad down there with Mom at eight o'clock on a Saturday morning, no Leo. Just Dad and Mom talking in hushed voices while coffee burbled in the pot, as if it were three years ago and not now. A general sense of uneasiness hit Ivy like the rush of heat when Nana opened her oven, but the pieces didn't click into place.

Ivy and Will came out of their rooms at the same time, and Will rubbed down the top of his sleep-fluffed hair.

"What's Dad doing here?" he asked.

Ivy shook her head. "No clue."

Mom and Dad were still close even though they weren't married anymore, and Dad lived eight blocks away, in a brand-new townhouse development that was pretty much the opposite of the skinny old row house where Mom, Will, and Ivy still lived. It wasn't unusual for Dad to be at their house in general, but it *was* unusual for him to show up early on a Saturday morning when he and Leo should have been at their favorite spinning class at the gym.

As Ivy followed Will down the creaky stairs, her heart started thumping and her brain raced to keep up. Something was wrong. It had to be. The last time Dad had been here when they woke up, it was to break the news that their great-grandfather had died.

But when Will and Ivy got downstairs, Dad said, "Hey! My two favorite kiddos!"

Some of Ivy's dread dissolved because Dad's voice was even more cheerful than usual. And he sat there across from Mom at the round kitchen table with his dark blond hair neatly parted and a big bag of bagels from Kepners' in front of him. Nobody would take the time to comb their hair that neatly and pick up bagels if something truly awful had happened.

Mom clasped her hands together, separated them, and tapped her fingertips against the edge of the table. "Morning, sleepyheads! Dad's here!"

"Um, yeah," Will said, raising his eyebrows at Ivy. "We caught that."

"You hungry?" Dad asked. "I brought sustenance."

Will and Ivy exchanged one more look, but then Will helped himself to a bagel, poured himself a glass of orange juice, and sat down in his usual seat. It would have taken a stranger situation than this one to keep Will away from bagels.

"How's it going, Ivester?" Dad picked up a plastic container and waved it around. "The bagels are still warm and I even got whitefish, because that's how much I love you." He pinched his nose as if he could smell the whitefish through the sealed lid, the same way he used to do when he still lived here and the four of them always got bagels on Saturday mornings. Ivy pushed away the nostalgia that pressed down on her ribs and laughed. Then she tore open a perfectly doughy sesame bagel, spread on plenty of whitefish salad, and held out the container toward Mom.

Bagels with whitefish were a tradition on Mom and Nana's side of the family, and Mom loved whitefish, too. She took the container from Ivy, but then she just set it down.

"You didn't want any salty fish spread for breakfast, Rachel?" Dad joked.

Mom fidgeted with her hands some more and then ran her fingers through her hair—curly and dark brown, just like Ivy's and Nana's, and damp and citrus-smelling from the shower. "I don't think I'm supposed to have . . . because it's smoked, so I'm not sure if . . ."

"Oh!"

Dad smacked himself in the forehead as if he should have realized, and then Mom said, "I have some news."

And finally, *finally* Ivy began to understand why Dad was here and what Nana had been talking about yesterday.

This was it.

This was happening.

Mom leaned forward to pat Ivy's arm with one hand and ruffle Will's bedhead with the other. Will's hair used to be so much lighter than Dad's, but now it was the same exact color, Ivy realized. When had that happened? And why was she focused on hair color when she knew what Mom was about to say?

"The IVF . . . the medical treatment, for the surrogacy. The third time we tried it, in June . . . it worked. I'm pregnant. Erin and Christopher are going to have their baby."

Mom's voice was bright, but her eyes were kind of

panicky. She glanced from Ivy to Will and back again. She was checking their reactions, making sure they were okay.

Ivy needed to be okay. She needed to be a whole lot *more* than okay.

Erin was Mom's best friend, and she and her husband, Christopher, desperately wanted a baby. Last year, after they'd tried everything else, they'd decided to try gestational surrogacy, which meant implanting an embryo with Erin's eggs and Christopher's sperm into another woman's uterus. So somebody else would carry their baby, but the baby would have their genes.

There were agencies that helped people find gestational carriers, but Erin and Christopher couldn't afford them. So they'd asked Mom last year if she might be willing to be their surrogate, and Mom had gone through a whole screening process with a doctor and a therapist to make sure she could do it. Then she'd asked Ivy and Will whether they thought they'd be okay with it if she said yes.

Will had kind of freaked out at first, but Ivy had been a hundred percent on board. For Erin and Christopher's sake, and also because Mom needed this. Ivy knew—because Mom had confided in her—that Mom was frustrated with her job at the historical society but nervous to leave. Mom wanted to do something "meaningful and fulfilling," and what could be more meaningful or fulfilling than this?

But then there had been two unsuccessful rounds of IVF last spring. Mom had said they thought they'd try again, but she'd never told Ivy they *had*.

June. They'd tried again in June. Mom had been pregnant since *June* and hadn't said a word.

Across the table, Will took an enormous bite of his bagel, and a blob of cream cheese clung to one corner of his mouth.

"Big news, huh?" Dad said. "Pretty amazing."

Will wiped the cream cheese off his face with the back of his hand, then wiped the back of his hand with a napkin. He glugged down half his glass of orange juice and said, "Wow. Congratulations! I mean . . . congratulations to Erin and Christopher? But . . . wow."

Ivy needed to say something, too. She tried to form her mouth into a smile, but her cheeks were too stiff and the corners of her mouth kept shaking.

"How long have you known?" she finally asked.

Her words sounded off, like when she hit a wrong note on the piano.

This is amazing! Erin and Christopher are going to be the best parents! I'm so happy!

Those were the words she should have said. Those words would have come out in the right key.

"We've known for a little while now." Mom looked down at her plain, dry bagel and tore off a tiny piece. "The pregnancy is almost fourteen weeks along," she told that miniscule bagel morsel. "The baby's due March twenty-second. I had some hormone levels that were a little bit off at first, so we didn't want to take anything for granted. But we just got some test results, and everything looks good."

"Fourteen *weeks*?" Ivy echoed.

"At the beginning of a pregnancy, there are risks," Dad chimed in, using his knowledgeable pediatrician voice, not his goofy dad one. "We didn't want to send you guys on an emotional roller coaster with all this. We wanted to wait until we were sure."

We.

Dad and Mom weren't married anymore—Dad had been with Leo for more than two years. But Dad had gotten to be part of this "we," and Ivy hadn't. Nana, too, clearly.

Ivy thought about all the time she and Mom had spent together over the last few days. They'd gone for a walk down to the river. They'd chopped vegetables for a stir-fry. They'd sat next to each other at Will's soccer game and gripped each other's hands when

Josh Miller crumpled to the ground and screamed because he blew out his knee.

Mom had known she was pregnant for all of that. Way before all of that, and she hadn't said a word. At the beginning of August, she'd claimed she had a "summer flu," and stayed in bed eating nothing but saltines.

She'd been *pregnant*. Mom and Ivy had always told each other everything, but Mom hadn't said a word. She'd *lied*.

Ivy needed to say something, but her tongue was too thick to fit inside her mouth. She'd never stopped to think about how she *had* tongue muscles before this moment, but now she couldn't figure out how to make them relax.

A tiny baby was there, growing inside Mom's body, and it had been all this time.

"Ives?" Mom said. "You all right?"

Ivy needed to get it together. She needed to loosen her tongue and relax her cheeks and curve her mouth into a smile—a convincing one, not fake like the one Will forced when he said thank you for a gift he was only pretending to like.

"That's amazing!" she finally managed to say. "Erin and Christopher are going to be the best parents! I'm so happy!"

Mom was still watching her too closely, and Dad was, too.

"This is complicated," Dad said. "However you're feeling right now is absolutely okay."

"Absolutely," Mom agreed.

Ivy shook her head, hard. "I'm great! Seriously. This is great!"

Mom's warm fingers squeezed Ivy's, and Ivy ordered her own fingers to squeeze back.

"It's completely understandable if this feels different than you thought it would. It feels different than *I* thought it would," Mom said.

But it *wasn't* understandable, this feeling Ivy had right now. She couldn't make sense of the unkind thoughts that were spinning around in her brain.

Ivy was imagining Mom showing up at school with her belly popped out as if she'd swallowed a basketball and random people saying, "Whoa, are you so excited to have a baby brother or sister?" when actually she *wouldn't* have a baby brother or sister. Or people asking, "Aren't your parents divorced? How is your mom *pregnant*?"

She was remembering what Will had said last February when Mom first brought up the surrogacy.

"This is *so weird.* Aren't we weird enough already? How are we supposed to explain this to people?"

They weren't "weird," exactly—but they were sort of *visible*, mostly thanks to Dad. A lot of Ivy's and Will's classmates went to Rittenhouse Pediatrics, where Dad was a doctor, and a lot of their parents watched his Doctors Dish YouTube channel, where he posted videos answering people's questions about raising "physically and emotionally healthy" kids. Everybody knew him, and everybody was always excited to run into him at the grocery store or the Greek restaurant or wherever, so people noticed pretty quickly when he started showing up places with Leo. And it was obvious that people thought it was unusual that Mom and Dad were still so close. That they'd sit together at school stuff—with Leo, too—and sometimes the five of them would go places all together. Other people's parents would say, "How wonderful! What a special family you are!" And technically it was *nice*, but it could be kind of a lot.

This thing Mom was doing was "wonderful" and "special" and unusual, too. This was another way they'd draw attention.

That didn't matter, though. That wasn't important.

"I'm seriously great," Ivy said again.

She inhaled a Will-sized bite of bagel, and that helped. Chewing loosened up her cheeks and tongue and gave her something to focus on.

"Can we call Erin and Christopher to congratulate them?"

Ivy had seen how devastated they were a couple of years ago, when Erin had finally gotten pregnant and they'd lost the baby just when they'd started to believe it was really coming. If she could hear how happy they were now, that would help.

Mom and Dad shared a look that lasted way too long.

"Sweetie," Mom said, "that's a really lovely thought . . ."

She trailed off and Dad picked up her sentence. "It's just that it's still relatively early in the pregnancy, and they aren't quite ready for congratulations."

"But I thought you said the risks are done," Ivy said.

Mom nodded, but it was that slow, I'm-deciding-what-to-say-next kind of nod that didn't actually mean yes. "Everything's going really well, and the chances of things going wrong are extremely small."

"But there's still a chance?" A tiny, terrified part of Ivy worried that she could somehow *make* things go wrong by not being happy enough about this baby.

"There's a detailed anatomy scan halfway through the pregnancy, at twenty weeks," Dr. Dad said. "That's when things didn't look so good for their baby the other time. But that was incredibly rare. We're talking about a less than one percent chance of something being significantly wrong at that stage."

"So as long as everything's okay this time, which we're sure it will be, then they'll be ready for congrat-ulations," Mom said. "And for now, we can focus on taking care of ourselves, okay? Because this is a lot for all of us to adjust to."

"Sure. Okay, yeah," Ivy said.

She nibbled her bagel and ordered herself to react the right way. The *Ivy* way.

Don't be selfish. This is happy news. Be happy!

She repeated those words over and over inside her head, willing them to hurry up and come true.

CHAPTER THREE

After breakfast, Dad drove Will to soccer practice, and Ivy went upstairs to start her homework. So far, eighth grade meant about eight times as much homework as seventh grade—especially in history class.

Ivy's history teacher, Ms. Ramos, was new and super enthusiastic, and apparently she hadn't gotten the memo that other classes gave homework, too. Ivy had worked hard on the rough draft of her first essay, but Ms. Ramos had given her a huge list of things to "develop and refine" before the revision was due on Monday. The feedback didn't upset Ivy as much as it would have two years ago, when she first started at Leland Magnet Middle School and wasn't used to getting *any* criticism from teachers. But it still stung a little, the way the baby toe on her left foot ached if she stubbed it, since she'd broken it when she was nine and the bones had stayed tender.

And right now, Ivy couldn't focus on any of the things she was supposed to improve in her essay. Before she realized what she was doing, she'd opened a search window in her computer browser, typed the words *Fetus at 14 weeks*, and clicked on the first link.

Your baby is the size of a lemon! the description read. But that first word, *your*, burned the lining of Ivy's stomach. This baby *wasn't* hers. The baby wasn't even Mom's. Not really.

There was an illustration of the fetus—curled up and a little bit alien-like, with a disproportionately giant head.

Baby's fingers and toes are beginning to grow. No more webbed hands and feet now! As the kidneys develop, Baby will begin to release urine into the amniotic fluid.

Yuck.

Ivy typed in a new search: *What can go wrong after 14 weeks of pregnancy?*

But then she closed the window before she could look at any of the results.

Mom knocked on the door and Ivy toggled back to her essay.

"Come in!" she called.

Mom tilted her head from one side to the other, stretching out her neck. That's what she did when she was stressed out, because her neck and shoulders got tight. Was she stressed out because of Ivy? Because she could tell Ivy wasn't as happy as she should be? As happy as she'd *promised* she'd be?

Mom sat down on the corner of Ivy's bed. "That big house on Eighteenth Street is on the market. Did you see? The one with the stained-glass windows? They're having an open house today. We could take a look if you want."

Ivy and Mom loved checking out the beautiful old row houses in their neighborhood when they were listed for sale. Mom knew a ton about the history of architecture, and she always pointed out all sorts of interesting things—the type of wood the floors were made of, the thick glass in the windows, the style of molding on the walls. Ivy and Mom would imagine what they'd do if they bought the house—which room would be Ivy's, where their furniture could go, what colors they'd paint the walls. But the truth was, whoever bought the house usually tore it down and started over, like the developers who'd made the luxury townhouses where Dad and Leo lived.

Mom rested a hand on her belly, and there *was* a

little bump there under her loose green shirt, now that Ivy was really looking.

"I should probably finish this essay before I go to Kyra's later," Ivy said.

Mom pressed her lips together, and Ivy almost changed her mind and said she'd make time for the open house after all. But then Mom took in a slow breath and said, "Okay, sweet pea. Well . . . we can talk later, then. Or you don't have to talk to me, if that feels awkward. But I want you to be able to talk to somebody. Dad, or Nana, or your friends. This isn't a secret. It's only going to get more and more obvious." Mom rubbed her hand in a little circle over her belly, the same way she rubbed circles across Ivy's back when Ivy couldn't fall asleep. "And talking to Dr. Banks is always an option, too," she added.

Dr. Banks was the therapist Ivy and Will had gone to back when Mom and Dad had separated. Will still saw him every other Thursday, and Mom had asked Ivy to talk to him one time last spring, too, before she decided to move forward with the surrogacy. Dr. Banks was nice, and Ivy knew therapy was a great thing, objectively speaking. But she didn't need therapy just because Mom was carrying Erin and Christopher's baby. Other people had way harder stuff to work through. Like Peyton, whose mom had died when she was little. And Erin and Christopher, who'd lost their last baby five months into the pregnancy. Those were difficult things. Ivy's problems were tiny in comparison. They weren't even *problems*, really.

"Or if you'd like us to find another therapist, if Dr. Banks wasn't the right fit. To help you process— "

"*Mom*," Ivy said, too sharply. She tried again. "I don't need help processing anything. I'm good."

Mom smiled. "You're *wonderful*. But that doesn't mean you don't need someone to talk to. Think about it, okay? This is amazing, what I'm able to do for Erin and Christopher. And it's also a lot."

"Okay," Ivy said, because that was the quickest way to end this conversation. "Love you."

Mom kissed Ivy's forehead and headed downstairs.

It's also a lot.

Mom had said pretty much the same thing when she first brought up the idea of being a surrogate.

"I'd be pregnant for forty weeks. You'd have a pregnant mom for all that time. That's a lot."

But it wasn't *that* much. Not when it meant giving Erin and Christopher their baby. Not when it meant giving Mom something meaningful and fulfilling.

Downstairs, the faucet turned on in the kitchen, and then the garbage disposal whirred.

Ivy still couldn't focus on her essay, so she went back to that anonymous email from the day before. She read it again, letting the words fill up her heart and straighten her spine into Nana-approved posture. This is who she was, deep down. A person who made other people's days better. She just needed to remember that.

She clicked *Reply* and began to type.

To: <downbythebay5@mailme.com>
From: Ivy Campbell <ivy.campbell@leland
magnet.org>
Subject: Re: Thank you

Hi!

It's a little strange to have no idea who I'm writing to! But I guess you probably have a good reason for wanting to stay anonymous? Or maybe you just thought it would be kind of fun, which is a good reason on its own, I guess.

I'm glad I could help you yesterday, and I'm sorry you were having such a rough day. I hope things are better today.

Can I do anything else to help you? If you ever want to talk, I'll always listen! (Or . . . read

what you type, I guess. And type something back
if you want.)

I don't know who you are, but I'm here
for you.

And as she clicked *Send* on the email, she noticed two clues she'd missed before.

The emailer was Sydney DelMonte—she was almost a hundred percent sure. And she was so, so glad.

CHAPTER FOUR

Downbythe*bay*. That was the first clue. The second clue was the number 5.

Sydney DelMonte's family went to the shore for two weeks every August, to a town called *Bay*view. Ivy knew because she and Will had been in charge of watering their plants last month when they were away. And Sydney DelMonte's field hockey number was 5. Ivy had seen her in her uniform.

Ivy had met Sydney right before the start of sixth grade, when the townhouses were ready and Dad and Leo and the DelMontes all moved in. Sydney's younger brother, Blake, was in Ivy's class at Leland Magnet, and he was always complaining about something or insulting someone. But Sydney was his polar opposite: always cheerful and friendly and smiling.

Except for yesterday morning, when Ivy had gotten to school late because she'd had an orthodontist appointment, and Sydney had been sitting on the little bench behind the middle school, crying.

Sydney was supposed to be at her high school, which was several blocks away, and Ivy was supposed to go straight inside the middle school to get her excused lateness pass at the front desk. But she couldn't just leave Sydney out there by herself, so she walked over.

"Sydney?" she said. "Are you okay?"

Sydney looked up. "Oh. Ivy, hey." Her face was pink and puffy, with grayish streaks of makeup under her eyes. She swiped at her eyes with her forearm, which meant the gray makeup streaks striped her arm, too.

"Did something happen?" Ivy asked. "Should I get somebody for you?"

Sydney shook her head. "No. Please don't get anyone. I'll be okay."

"Are you sure?"

Sydney sighed. "I don't know. I don't have any idea what I'm doing here. I had a free first period, and I was wandering around because I couldn't face school yet, and for some reason I came here." She kicked a rock with the toe of her brown boot and let out a sound that was half sniffle, half laugh. "I'm a mess. Everything's a mess." She flung her arms wide enough to indicate the whole area behind the school, the whole city block, the whole city, maybe. "And it's just going to get worse."

Ivy sat down next to Sydney and patted her knee because she didn't know what else to do. "I'm really sorry you're having such a hard time," she said.

Sydney didn't even seem to hear her. "I miss middle school. Maybe that's why I came here. Patrick and I got together in eighth grade. Did you know that? I liked him so much then. I was so, so happy."

Ivy noticed the past tense. *Liked* him so much. *Was* so happy. "I knew you'd been together a long time," she said. "But I didn't know it was since eighth grade."

Patrick was tall and good-looking and quiet, and he was at the DelMontes' house all the time. Will idolized him because he was the star goalie on his high school soccer team, and he was already getting recruited by Division 1 colleges. He'd been a counselor at the soccer camp Will went to over the summer, and for weeks Will started almost every sentence with "Patrick says . . ."

"Are you . . . Are you and Patrick having relationship problems?" *Ack.* Ivy cringed when the words left her mouth.

Sydney looked up in the sky, where an airplane glided through the clouds. A squirrel scampered up the trunk of a tree at the edge of the school's back patio, and a siren wailed in the distance. "I don't need to burden you with all the drama."

Drama. Nana didn't like that word. Ivy had used it once in front of her—she couldn't remember why—and Nana had said it "minimizes legitimate feelings and conflicts, and people only use it when they're talking about girls."

"I'm sure it's not drama. I'll listen if you want me to."

"You're sweet," Sydney said.

"Well, so are you," Ivy blurted. "You're nice to everybody. You invited Will and me to have cake with you on your birthday last year. Remember that? And that time I forgot my key and couldn't get into Dad and Leo's, you let me come inside until they got home and hung out with me even though you were probably busy."

The truth was, Ivy looked up to Sydney at least as much as Will looked up to Patrick. She had ever since sixth grade, when she started middle school at Leland with all the other kids who had good enough grades and test scores to go there, and suddenly it was so obvious that she wasn't as smart as she'd thought. It helped to see Sydney around the neighborhood—to notice that whenever Sydney's name came up, the first word people said was *nice*. Ivy wanted to be that way, too.

"I used to be like that," Sydney said. "I don't think I am anymore."

"I'm sure you are!" Ivy replied.

Mom had a framed calligraphy print on her wall that said, *Wherever you go, there you are*. She'd bought it at a craft fair not long after Dad moved out, and she said it meant that wherever you were, whatever was happening, you were still yourself, no matter what.

"I just think . . . whatever's going on," Ivy said. "You're still you. And you're awesome! So you'll get through it."

Sydney smiled. A sad smile, but still.

"I'd better go," she said. "I'm sure Patrick's looking for me, and you should go inside—I don't want you to get in trouble. But thanks for coming over to sit with me."

And then Sydney walked south, toward the high

school, and Ivy went to the front desk to get her late pass and headed to second period.

She was only about five minutes later than she would have been if she'd walked straight into the building. Five minutes that must have made a big difference for Sydney DelMonte.

CHAPTER FIVE

Kyra had invited both Peyton and Ivy over, but when Ivy arrived later that afternoon, exactly on time, Peyton was already there.

Peyton and Kyra were lounging on Kyra's bed talking in hushed voices, and they both straightened up when they saw Ivy, as if she were a teacher who'd caught them passing notes. Peyton gave Kyra an almost invisible headshake that made her shiny, shoulder-length black hair swish once before settling back into place.

This wasn't the first time Ivy noticed a tiny signal pass between her two closest friends. Ever since Kyra and Peyton had gotten home from sleepaway camp in August, it had felt like the two of them were perfectly in sync and Ivy was a beat behind. They hadn't even gone to the *same* sleepaway camp, but somehow that didn't matter. They bonded over all sorts of camp experiences and traditions, and Ivy didn't understand any of them.

"Ivy! Hey!" Peyton said. Not loudly, because Peyton was never a loud person, but nowhere near as quietly as she'd been talking to Kyra.

And they were both wearing skinny, shiny hoop earrings. Peyton's were silver and Kyra's were gold, but they were the same size and shape. Had they been hanging out all day, just the two of them? Had they bought matching earrings without her?

"Ooh, what's that?" Kyra pointed to the container of rugelach Ivy had brought to share, and Ivy pried the top off.

"Rugelach? Yum!" Peyton cheered, and she and Kyra jumped off the bed to help themselves.

"I am *such* a fan of your new baking hobby," Kyra said.

Peyton and Kyra both plopped back down against the pillows with two pieces of rugelach each, and Ivy sat down at the bottom of the bed, feeling much better than she had the moment before.

"These are so good!" Peyton said.

"Mmm," Kyra agreed.

Nana said baked goods could fix the majority of all problems, and maybe she was right.

"What's new, Ives?" Kyra asked. "How was your day?"

"Oh. Um." Ivy's tongue did the tightening thing, swelling to fill up her mouth, but she bit down on the edges to make it stop.

"Ivy?" Peyton said. "You okay?"

The thing was, Ivy hadn't told Kyra and Peyton anything about Mom trying to be a surrogate for Erin and Christopher. She wasn't actually sure why. But now it was like Mom had said: The surrogacy couldn't stay a secret for long. It would be way weirder if they noticed Mom's baby bump before Ivy had said something.

"I have some news, actually." Ivy pointed her toes out and pulled them back, then out, then back, watching the little hearts on her socks bob. "Well, my mom has some news. She's pregnant."

Kyra let out a startled "What?" then cleared her throat. "But she's not . . . I mean, does she have a boyfriend, or . . . ?"

"Oh!" Ivy shook her head. She wasn't explaining this right. "No. You know Erin?"

Ivy had only met Peyton when they'd started middle school, but she'd known Kyra forever—their moms had become friends at a breastfeeding support group when Kyra and Ivy were only a few weeks old. Kyra had met Erin a bunch of times over the years, so she nodded, but she didn't look any less confused.

"Erin's my mom's best friend," Ivy told Peyton. "She and her husband can't have a baby on their own, but they really, really want one. It's their baby my mom's pregnant with. She's a gestational surrogate—that's what it's called."

Kyra and Peyton caught each other's eyes. A song Ivy had never heard before was playing over Kyra's speakers, and it bothered her suddenly that Kyra listened to all different music ever since she'd come back from camp. What was wrong with the music Kyra had liked before? The stuff Ivy still listened to?

Kyra and Peyton were silent for too long, and those matching hoop earrings were so *shiny*, and the distance between the two of them at the head of the bed and Ivy at the foot felt enormous.

"Wow, Ivy," Kyra finally said. "That's amazing."

"Really amazing," Peyton agreed. "Are you surprised?"

"And, like . . . are you okay?" Kyra finished, her voice so soft and concerned that it made Ivy's whole body itch.

That's what Kyra had kept asking, over and over, when Dad and Leo had moved into the townhouse together the summer before sixth grade, even though Ivy kept insisting she was fine.

"I'm good!" Ivy said. "It's actually not a big deal. The baby isn't related to me. This is just something my mom's doing to help her friend."

Ack. This was a baby. A human being. Why had she said this wasn't a big deal?

"I mean, it's a huge deal for Erin and Christopher, obviously. And, uh, for the baby. It's exciting!"

"Okay," Peyton said slowly. "Well, if you want to talk about it more, we can."

"Yeah," Kyra agreed. "We're here for you, Ives."

We.

It was nice, what Kyra and Peyton were saying, but Ivy felt the same way she had with Mom and Dad this morning.

Dad got to know Mom was pregnant so much earlier than Ivy and Will did. He and Mom were a *we* that Ivy was stuck outside of, and Kyra and Peyton were, too.

This was yet another thing that separated her from her two closest friends—another thing that knocked her further off their beat.

She wanted to change the subject. She wanted

to say something that would bring them all back in sync. "Oh! Will said Josh Miller's knee surgery is a week from Monday," she announced.

That fact didn't have anything to do with anything, but Peyton's cheeks flushed the way they always did when anybody said Josh's name.

"Aw, poor guy," she cooed in that high-pitched voice people used to talk to little kids. As if Josh were a toddler with an adorable lisp instead of a tall, cute, confident guy who scored almost all the soccer team's goals.

"Maybe you can do something nice for him while he's recovering," Ivy suggested. "You have English together, right? You could offer to give him your notes? Or I could help you bake something for him?"

This was more comfortable territory now, helping Peyton. Usually Kyra was the one who gave Peyton advice about Josh stuff, since Kyra had a boyfriend for a couple of weeks at camp, and Ivy helped when Peyton wanted to practice a song or vent about her stepmom. But helping was helping, and Ivy's body relaxed.

Peyton shook her head hard. "That would make it so obvious I like him."

"Yeah, baking for him's a little cringey," Kyra said. "But I don't think it's a bad thing if he finds out you like him, Pey. You're fun and easy to talk to. And have you *seen* yourself lately? You're gorgeous!"

When Kyra said the word *gorgeous*, Peyton hugged a pillow to her chest as if she needed something physical to absorb her embarrassment so she wouldn't burst.

Peyton *was* pretty. Everybody suddenly seemed to notice that last spring, after she got her braces off, switched from glasses to contacts, and started wearing the clothes her stepmom picked for her. All at once, people paid a lot of attention to her, and sometimes she seemed to like the attention and sometimes she didn't.

She definitely *didn't* like it when Chloe Casperson, queen of inappropriate, backhanded compliments, said Peyton was so pretty because she was half Chinese and half white, and mixed-race people are always attractive. Josh was friends with Chloe, but he told her that was offensive, and then he sat down next to Peyton in study hall and said not to listen to Chloe when she said stuff like that, and who cared *why* Peyton was pretty. Peyton had liked him ever since.

"Seriously, Peyton," Kyra said. "Just, like, channel Ivy and jump out of your seat to help him every time he comes near you. You'll be together in no time."

She was using the sarcastic voice she used to only use with her sister or her mom. Lately, she sometimes used it with Ivy, too. But then she laughed as if she were joking around, so Ivy tried to laugh, too, even though she felt like she'd been punched.

Kyra was talking about what had happened yesterday when Josh had dropped all his stuff. The thing that had made Ivy wonder for a split second if Josh could be the anonymous emailer.

Peyton's eyes darted from Kyra to Ivy and back. "Wait, what?"

"Nothing!" Ivy said. "His bag wasn't closed all the way and stuff spilled out when he walked into history class, so I helped him."

"Omygosh, when he sat next to you after you picked up his stuff, I thought Chloe was going to knock you out of your chair and fight you for it." Now Kyra's voice was friendly. It was impossible to keep up.

"Josh sat next to you?" Peyton asked.

"It wasn't a thing," Ivy insisted.

And it *wasn't*. Ivy was almost positive. Except that when Chloe had rushed over after class and offered to carry Josh's bag to art, he'd told her Ivy was going to carry it for him, and Chloe had huffed off.

"I just want like five seconds of quiet," he'd said,

and then Ivy had walked next to him, carrying both their bags.

But then in art class, he'd sat with Chloe and her two friends, Morgan Elliott and Nora Kim. Chlo-Mo-No—that's what Josh and the other soccer guys called them. Three syllables, one entity. And he'd laughed and flirted with all three of them, and it was hard to believe he was the same kid who'd said he wanted quiet as he hobbled down the hallway.

Peyton sighed. "Okay. Maybe I'll text him or something, to say I heard about the surgery. But really, Ivy. If you want to talk more about your mom—"

"I don't," Ivy said. "I was just updating you. But thanks."

Peyton glanced at Kyra...and Ivy was almost positive Kyra rolled her eyes. But then Kyra asked what kind of pizza they should get, and the three of them watched a movie they'd seen a bunch of times and chatted throughout the whole thing and everything was fine. Good, even.

Peyton's dad picked her up because she had youth group at her synagogue the next morning, but Ivy spent the night. They set up Kyra's trundle bed, just like always, and when they got under the covers, Kyra rolled over to face Ivy.

"Is it okay if I tell my parents?" she asked. "About your mom and the baby, I mean?"

"Oh." Ivy's parents and Kyra's parents used to be really close friends. They hadn't spent as much time together since Ivy's parents had split up, but it made sense they'd want to know. "Sure, yeah. My mom said it's not a secret."

"Cool." Kyra propped her head up on her hands. "Hey. I don't think I told you. I got my period at camp."

"Whoa!" Ivy sat up.

"*Finally*, right?" Kyra laughed. "I thought the pads my mom bought me were going to disintegrate by the time it came."

Both Ivy and Peyton had gotten theirs in seventh grade, and Kyra was the only one of the three of them who was prepared. She'd given them both pads from the stash she'd kept in her locker, and she'd had all sorts of questions about whether pads were uncomfortable and whether they might switch to tampons and what the bleeding felt like.

"Was it everything you'd hoped for?" Ivy was joking, but Kyra didn't laugh.

"Eh, it's kind of messy and annoying and cramps suck. But do you ever think about what it *means*? We get our periods because our bodies are capable of getting *pregnant* and growing babies. I feel like nobody talks about it, but that's literally why we menstruate."

Ivy's brain flashed to the baby development site she'd found—that image of a fourteen-week-old fetus growing inside a uterus. She touched her own abdomen. "You're right. I never think about that, but geez. Yeah."

Kyra sat all the way up. "And also, we're born with all the eggs we're ever going to have, already there in our ovaries. We lose one every time we have a period, but they're all just *there*, these things that could someday turn into babies that we'd grow in our own bodies. Or in someone else's body, I guess, like with your mom."

Ivy loved this part of Kyra—how curious she was, all her big ideas and questions. Lately, being with Kyra made Ivy feel smaller most of the time. But conversations with Kyra used to make the whole world feel bigger and more exciting and full of wonder.

"It's super strange but also kind of amazing, right?" Kyra started giggling. "Omygosh, remember when your dad recorded that Doctors Dish video responding to some parent's question about whether they should buy their kid pads or tampons when she got her first period?"

Ivy winced. "That was so awkward."

"He was like, 'I've heard the process of inserting a tampon can take some getting used to.'" Kyra was laughing so hard she could barely get the words out.

"Stop! Please, stop!" Ivy pleaded, but she was laughing, too.

Kyra lay back down. "Anyway. You don't like Josh, do you?"

Ivy blinked. Where had *that* come from? "I . . . He's fine? I don't like him the way Peyton does, if that's what you're asking."

"Okay. Good." Kyra yawned, which made Ivy yawn, too. "Do you want to go to sleep? Or did you want to talk more?"

Ivy was about to say *yes*, she wanted to talk a lot more. She wanted to know more about Kyra's camp boyfriend, Noah, and how their first kiss had happened—where they were and who started it and whether they talked about what they were about to do before they did it. She both wanted to know and *didn't* want to know when Kyra and Peyton had gotten those matching earrings and whether Kyra still thought of Ivy as her best friend.

But then Kyra added, "It seemed like you didn't want to talk about your mom, but I'll stay awake if you do."

Oh. "We don't need to talk about that," Ivy said.

"Okay, then," Kyra said, rolling over toward the wall. " 'Night, Ives."

"Good night," Ivy echoed, and within seconds, Kyra's breathing evened out and she began to snore softly.

It was barely 11:00. They used to stay awake *way* later than this at sleepovers.

But maybe Kyra was just really tired, Ivy told herself. She'd been acting like the old Kyra for a little while, at least, and that was something.

CHAPTER SIX

When Ivy got home the next morning, she saw the new email from downbythebay5@mailme.com, sent late the night before.

> **To: Ivy Campbell <ivy.campbell@lelandmagnet .org>**
> **From: <downbythebay5@mailme.com>**
> **Subject: Hi again!**
>
> Dear Ivy,
>
> I do have a good reason to want to stay anonymous, but I can't tell you what it is, because

then you'd be able to figure out who I am. So you'll just have to trust me.

I appreciate you being here for me—metaphorically, at least. You are not actually here in my room with me right now, which is lucky for you because my room is not a fun place to be at the moment. My parents said some things that made me mad and then I said something that made them mad, so they told me to come up here and cool down. But I'm not cooling down at all. I'm getting madder and madder.

I know this is a totally clichéd thing to say, but UGH, SAINT IVY, MY PARENTS DO NOT GET ME! They act like they think I'm somebody I'm not. Or maybe they want me to be somebody I'm not.

Sometimes I want to stomp my feet and pound my fists like I'm a little kid and scream, "I'm not you! You can't make me be like you!" But I know that wouldn't do any good. So I'm complaining to you instead, which helps a little bit.

Sincerely,
Your whiny anonymous friend

Ivy imagined Sydney typing this from her bedroom, which was identical to the room at Dad and Leo's where Ivy occasionally spent the night because all the townhouses had the same layout.

She could definitely picture Sydney fighting with her parents, especially her mom. She didn't really know Sydney's dad, but Mrs. DelMonte was intense. Ivy had heard her talking to Leo one time about how Sydney needed to "step it up" and improve her grades and test scores if she was going to get into a good college.

The other day it had seemed like Sydney was upset about Patrick, not her parents . . . but it's not like there was a limit on the number of things that could go wrong at the same time in a person's life. Sydney could be having boyfriend issues *and* parent issues. The tone of the email didn't strike her as a hundred percent Sydney-like, either. But it's not like Sydney and Ivy had ever exchanged emails before.

Ivy sent a quick reply:

To: downbythebay5@mailme.com
From: Ivy Campbell <ivy.campbell@leland
magnet.org>
Subject: Re: Hi again!

That sounds really hard with your parents.
I hope things are better this morning. I'm
(metaphorically) here for you anytime. Complain
away if it helps!

Then she went back to that fetus development site she'd looked at the day before and picked up where she'd left off, after the fetus pee.

You're likely past the worst part of the first-trimester nausea. Morning sickness (which should really be called all-the-time sickness) and first-trimester fatigue are no joke, and you've made it past a big hurdle, Mama! Enjoy the relative comfort of the second trimester as you prepare to meet your baby. And eat up! Now that you're probably feeling better, try some of these yummy pregnancy superfoods to make sure you and Baby are getting all the nutrients you need.

A bunch of the superfoods were things they had in the kitchen—oats and bananas and almonds and Greek yogurt. Maybe what Ivy needed was to *do* something for Mom and the baby—something to show her support. She found a healthy muffin recipe Nana wouldn't approve of, headed down to the kitchen, and fell into the calming routine of lining up ingredients and mixing up batter.

Soon, she put the muffins in the oven, and they filled the whole house with their warm, sweet scent as they baked.

Will came downstairs as Ivy took them out of the oven.

"Did you make Nana's cinnamon–chocolate chip muffins?" he asked, reaching for the pan.

"They're oatmeal-banana-almond," Ivy told him. "And they need to cool."

"Oh." His nose wrinkled in disappointment as he pulled his hand away. "Were we out of chocolate chips?"

Ivy laughed, because this was typical Will. Whatever he was feeling, he let you know.

Or . . . that's how he used to be, anyway. He'd been working hard with Dr. Banks at strategies for managing his frustration, especially when he was playing soccer, so now he didn't get as mad as he used to. And he'd stayed pretty calm and private since Mom's big announcement, too.

"I made them for Mom. They have ingredients that are supposed to be good for pregnant people. Speaking of which—"

Will's cheeks flashed red. "I don't want to talk about it."

Yikes.

"Okay. But . . . are you doing all right? Are you going to tell your friends? I told Kyra and Peyton last night, just so you know."

"Ivy. I don't want to talk to you about this."

The *you* stung. Ivy was used to being the person Will *did* want to talk to. When Mom and Dad had gotten divorced and Dad and Leo had moved in together, Will had shut down from Mom and Dad, but he'd opened up to Ivy.

"Well, maybe we can watch the Eagles game later? Or kick the soccer ball around, or make popcorn?"

Those were things they'd done together when Will was having a hard time before.

But he shook his head. "I'm watching the game at Dad's with my friends." He must have seen the hurt on Ivy's face because he added, "I'm not trying to make you feel bad. But we worked this out last spring. Me and Mom, with Dr. Banks. If I don't want to talk about stuff, I'm just supposed to say I don't want to talk about it, and that's supposed to be that. People are supposed to let it go."

Ivy took a deep breath. "Oh. Okay. I get it," she said.

"Thanks." Will dashed upstairs without waiting for a muffin.

Here was yet another *we* she'd gotten boxed out

of. But she wanted Will to be okay. She wanted to do whatever he needed, even if that meant leaving him alone.

Once the muffins had cooled, Ivy brought two of them up to Mom's room, where Mom was sitting at her antique desk, working on her laptop.

"I made these, if you want one," Ivy said. "For you and the baby. They have pregnancy superfoods."

Mom's eyes filled with tears.

"Oh, honey. Thank you. That's so sweet. I've been up here for way too long, trying to get this grant proposal finished, and these days I have to eat every two hours or I start to feel sick. You're a lifesaver."

Ivy sat in Mom's reading chair, relieved she'd done something right, and they ate their muffins together.

"Delicious!" Mom raved.

They weren't as good as the rugelach Ivy had baked with Nana, but they were decent: hearty and comforting and not too dry. And they were obviously making Mom happy. *Ivy* was obviously making Mom happy, which was the whole point.

"So. Tell me things," Mom said. "How did it go at Kyra's last night?"

Tell me things. That's what Mom always said, and then Ivy would be off, filling Mom in on everything that had happened since the last time they'd talked, which was never very long ago. And then Mom would tell Ivy things, too.

But now Ivy *didn't* tell Mom everything. She told Mom which movie they'd watched and what kind of pizza they'd ordered and how Peyton had gotten picked up early. But she didn't say anything about how Peyton had already been there when she showed up, or the matching earrings, or how explaining about the surrogacy only made her feel more out of sync with her friends.

"I'm glad you and Kyra got some time just the two of you," Mom said.

"Yeah. It was good. I think we're good." Ivy wanted that to be true, but she wasn't a hundred percent sure it was.

"And . . . you're really feeling okay about everything? The pregnancy?"

"I'm good," Ivy insisted.

Good, good, good. How many more times in one conversation could she say the word *good*?

"Anyway. How are *you*?" Ivy asked.

She told herself that if Mom answered this question for real—if Mom really told her what this felt like right now, to have Erin and Christopher's baby growing inside her body, or what she'd meant yesterday when she'd said things felt different than she'd expected, or which hormones had been off at the beginning of the pregnancy and what that meant—if Mom said any of that, then Ivy would talk to Mom for real, too.

But all Mom said was "Oh, I'm doing fine. Tired, and behind on this grant application. But much better now, after this muffin. That hit the spot." Nothing else. Nothing real.

Ivy stood up and made herself smile. "I'll let you work, then."

"Thanks, Ives. I'm here if you need me. Work is work—you're way more important."

"Yeah. Okay thanks," Ivy said.

But right now, Ivy didn't *feel* important.

Not the way she used to, when Will needed her, and Kyra told her everything, and Mom did, too. At least downbythebay5@mailme.com wanted her help . . . sort of. In a very vague and mysterious way, but still.

CHAPTER SEVEN

The next morning, Ivy brought three superfood muffins to school: one for her, one for Kyra, and one for Peyton.

As soon as she walked into the building, she noticed Lila Britton sitting on a bench outside the auditorium, her sketchbook on her lap.

Lila was new this year, and Ivy was her official New Student Buddy. That meant Ivy was supposed to show Lila around on the first day of school and sit with her at lunch and make sure she was "settling in okay." Except that Lila had made it very clear that she had no desire to settle in and no desire to be buddied, especially by Ivy.

But last Friday, Lila had forgotten her math book

for the third time, which meant her teacher was going to email her parents. She was surprisingly panicked for someone who always acted like she didn't care about school, so Ivy had offered up her own book. It didn't matter so much for Ivy to be unprepared, since she'd never forgotten anything before, and Lila had seemed genuinely grateful.

Ivy stopped next to the bench. "Hey, Lila! How was your weekend?"

"Fantabulous." Lila's voice was just as exasperated as usual, and she didn't look up from her sketchbook. Maybe they hadn't had much of a breakthrough on Friday, then.

"Well, have you checked out any of the artsy stuff I told you about yet? The museum, or the mosaics in South Philly, or any of the murals?"

Lila began to move her pencil faster, shading in a shape at the top of her page. "Nope."

"How about the art club? Are you going to join?"

Now Lila finally glanced up. Her face was round and freckled, and her light brown hair was cut asymmetrically, with one side super short and the other side almost to her chin. She tucked the longer side behind her ear twice, but it came loose both times. "Look. This year is something I plan to survive. Not something I plan to enjoy. I don't need to join clubs or discover special Philadelphia places, okay?"

Ivy blinked. "Why not?"

Lila started drawing again, pressing hard enough that the tip of her pencil snapped off.

"I have one year at Leland, and then everything's going to reset when high school starts," she said. "And I'm hoping somehow or another I can be back in New York for high school, which means there's no point in forcing my way into the social scene at this strange little school or searching for things to like in this strange little city."

"Philadelphia isn't a little city," Ivy pointed out.

Lila narrowed her eyes, which were rimmed in dark green eyeliner. "Why do you care so much if I like it here?"

"I don't know," Ivy admitted. "I guess I don't like to see people be unhappy."

Lila groaned as she pulled a pencil sharpener out of her bag. "If you tell me I can choose to be happy, I'll throw this pencil sharpener at your head, I swear. I'm tired of people saying things like that. That's not how emotions work."

Yikes. "Okay, I won't say that," Ivy promised.

Lila eyed the container Ivy was carrying. "What's that?"

"Oh. Uh, muffins? I was gonna share them with my friends." That felt a tiny bit harsh, like she was rubbing it in that Lila didn't have friends here, even though Lila had just said she didn't want any. "You can have one."

Lila raised her eyebrows. "You want to give *me* a muffin?"

"Sure! They're, well, they're kind of healthy, though. They have lots of superfoods," Ivy babbled. Why was she still talking? "Anyway, you don't have to take one. I was just—"

"No, okay. I'll take a muffin."

She said it like she was doing Ivy a favor, but it wasn't as if Ivy could take back the offer because Lila wasn't acting grateful enough. So Ivy opened up the container and Lila helped herself.

"Okay, well, have a good morning," Ivy said.

"Mmm, you too," Lila said through a mouthful. "Thanks."

Ivy started toward the staircase, but then somebody behind her called out, "Hey! You're giving out muffins?"

She heard the click-clack of crutches, and there was Josh Miller, right next to her.

"They're healthy and they got a little smushed," Ivy said. "But if you want one, sure."

"Really? Because it was kind of an intense morning. I didn't get a chance to eat anything yet."

"Go for it," Ivy said.

Josh took one of the two remaining muffins. "Mmm. These are good. You made these?"

Ivy nodded. "Yeah. I bake a lot."

Josh's eyes lit up. "You made those chocolate chip cookies for that student council bake sale, right? Those were epic."

Ivy looked down at the rubbery gray hallway tile because it was too much, actually making eye contact when Josh was standing this close *and* complimenting her. "Dark chocolate chunk with sea salt. Yeah."

"Miller!" someone shouted from the top of the staircase. It was Blake DelMonte, Sydney's younger brother and Josh's best friend. "Dude, finally. Come on!"

"Coming!" Josh called, and then smiled at Ivy. "Thanks again, Opi. You're the best."

He crutched down the hall toward the elevator.

Opi. That's what Josh and Blake had called Ivy for like three weeks last year, when they were all about giving people nicknames. Blake had suggested "Poison Ivy," but Josh had said Ivy was the opposite of poison. "Opposite-of-Poison Ivy" was kind of a mouthful, so for a few days she was O.P.I., even though Kyra pointed out that was a nail polish brand. Then the three letters got blurred together into a two-syllable word instead, and then they'd moved on and stopped calling her anything. She was sort of flattered that Josh remembered.

And he'd told her she was the best. Ivy knew that was just something people said, but still. It felt good to know that she'd cheered him up from whatever had been going on that morning.

Ivy ate the last muffin on her way up the stairs, stashed the empty container in her bag, and found Peyton and Kyra sitting cross-legged on the ground by Kyra's locker. Those matching hoop earrings glimmered in their ears, and their hairstyles matched today, too.

They both had their hair down, with a tiny clip pulling back the front. Kyra had blown out her wavy, dirty-blond hair, so hers was as straight and shiny as Peyton's. Ivy touched the top of her curls, which she'd pulled into a tight bun. Kyra had tried to straighten her hair once for a dance last year, but it had been a disaster.

Kyra and Peyton paused what they were doing to say hi, but then went back to studying for their Mandarin quiz. Ivy took Spanish, and she didn't have anything to study. She sat on the ground next to them anyway.

Lila walked by, wearing big headphones and clutching her sketchbook to her chest as if it were armor.

If you tell me I can choose to be happy, I'll throw this pencil sharpener at your head, Lila had said. *That's not how emotions work.*

One time, when Kyra was turning ten, Ivy was supposed to go with Kyra's family for a special camp-out sleepover at the zoo. They were so excited, and then Kyra got a stomach bug and they couldn't go, and Ivy was so, so sad, even though she knew Kyra was the one who really deserved to be disappointed. Ivy was moping around, and Mom had told her that sometimes when you were feeling grumpy, you could try to act happy on the outside and that might trick your insides into catching up. It had worked for Ivy that night—she decided to pretend she was happy to get pizza and play board games at home, and pretty soon, she actually was.

But then the next year, after Dad left, when Will was having a hard time, Ivy had asked Mom if she thought Will should try to act happy on the outside, and Mom had said that didn't work with big stuff—when you were sad about something big, you had to let yourself feel it.

It was easy to take it personally when Lila acted sort of rude, but maybe Lila was having a hard time because of something big. Maybe she acted angry and annoyed with everything because she didn't want her sad, private feelings oozing out like rugelach filling.

The bell rang, so Ivy and Kyra said goodbye to Peyton and walked together to history class. They took their usual seats, and then Josh Miller crutched past them, grinning at Ivy.

"Thanks again for the muffin, Opi," he said as he headed toward the seat Chloe had saved him in the back.

Kyra had been writing out her daily to-do list in her special bullet journal, but she stopped writing mid-word. "Wait. What? You gave *Josh* a *muffin*?"

It sounded like a terrible thing, the way Kyra said it.

"It was nothing. I made some at home, and I had some extras."

"Oookaaaaay." Kyra stretched out the syllables, as if the word didn't fit the situation. As if she *didn't* think it was okay, what Ivy had done.

At the back of the room, Chloe made a fuss over Josh's knee and propped his crutches against the wall for him. Josh ducked his head and maybe smiled, but to Ivy it looked more like a wince.

"I brought in a few extras," Ivy tried to explain. "I was going to offer them to you and Peyton, but then

Lila saw them. So I gave one to her, and then Josh wanted one, too. And he hadn't had breakfast."

Kyra rolled her eyes, and when she spoke, her voice was unbearably harsh, like the sound of two pieces of Styrofoam rubbing against each other.

"You know Josh is capable of getting his own breakfast, right? All of us are. Josh could have gotten food at the cafeteria if he hadn't eaten at home. You don't have to bring food for people. It's not your job to take care of everyone, Saint Ivy."

Ivy's throat tightened. She wasn't always sure whether Kyra was teasing her in a friendly way or not when she called her Saint Ivy. This time, it definitely wasn't friendly.

"I wasn't trying to take care of anyone. The muffin wasn't even supposed to be for him, but he asked. I was only trying to be nice."

Kyra looked down at her notebook, where her pink pen had left a bright, wet blob when she'd stopped writing but had kept the tip pressed against the page. She let out an enormous sigh. "Sometimes you're so worried about being nice that you're not that good a friend," she said. Then she tore out the page with the pink blob and started copying her to-do list over on a new, clean sheet.

Ms. Ramos started class, but Ivy couldn't pay

attention. What did that even mean, that she cared more about being nice than being a good friend? Didn't those two things go together?

Did Kyra really think she should have refused to give Josh a muffin out of loyalty to Peyton? And why did Kyra suddenly find Ivy so exasperating almost all the time?

As Ms. Ramos went over the homework and Chloe giggled at something Josh had said, a terrible thought occurred to Ivy. What if Kyra found her so annoying that *she'd* written the anonymous emails as some kind of cruel prank? But that couldn't be. Kyra had been sleeping right next to Ivy when the last email came in. Unless she'd woken up?

No. Ivy shook off the idea. She couldn't imagine that Kyra would be that mean. They were going through a rough patch, but they'd been friends so long that Ivy was sure they'd be okay. It was like . . . when you took a quiz with only ten problems, a few mistakes meant a bad grade. But when you took a hundred-question test, each individual answer didn't count for that much. You could mess up a little and still be fine.

CHAPTER EIGHT

When Ivy got to lunch, Kyra and Peyton were already sitting at their usual table, whispering with their heads close together and their smooth, straight hair framing their faces. Ivy's heart sped up. Was Kyra telling Peyton about the muffin? Even if she wasn't yet, she probably would soon, so Ivy plopped her tray down and told Peyton her side of what had happened, as fast as she could blurt it out.

"I'll never give him another baked good again, though. Even if he asks for one. No more pastries for Josh if it bothers you, I promise."

Ivy held up her palm like she was doing a pledge. She was trying to lighten the mood, but no one laughed.

Peyton glanced over to the table in the corner

where Josh and Blake were sitting. "Okay. Thanks, Ivy. I'm sure you didn't mean anything by it."

Will was at Josh's table, too, with his best friend, Langston, and a couple of other seventh graders from the soccer team.

Ivy waved at Will, but he either didn't see her or pretended not to see her. Josh saw, though, and shot her a smile that dimpled his right cheek and squinched up his eyes.

"Let's talk about something else," Kyra suggested. "Let's talk about auditions for the musical!"

"Oh! You decided to try out, Pey?" Ivy asked. "That's great."

The show was *The Wizard of Oz*, and the director had practically begged Peyton to audition, since she had such a beautiful voice, but Peyton liked chorus better than drama. She wasn't into dancing or acting—she just loved to sing.

"My dad and Monica said it was either the musical or the swim team," Peyton said. "They want me to 'try new things and expand my horizons,' direct quote. So."

Ivy's breath caught.

My parents do not get me! They act like they think I'm somebody I'm not. Or maybe they want me to be somebody I'm not. That's what the last anonymous email had said.

It sounded like something Peyton might say. And Peyton had gone home on Saturday night. Technically she *could* have sent it. But this was getting silly. Ivy could probably talk herself into thinking *anybody* was the emailer.

"I'm going with 'Better' from *Legally Blonde* for my audition song, I think," Peyton said.

"Ooh, that's good," said Kyra. "What do you think I should do?"

"Wait," Ivy said. "*You're* trying out?"

Kyra snorted a laugh. "Gee, thanks for the vote of confidence."

"No, I mean . . . I thought you had debate team after school. And you love debate. I didn't think you were into musicals."

Kyra shrugged. "I'm bored with debate. And I did the big show at camp, and I had fun."

Ivy gulped. "That's great. I just thought you were really into debate."

Kyra took a bite of her mom's pasta salad, which her mom used to make without black olives when Ivy was over. "Last year. Not anymore."

"You could try out, too, if you want," Peyton offered.

But Kyra didn't jump in to agree. And how was Kyra just not into debate anymore? Ivy distinctly remembered sitting next to her last year when the cast of the musical did a little preview during assembly. *I don't get the appeal of musical theater at all*, she'd said. *It makes no sense for people to randomly break into song in emotional moments. Like, either do a play or sing songs. Pick one.*

"Oh, or maybe you could play piano!" Peyton said. "They might want a student accompanist."

Ivy shook her head. "I'm nowhere near good enough at the piano for that." She didn't even take lessons anymore.

"Stage crew, then?" Peyton suggested.

But Kyra didn't say a *word* and those matching earrings were so distracting, glimmering under the fluorescent cafeteria lights. Ivy touched her own earlobes. Her star-shaped studs were so babyish! Why was she still wearing those?

"I don't think musical theater is really my thing," she finally said. "But I can help you practice your songs if you want. And I'm sure you'll both be great."

Kyra held up a hand to high-five Peyton. "We'll be *amazing*!" she corrected Ivy, as if Ivy couldn't even give a good enough compliment, suddenly.

One table over, Lila sat by herself. When Ivy looked her way, their eyes met, and she gave Ivy a sympathetic half-smile, as if she were listening to this whole conversation and she felt sorry for Ivy.

• • •

The next day at recess, Ivy went to the music room with Peyton and Kyra to play their audition songs on the piano while they sang. She couldn't do the full piano accompaniment—that was way too hard. But she could play the basic melody and help them stay on key.

Ivy knew Peyton would sound incredible, but Kyra was better than she expected. Her voice wasn't as impressive as Peyton's, but she was so confident— she went for every note, not doubting herself at all. A tiny, jealous part of Ivy didn't want Kyra to be this good. She already did so many things so well. Rationally, Ivy knew that talents didn't get doled out evenly like portions of tater tots in the cafeteria—two scoops per person, no extras. But sometimes it felt like they *should*.

When they left the music room, Elias Young was waiting to go in. Ivy and Elias were in student government together, and they used to take piano lessons from the same teacher when they were in elementary school. Elias's lessons had been right after Ivy's, and they would talk sometimes when Mom was a little late to pick up Ivy and Ms. April had to take care of something before she was ready for Elias.

"Oh, hey," Ivy said, and he smiled.

"Hey. That sounded great."

He was looking at Ivy, not Peyton or Kyra, even though they'd been the ones singing. Maybe he didn't realize?

"They're trying out for the musical," Ivy explained.

"Nice. Break a leg," Elias told them. And then he looked right back at Ivy. "The piano sounded good, too, though. I didn't know you were still playing."

Ivy's cheeks burned. "I'm not really playing. I mean, not like you. I just mess around."

Ms. April had always put her most advanced students at the end when she hosted recitals for everyone's families, and by fifth grade, Elias was the last one, the grand finale. When Ms. April moved away, Ivy had stopped taking lessons. She wasn't getting that much better anymore and didn't love piano enough to practice the way she should. Elias had switched to a new teacher—a really big-deal, super-selective one. Ivy had watched his fingers fly across the keys at last year's spring concert and for a second she'd had the same feeling she'd had when she tried out for the girls' soccer team last year and watched Nyeema Jackson play. That it would have been fun, to be that good at something people could sit there and watch you do.

"You could probably pick up another instrument fast, if you ever wanted to," Elias said. "Did you hear about the new percussion ensemble? I'm in it, and it's pretty fun. I do xylophone."

"Oh. Nice," Ivy said.

"We could use more people. If you're ever interested, let me know."

Then he said goodbye and went inside the room, and Peyton grabbed Ivy's arm.

"That was adorable!" she said.

Ivy was genuinely confused. "What was?"

"Elias! He likes you, don't you think? He's cute, in kind of a dorky way. I never noticed."

Was he? Ivy wasn't quite sure. "I don't think he likes me. We're friends, sort of."

"But he was *so* focused on you and he wants you to join percussion!" Peyton insisted. "He didn't look at me or Kyra at all. Right, Kyr?"

"I didn't really notice." Kyra shrugged. "But he might like you! I don't know. Although I heard the percussion ensemble is all guys and Mr. Shah wants girls to join."

And even though Ivy didn't think Elias liked her—had never even stopped to wonder if he might—something inside her deflated.

"Practice again tomorrow?" Kyra asked.

"Of course," Ivy said. "I'll help anytime."

The three of them linked arms as they walked to their next class, and Ivy told herself there was absolutely no reason to be disappointed.

CHAPTER NINE

On Sunday morning, Ivy and Will were at Dad and Leo's house, eating brunch and talking about Will's soccer game that afternoon.

Ivy hadn't gotten another anonymous email that week, and the more days that went by without one, the less she thought about them. Until now, when she was sitting *so close* to where Sydney DelMonte lived.

Was Sydney still fighting with her parents, if she really was the emailer? Had she and Patrick broken up?

Nana always said Ivy had good instincts and she should listen to them, and right now, Ivy's instincts were telling her that Sydney needed a friend—a friend who wasn't all caught up in whatever was going on with Patrick. A friend like Ivy, maybe.

So after brunch, Ivy offered to take the trash out to the communal dumpsters behind the townhouses. And then, slowly, she headed toward Sydney's house.

Her knuckles had just made contact with the door when it swung open and Sydney appeared. Her dark hair hung wavy and loose down her back, and she wore a bright pink shirt, dark jeans, and black eyeliner that made her amber eyes sparkle. No splotchy, mascara-stained face today.

"Oh! Ivy! Hey!" she said.

It was pretty clear that she had been expecting *someone* to knock, and it was pretty clear that someone wasn't Ivy.

"Hey! Uh, I was just at my dad's." Ivy turned around to point, even though Sydney obviously knew where Dad and Leo's house was. "I was thinking of you and wondering if you're okay."

Sydney flashed a quick, definitely fake smile and raked her fingers through the front of her hair, checking her reflection in the glass part of the door. "I'm sorry I was a mess that day you saw me. I was freaking out, but I'm good now. Everything's okay." She was talking really, really fast. As if the faster she said these words, the truer they'd be.

"Oh. Okay. Um . . . So you and Patrick . . ."

"We're good! Together. Happy. Fine. He's coming to pick me up, actually, so . . ."

Good.

Sydney hadn't seemed good the other day. She didn't really seem good now, either.

"And things with your parents? They're okay, too?"

Sydney's face crinkled in confusion. "My parents?"

"I . . . I got this email." Ivy's heart pounded. She hadn't planned to bring up the email. She didn't know why she had.

Sydney shook her head. "What email?"

Just like that, the idea of her sending a middle school kid like Ivy any kind of anonymous email sounded so ridiculous that Ivy couldn't believe she'd ever thought it was possible.

"I guess I got confused," Ivy mumbled.

"Okay. Well, no problem," Sydney said, her voice cheerful again. "Thanks again for stopping by. I'm really fine, I promise."

She closed the door, and embarrassment smacked Ivy in the chest.

Sydney hadn't sent any emails. Sydney didn't need Ivy's help.

But then who did?

That afternoon, Leo was busy with work, and Dad, Will, and Ivy went to Will's soccer game.

When they got to the field, Will joined his teammates for warm-ups and Dad joined the superfan crew—a cluster of super-enthusiastic parents who stood as close as possible to the field and walked up and down the sideline with the action as if they could impact the outcome of the game through their proximity.

Ivy took a seat halfway up the mostly empty bleachers by herself, since Mom was out with Nana. It finally felt more like fall than summer. The sky was a deep, cloudless blue, but chilly air shot through the thin cotton of Ivy's long-sleeved T-shirt, making her shiver.

She watched Will stretching on the field and wondered if he was relieved Mom wasn't here. She wondered if he'd asked her not to come, even—if that was another one of their ground rules: that Will could tell Mom to stay home from things, and she would.

Blake DelMonte showed up with his parents, who joined Dad and the superfan crew. At least Blake hadn't been there when she'd knocked on the Del-Montes' door that morning. He would have found some way to make Ivy feel even more foolish.

At the edge of the field, Josh Miller sat on the bench by himself. His crutches lay crisscrossed on the ground, and his injured leg was propped up on a pile of soccer bags.

Poor guy. His surgery was tomorrow, and here he was, sitting alone on an uncomfortable bench, his shoulders slumped as he watched other people get ready to play his favorite sport. He took his phone out of his pocket and stared at the screen, and then someone stepped up on the bleacher right behind Ivy, covering her in shade.

"Hey there."

It was Lila, wearing cropped, wide-leg black jeans that left a strip of bare skin above her ankle boots and a faded maroon T-shirt from a Brooklyn music festival. She must have been even colder than Ivy was, but she didn't show it. The leather satchel she used instead of a backpack at school was slung over one shoulder, and she held her sketchpad in her free hand.

"What are you doing here?" Ivy asked, and Lila's eyebrows shot up.

"Thanks for the warm welcome," she said.

Oops. "I just mean I didn't know you were a soccer fan."

Lila lowered herself down next to Ivy and kicked the bleacher below them with the heels of her boots, making a hollow clang. "I'm definitely not a soccer fan."

She opened up her sketchpad and started drawing something that was all slanted lines and angles.

"How come you're here if you don't like soccer?" Ivy asked. "Feeling so much school spirit you couldn't stay away after yesterday's pep rally?"

Lila smiled. "How did you know? I have a major thing for mascots, especially of the winged variety."

Ivy had helped organize the assembly, since she was on student government, and the plan had been for Josh to wear the Hawk mascot suit and shimmy around with the dance team like he'd done last year. But Blake had done it instead, since Josh was too hurt to shimmy.

"Also, my brother," Lila added.

"Wait, what?" Ivy asked, and Lila laughed.

"No, no, sorry. I don't have a thing for winged mascots and my brother. I don't have a thing for winged mascots *or* my brother. But my brother's the reason I'm here. My parents dragged me to watch him sit the bench."

She gestured toward some of the non-superfan parents, who sat toward the front of the bleachers, and Ivy wondered which ones were hers. The dad with graying black hair? Ivy hadn't seen him around at games before this year. Or maybe the woman with the blond highlights. She looked stylish enough to have moved from New York City.

Lila went back to her sketch, and Ivy scanned the field, trying to figure out which of the new players was her brother.

"Number seventeen. Harrison," Lila said without looking up from her sketchpad, even though Ivy hadn't asked.

"Oh. Huh." Ivy glanced between Lila and Harrison, who was in sixth grade. Lila was short and sort of roundish, with white skin, blue-gray eyes, and light brown hair. Harrison was tall and lanky, with light brown skin and thick, black hair. His last name was Vanguri, not Britton.

Lila sighed. "Lila Vanguri Britton. Harrison Britton Vanguri. We don't have the same last name and he doesn't look like me. Didn't you get the 'All families are different and different is great!' lessons in elementary school?"

"Sorry. Yeah. I know families are different." Ivy's

eyes drifted over to Lila's sketch. "You're drawing Josh?"

Lila groaned. "Don't get worked up. I have no interest in Josh Miller. You don't have to worry about any more competition."

"Shh!"

Ivy checked the area around them to see who was close enough to have heard what Lila had just said. A few younger kids, but they were busy having a fake sword fight with twigs.

"I'm not worried about competition," Ivy whispered. "I don't like Josh."

Lila shrugged. "If you say so."

"I *don't*!" Ivy said, louder this time.

Now Lila raised one eyebrow.

"If you think that because you saw me give him that muffin, that was nothing. He just *asked*."

Lila's mouth quirked into an infuriating half-smile, the kind that said, *I find you amusing right now*, when Ivy wasn't trying to be amusing at all.

"Whatever. The game's starting," Ivy said, pulling out her touch tally notebook.

Lila added some shading underneath the bench in her sketch and twirled one finger in the air. "Woo-hoo."

The ref blew the whistle, and Ivy turned to a fresh page. Blake lined up for the kickoff in Josh's usual spot. He tapped the ball to the other kid playing forward, who passed it back to Will. Will dribbled a few steps to pull a defender his way before smacking a hard pass to the other center midfielder. Ivy added the first mark on her tally.

"Uh, what are you doing?" Lila asked.

Ivy glued her eyes to the field, even though the other center mid launched the ball down the sideline, way ahead of where Will was positioned, so he wasn't likely to touch it again soon.

"I keep track of how many times my brother touches the ball," she explained. "Like, every time someone passes to him or he steals the ball or whatever."

"Well, now I feel like a crappy sister," Lila said. "Go, Harrison! Way to be there!"

Harrison, who was sitting on the bench, turned around and shushed her.

Ivy laughed hard enough that a woman with long black hair and skin about the same shade as Harrison's turned around. Lila put on an exaggeratedly cheerful smile and waved, and the woman smiled back before turning around to face the field.

Ivy caught herself watching the woman too intently, wondering how she and Lila were related, before she reminded herself how it felt when people stared at Mom and Dad and Leo when they were all together, trying to figure her family out. And now that Mom's belly was growing, people would try to figure *that* out, too. Ivy didn't need to understand the inner workings of Lila's family or anybody else's.

The other team took a throw-in, and Will headed the ball away from the kid he was defending, so Ivy made another mark.

"*Why* do you do that, exactly?" Lila asked.

Ivy sighed. "Will's a defensive center midfielder. So he's not going to score a ton of goals, but he sets up the offense and supports the defense. He should be involved in every stage of the game, so he should touch the ball a lot. It shows him how well he's doing, if he can see how many touches he has."

It was Dad's idea, but Ivy liked doing it. She came to all Will's games anyway—she had ever since Dad moved out, because for a while there, Will was mad at Dad and didn't want him to come.

"And . . . that's fun for you?" Lila asked.

"Yep."

Will stole the ball and dribbled down the sideline, so Ivy made another mark, and then he took a shot that curled left of the goal. As the other team's goalie ran after the ball, Lila went back to sketching.

Her drawing was good. Like, really good. But she'd stretched out the space between Josh and the next closest kid, making Josh look even more isolated than he was, and she'd captured how everybody else on the bench was looking up, watching the game, but Josh's head hung low, studying the screen of his phone. The picture made Ivy feel so sad for Josh that she had to look away.

She'd felt this sad for Josh another time, too. Right at the beginning of the season, when his dad wouldn't stop yelling at the ref about a call he didn't like and the ref finally made him leave, so he took off, cursing under his breath.

Josh's dad had seemed like a jerk. *Josh* could be the one struggling with his parents.

The breeze kicked up, ruffling the pages of Ivy's touch tally notebook, and goose bumps covered her arms.

"Wait, so why don't *you* play?" Lila asked. "Since you're so into soccer."

Ivy shrugged. "I like the game, but I'm not any good."

Dad and Will had convinced her to join the girls' team last fall, but it had been way too frustrating. She understood the game so well that she knew what she *wanted* to do on the field, but she didn't have the skills to do it. At tryouts, she'd known exactly where she should pass the ball when they scrimmaged, but she hadn't kicked it hard enough. Nyeema Jackson had intercepted her pass easily and scored a goal that was completely Ivy's fault. That kind of thing would just keep happening and happening, she could tell. Those other girls had been playing for so long already. She wouldn't ever catch up.

"Uh, Harrison isn't any good either, trust me," Lila said.

Ivy shifted in her seat. "Soccer's just not my thing."

"So?"

"What do you mean, *so*?"

"I mean, you don't have to be good at something to do it. And not everything you do is going to be your *passion*. Like, what even *is* your thing?"

"I'm . . ." Ivy started, but the rest of the sentence sputtered out.

"See?" Lila said. "No one has only one *thing*. And people do tons of stuff that *isn't* their thing. Like, school isn't my thing. Living in Philadelphia definitely isn't my thing. But here I am, you know? You're the one who's always encouraging me to make the most of it."

"I guess," Ivy said. But Lila was missing the point. Sure, people did all sorts of stuff they didn't love, but almost everyone Ivy knew had one main thing they were really into and really good at—usually something they'd already been doing for ages. Like art for Lila.

Lila stood up as another woman—the glamorous one with highlighted hair—stood, too. She looked back at Lila and tilted her head toward the parking lot.

"I have to go," Lila said. "Speaking of activities that are not my thing, I have a violin lesson."

Then she ripped the drawing of Josh out of her sketchbook, handed it to Ivy, and hopped off the side of the bleachers, landing with a thud.

"My gift to you," she called up. "Even if *he's* not your thing, either."

Ivy flipped the paper over fast and glanced around again to check that nobody had heard that.

"See ya, Saint Ivy!" Lila called. "Happy touch tallying!"

Ivy found herself smiling, even though she knew Lila was making fun of her. It had been nice, actually, having Lila's company.

Pretty soon, Will's team scored, and his coach took him out for a rest, which meant Ivy had nothing to keep track of. She slipped Lila's picture of Josh into her bag and pulled out her phone . . . and there it was in her inbox. A new message from the anonymous account, sent fifteen minutes before the beginning of the game.

> **To: Ivy Campbell <ivy.campbell@lelandmagnet .org>**
> **From: <downbythebay5@mailme.com>**
> **Subject: Argh**
>
> Me again!
>   Ready for some more venting? Here goes.
>   I should be used to people disappointing me by now, but I'm not. And right now I can't do anything except suck it up and pretend everything's okay. So that's what I'm going to do. But first I'll just say it.
>   People are the worst sometimes.
>   A lot of the time, it feels like.
>
>   Thanks for "listening," Saint Ivy.

Saint Ivy. Like Lila had just called her. Ivy stared at the parking lot where Lila had gone. Could the emails possibly be from her? She didn't seem particularly sad today, though. And she didn't seem like she'd confide in Ivy even if she were.

Down on the bench, Will was sitting next to Josh, who nodded at something and pointed out at the field. Goose bumps sprung up on Ivy's arms again even though the wind had died down.

Josh had been on his phone right up until the game started. He could have sent that email.

Well, whoever had sent the email needed to know *she* wouldn't disappoint them, so she typed a quick reply.

To: <downbythebay5@mailme.com>
From: Ivy Campbell <ivy.campbell@leland magnet.org>
Subject: Re: Argh

Hi, I'm really glad you wrote to me again! I'm always happy to "listen."

I get that people can be disappointing, and I'm sorry somebody let you down. Or more than one somebody, maybe. I don't think it's possible to be used to that kind of thing, though. Because if we got used to people disappointing us, then that would mean we had really low expectations, and that would be pretty sad.

I think there are lots of people who *won't* let you down. There are lots of people you

don't have to suck it up and pretend to be
okay for.

You definitely don't have to pretend to
be okay with me, just so you know. Please write
me anytime you need to!

Your friend,
Ivy

Will had gotten up and was jogging along the sideline now, getting ready to go back into the game. Josh clapped when Blake stole the ball from the other team's defender, and then he stretched his bad leg out straight in front of him.

Ivy sent the email, and a moment later, Blake scored and everybody on the bench erupted in cheers.

Everybody except Josh, who pulled out his phone.

Because he'd just gotten Ivy's message—that had to be why.

It was Josh Miller. That's who needed Ivy's help. And she wasn't going to let him down.

CHAPTER TEN

Josh's knee surgery was on Monday, and he didn't come to school all week.

The cast list for *The Wizard of Oz* went up— Peyton was Dorothy, and Kyra was Auntie Em. They were distracted by the musical all week, and Ivy was distracted wondering how Josh was doing, and listening extra carefully when she was near any of his friends to see if they'd talk about him.

She had to do *something*, so she sent another quick message to downbythebay5 on Friday morning to say she hoped everything was okay. An hour later, she got a reply.

This week has been the worst. Please send
pictures of adorable animals ASAP.

So Ivy spent recess hiding out in the bathroom,
sending the cutest, silliest photos she could find.

She wanted to do more, though. She racked her
brain for things she knew about Josh—things that
might make him happy. And she thought of Nana, saying baked goods could fix the majority of all problems.

**If you haven't gone shopping for Friday
Afternoon Baking ingredients yet, can I
make a request?** she texted Nana, and Nana replied right away.

Anything for you, Ivy girl!

So the next Monday morning, Ivy showed up
at school armed with a bag full of brookies zipped
inside her backpack, just for Josh. Brookies were one
of Nana's specialties—half brownies, half cookies.
You made two separate kinds of dough—one chocolate chip cookie dough and the other double fudge

brownie batter—and you smushed together some of each and baked them on cookie sheets.

At the student government bake sale earlier in the year, Josh had bought one of her salted dark chocolate chunk cookies and a brownie, saying it was impossible to choose between the world's most perfect desserts.

Ivy was planning to slip the bag into the little cubby under Josh's locker when the hallways were clear. She'd do it secretly, so Josh wouldn't know she'd figured out his identity and Peyton and Kyra wouldn't get upset with her.

At recess, Ivy told Kyra and Peyton she had to meet a teacher and waited until the hallways were empty. But when she snuck back to her locker to get the brookies, there was Josh, standing in front of the closed door to the history classroom and peering in the little strip of window above the doorknob.

His right leg was bandaged from underneath his athletic shorts all the way down to his ankle and striped with Velcro bands that held a bulky metal brace in place.

"What's up, Opi?" he said.

Ivy cleared her throat. "Hey! Um, how are you doing?"

Josh glanced down at his leg. "I've been better."

Right. Duh.

"Are you waiting for Ms. Ramos?"

Josh nodded. "I was already behind on assignments before I missed a whole week of school. So . . . yeah. I'm not in good shape."

He winced, and Ivy's heart ached for him. "Ms. Ramos is a hard teacher," she said.

"Probably not too hard for you, though. You're smart."

Ivy blushed. "I'm, like, medium-smart."

"I wish *I* were medium-smart. Or I wish I could get myself switched to a different history section with a teacher who doesn't think I'm a lazy jock. My dad tried to get me moved, but the school said no."

Ivy was about to say she was sure Ms. Ramos didn't think he was a lazy jock. Ms. Ramos assigned a lot of work, but she didn't play favorites. She made a big thing about how it was her job to help every single person in the class succeed. How anyone could get an A, as long as they put in the work.

But Ivy didn't want to make Josh feel worse, and then his stomach rumbled loudly.

"Did you not eat breakfast again?"

"No, I did. It was just a while ago. My knee hurts too much to stay asleep." He straightened his crutches and winced again, and there were purplish circles under his eyes.

"Actually, you know what?" Ivy said. "I have something for you!"

Her words hung there in the air between the two of them, and her heart rate sped up. Maybe this was too much, giving Josh brookies. But she took the bag out of her locker, ripped off the little note that read *Here's a little pick-me-up from an anonymous friend*, and held it out to him.

"They're called brookies," she explained. "Half brownies, half cookies."

And then the door across the hall swung open. It was the door to the guidance counselor's office, and Lila walked out. Ivy willed Lila to keep walking, straight past them, but she stood there, still.

"Wait. You made these for *me*?" Josh said. "I love brownies. And cookies!"

Ivy was way too embarrassed to hold eye contact, so she stared down at the hallway carpet. She would have said it was maroon, if somebody had asked her before this moment, but it had tiny flecks of blue, black, and yellow all mixed in.

"I heard you say that, at that bake sale. And I was baking with my nana anyway and brookies are one of her specialties. I thought they might cheer you up."

The words tumbled out in a rush. *Yeesh.* Did Ivy really have to bring up her *nana*?

But Josh smiled that cheek-dimpling, eye-squinching smile and then he leaned his torso down toward her. It took a second for her to understand that he was leaning down for a *hug.*

Josh Miller was hugging Ivy right in the middle of the hallway with Lila Britton looking on. Or . . . as close to hugging as possible, when one person is propping himself up on crutches and the other person freezes and doesn't do anything with her arms. Josh smelled like minty shampoo and laundry detergent, and Ivy's skin flushed, being that close to him. But it was just an automatic physical reaction to an unexpected hug from a boy like Josh, she figured—like shivering when the temperature drops, or sweating on a muggy day.

Then Josh took a bite of brookie, and his face lit up with delight. Ivy's heart surged because *this* was the real magic of baking. The chance to give someone else this much joy for a few seconds, even when everything else was a mess.

"These are awesome," he said. "*You're* awesome."

Ivy gulped. "Thanks. Or . . . you're welcome, I guess?"

Lila was gone now, at least. Ivy wasn't sure when she'd walked away.

Josh looked back at Ms. Ramos's door and sighed. "I have to go to the nurse to get pain meds. I guess Ms. Ramos isn't coming."

Ivy liked Ms. Ramos, but right at this moment, she was furious with her. How could she not show up when Josh was already having such a hard time?

"I'm really sorry she bailed on your appointment."

Josh adjusted his weight on the crutches. "Well, I didn't technically make an appointment. But she makes such a huge thing about how she's always available."

"Oh. Uh, yeah. I guess she does."

But what Ms. Ramos really said was that she'd always *make herself* available, so kids should email to set up a time—not that she'd just be in her room, waiting indefinitely.

Josh slid the bag of brookies into his backpack and turned so Ivy could help him zip it up. "Thanks again, Opi. This was really cool of you. Today sucks, and you made it suck less."

Today sucks, and you made it suck less.

That was almost a direct echo of the first downbythebay5 email, wasn't it? Ivy looked Josh right in the eye, searching for some kind of . . . Well, she wasn't sure what she was searching for. An acknowledgment that he was repeating what he'd written?

An inside-joke sort of smile? His face looked pretty much the same, though. Cute, tired, uncomfortable. *Poor guy*.

"I'm glad I could help," she said. "If there's anything else I can do, let me know. I'm here for you."

He smiled. "Thanks, Ivy. I might take you up on that." Then he lifted up one crutch and sort of pointed it at her. "You're awesome."

You're awesome. The words looped inside Ivy's head, making her dizzy, but in a good way.

CHAPTER ELEVEN

When Ivy joined Kyra and Peyton at lunch, Kyra was in what Will used to call Turbo Mode, talking ten miles a minute and gesturing wildly with her hands.

She was describing something funny that had happened at yesterday's rehearsal and then complaining about a fight she'd had with her sister. Peyton laughed and groaned and "Mmm-hmm'd" in all the right places, and Ivy just sat there, dunking oyster crackers into her broccoli-cheese soup and waiting to see how many minutes would go by before either of them said anything to her at all. Finally, Kyra took a breath and a big sip of lemonade, and then she turned to Ivy.

"My mom said she saw your mom at the grocery store and it's really obvious she's pregnant now, but the baby's doing well," she said.

"Oh!" Ivy had just scooped up a spoonful of soup, and she was so startled that she dropped the spoon and soup spilled all over her tray. She mopped it up with her napkin and said, "Yep. She's good. The baby's good. Everything's good."

She winced. Three *good*s in three sentences was overkill.

"My mom said your mom's tired all the time and that there's extra testing and stuff that she has to do since she's over forty. My mom said she seemed super overwhelmed."

Kyra was talking with her debate-team gotcha voice—as if she was trying to catch Ivy in a lie. Or showing off that she and her mom knew more than Ivy did. Which . . . did they?

Ivy's mom was definitely tired. But some of that was because she was so busy at work lately. The historical society had lost some funding, and there was a chance they'd have to stop some of their programming and lay off staff. So Mom was working extra hard, trying to find solutions and apply for more grants. But she hadn't said anything to Ivy about extra testing she had to have because of her age.

"How's everything going for *you*?" Peyton asked, her voice way too soft and sympathetic. Way too much emphasis on the *you*.

A moment before, Ivy had wanted Kyra and Peyton to pay attention to her . . . but not this kind of attention.

"You haven't talked about it at all," Kyra pointed out. She didn't sound triumphant or sneaky now. Just frustrated, and maybe even sad.

"There isn't really that much to say," Ivy replied. "It's an amazing thing my mom's doing. The baby's doing great. But . . . it isn't really about me."

Kyra threw her head back, as if she needed to search the cafeteria lights for some hidden source of patience before she could handle Ivy. "It *is*, though," she said. "There's no way this doesn't affect you. Why won't you talk to us for *real* for five seconds?"

But what did she expect Ivy to do? Confess every feeling she'd ever had in the middle of this loud, crowded cafeteria with her two friends who left her out of so many things so much of the time?

Ivy glanced up and saw Lila with her lunch tray, walking right toward them. She struggled to swallow. It had been the right thing to do, giving Josh those brookies. She knew it had. But it wouldn't sound like it if Lila said anything in front of Peyton and Kyra.

Was Lila going to sit with them *now*, after Ivy had invited her to join them every day for the first week of school, and every time she'd said no? What if Lila teased Ivy the way she had at the soccer game, making it seem like Ivy had a crush on Josh even though she didn't? She was almost sure she didn't.

But Lila kept walking past their table to the one behind them, and Ivy finally exhaled.

"You know what? Never mind," Kyra said. She finished her sandwich and then stood up. "Peyton and I actually have to go."

"But lunch isn't over," Ivy said. Peyton had only eaten half her bagel.

"Yeah, but we have to go to Mandarin early," Kyra said. "We have a question about the homework."

"It was really hard," Peyton mumbled. "You're lucky you take Spanish." She took a few more bites, and then they picked up their stuff and off they went.

Lila waved to Ivy from the next table and then pulled open a bag of chips. "Want one?"

Ivy watched Peyton and Kyra go, their heads angled together and their shiny, smooth hair swinging. "No thanks."

"Suit yourself. You have any more cookie-brookie-wookie things?"

Ivy's jaw tightened. She stood up and carried her tray to Lila's table, then set it down with a smack. Soup spilled over the edge of her bowl, but she didn't bother to mop it up.

"Listen. I know what you saw today, and it isn't what it looked like."

Lila raised one eyebrow. "What do you think it looked like?"

"Just . . . There's more to that situation than you understand, okay? There's a reason I baked for Josh. And it's *not* because I like him."

Lila tilted her head to the side. "Okay. What's the reason?"

Ivy sighed. "I can't really talk about it. But can you not say anything about the baking? Especially not around Kyra and Peyton."

"Sure," Lila said. "You give me some cookie-brookie-wookies, I won't say a word."

"They're called brookies and I don't have any more! I could make you some, though? Or I could make you something else. I'll bring something tomorrow. But please. Don't say anything."

Lila put down her bag of chips and held up her hands. "Whoa. I'm messing with you, Ivy. I won't say anything. I'm sorry."

Ivy's heart kept beating too quickly for a few moments, the same way it didn't slow down right away after she ran the timed mile in gym class.

"Oh. Okay. Thanks." Gradually, she started to relax.

Lila nodded. "Hey, so you were right about those magic gardens, by the way. They're nice."

"Wait, you went?" Ivy asked.

"I mean, don't get *too* excited. I didn't have anything else to do."

"But you liked it? The mosaics are amazing, right?"

"A-plus mosaics," Lila agreed. "But I also had the world's most disappointing bagel afterwards. They shouldn't be allowed to use the word *bagel* for what they sell in this city. They should call it . . . I don't know. Dry, mushy, donut-shaped bread."

Ivy laughed. "Somehow I don't think that name's going to catch on. You should try Kepners'. Their bagels are the best."

Lila raised one eyebrow again. "I have very high standards for bagels, Ivy. I'm a New Yorker."

Ivy faked a gasp. "You're kidding! I had no idea you were from New York. You only mention it *every other sentence.*"

Lila looked down. "So? I miss my city."

And . . . obviously Lila missed her city. But there

was something about the way she said it right now—no sarcasm, no bitterness. It hit Ivy in a different way, what Lila was going through. Starting eighth grade at a brand-new school in a brand-new city when eighth grade was supposed to be an ending, not a beginning.

"This must be really hard," Ivy said. "Moving here. Leaving your friends."

"Well . . . yeah." Lila opened her mouth like she was about to say something else, but then she groaned. "Busted."

Ms. Ramos was click-clacking over to their table in her low-heeled boots. Lila wasn't in Ivy's history class, but she must have been in one of Ms. Ramos's other sections, because Ms. Ramos stopped next to her and said, "Lila. We had an appointment. Did you forget?"

"Sort of?"

Ms. Ramos sighed. "Let's talk in the hallway, okay?" She gave Ivy a quick smile and walked out the cafeteria door.

Lila winced. "My parents are . . . not exactly happy about my history grades so far," she said. "Not living up to my potential and all that. Blah."

"Gotcha."

Lila rolled her eyes and stuck her tongue out to the side as if she were making fun of Ms. Ramos and herself and this whole situation. As if she didn't care about any of it. But as she followed Ms. Ramos to the hall, Ivy remembered how panicked she'd been the day she couldn't find her math textbook and didn't want the teacher to email home. And how she'd ordered Ivy not to tell her she could choose to be happy, because she couldn't. It was hard to remember sometimes, when Lila tried to look and act so tough. But she was just a person, struggling with her own stuff, doing the best she could.

When lunch was over, Ivy headed to the foreign language wing for Spanish class, and there, just ahead of her, the door to the girls' bathroom opened. Peyton and Kyra came out, their heads angled together, whispering.

They'd been in the *bathroom*, not at Mandarin.

Kyra had been so annoyed with Ivy that she'd lied to get away from her, and Peyton had just gone along.

"Ivy?" somebody said. Elias Young, filling up a bottle at the water fountain, then adjusting his glasses. Dorky-cute, Peyton had said. Maybe so. "You all right?"

"Yep!" Ivy replied.

"We have percussion ensemble at seven forty-five tomorrow morning, if you're interested."

Ivy remembered what Kyra had said. That they just needed girls.

"I'll think about it," she told him. "Thanks."

Elias smiled. "Mr. Shah usually brings donuts. In case that changes anything."

For a second, Ivy wished Peyton were here to help her make sense of this interaction. Did Elias really want *Ivy* to join percussion, or was he just being friendly or doing his part to recruit people?

But then she looked down the hallway to where Peyton and Kyra were walking into Mandarin together, arms hooked at the elbows.

She said goodbye to Elias and walked into the Spanish classroom, alone.

CHAPTER TWELVE

That night, Ivy got a text from a number she didn't recognize.

Hey Opi, it's Josh. Will gave me your number. I'm stuck on history homework. Can you video chat to help?

She smiled as she read his message and typed back, **of course!**

Instantly, her phone began ringing. She redid her ponytail, yanked on a headband to tame the frizzy front pieces, and answered.

Josh's face filled the screen. He was sitting on a couch with framed family photos on the wall behind him and the TV on in the background. Hockey, it sounded like. Ivy angled her desk chair so he wouldn't see her unmade bed.

"Thanks for saving my butt," he said.

"Sure! What are you stuck on?"

Josh took an exasperated breath that puffed up his cheeks. "This article we're supposed to read. It's so long, and I don't understand any of it. I have no idea what to take notes on."

"Okay." But . . . it wasn't *that* long, and Ms. Ramos had given them a bunch of background information in class so they'd understand the context. Maybe Josh had been in too much pain to focus? "Do you want me to go back over what Ms. Ramos said?"

"Nah, I know that stuff, but I still don't understand. If you could tell me the gist of what the article says, that'd be great. The main idea and supporting details and all that."

Oh.

That's exactly what they were supposed to take notes on. Ms. Ramos had rules about what was allowed and what wasn't if kids wanted to work together on homework. It was fine to talk through ideas, but it wasn't fine to give someone your answers. Josh was sort of asking for her answers.

"Well . . . we could read the article together, I guess? Like, I could read a paragraph out loud and then we could stop and talk about what it means, and then you could read the next? And then you could figure out the main idea and stuff on your own, once we're done."

"I don't have *time*, Ivy," Josh snapped. "I still have to finish my problem set for math, and I'm way behind in science, since I missed the lab last week. I need to do this fast, and I thought you wanted to help."

"I do! But I don't think I'm supposed to give you the answers?" Ivy wasn't sure why that came out as a question.

Josh groaned, and Ivy's heart rate sped up. He wasn't annoyed with *her*, she told herself. He was tired and hurting and frustrated that there was way too much homework this year.

"Did you read it already, but you just don't understand the details?"

If he'd already spent a lot of time on it, she could explain it a *little*. It wasn't his fault he'd hurt his knee and missed so much school.

"Yeah," Josh said. "Most of it. Yeah."

Ivy knew Ms. Ramos would want Josh to email her to tell her he was stuck. To set up an appointment tomorrow so they could go over it. Maybe that's what Ivy should suggest. But then there would be even more homework tomorrow, and he'd get even more behind.

"Look, forget it," Josh said. "It's just that you said you could help and I'm kind of desperate. I haven't done a couple of history assignments, and Ms. Ramos is going to call my parents again if I don't do a good job with this one."

His voice broke a little on the word *parents*.

In the background, the hockey announcer boomed, "Goal!" and there was a staticky burst of cheering.

This was Josh Miller, star of the middle school soccer team. Cutest boy in the eighth grade. The guy so many people had crushes on. He was letting Ivy into this private, vulnerable moment.

Other people had disappointed him—that's what the emails had said. Ivy wouldn't do that, too.

"I guess I could summarize what the article says, and then you could figure out what to write down pretty easily."

Josh's smile spread, dimpling his cheek and squinching his eyes. "Thanks, Ivy. I knew I could count on you."

Ivy dug in her backpack for the article, but the first piece of paper she pulled out was the picture of Josh that Lila had drawn at the soccer game. Yikes, she still had that in there? She put it down fast and found the right paper.

Then she went through it, telling him all the stuff that seemed most important. She told herself she wasn't exactly giving him the answers—she was just making them easier to spot. Like handing him a flashlight and telling him where to shine it.

"Thank you, Ivy," he said when she'd finished. "Seriously. Thank you so, so much."

It was only homework, she told herself. It wasn't like Josh was asking her to give him the answers for a test. He needed to know he had someone on his side, and that was more important than one night's history homework.

Ivy couldn't focus on the rest of her assignments, so she went downstairs to the kitchen for a snack. Will was there making microwave popcorn.

"You want some?" He held up the steaming bag.

"Definitely. Thanks."

He poured half the bag of popcorn into a bowl for Ivy, and she squeezed mustard into a dish for dipping. Will made a grossed-out face and poured the rest of the popcorn into his own bowl, adding Milk Duds Mom was probably saving to give out at Halloween.

"Are you really supposed to have those?" Ivy asked. "Won't the caramel stick to your braces?"

"I'll chew carefully," Will said. "You worry about you, I'll worry about me."

But that's not the way things had ever been with Ivy and Will. They worried about each other, not only themselves. Or . . . Ivy worried about Will, at least. And Will had always let her, before now.

Will sat down in his usual seat at the table and Ivy took hers across from him.

"Josh asked me for your number today." Will raised his eyebrows, which were a couple of shades blonder than the hair on his head. Ages ago, when they were little, Kyra had teased him that having blond eyebrows meant he was going to go bald someday, and he'd cried. Ivy had no idea where she'd come up with that and no idea why it had upset Will so much.

Now Will was at least three inches taller than Ivy, and Ivy hadn't seen him cry in ages. She hadn't seen him lose his temper, either. Not for months.

"Yeah. He wanted help with history homework," Ivy said.

Will didn't say anything, just ate another handful of popcorn and Milk Duds.

"Hey, does Josh know, by the way? Do Josh and Blake and the other soccer guys know about Mom and the baby?"

Will shrugged. "Probably. I don't really know."

"Wait. What do you mean, probably?"

"I told some guys on the team, right after Mom

told us. Josh and Blake weren't there, but people might have told them."

He said that offhandedly, as if he didn't care at all who knew. Even though *he* was the one who said this would make their family weirder back when Mom brought it up last year. He was the one who worried what people would think.

Ivy dropped a popcorn kernel in the mustard, submerging it completely, when she only liked to dip the top.

"You told 'some guys on the team'?" Her words came out sharp. Like an accusation. She tried to soften her voice. "I just . . . I thought you didn't want to talk about it. Like, with anybody. At all."

Will took another bite before he answered. He was more interested in this snack that *definitely* violated orthodontic protocol than this conversation, and that made Ivy want to rip the bowl out of his hands and dump it all over the floor.

"I don't want to talk about it with them," he said.

So calmly. Who was this calm giant, and where was her brother who never hid what he was feeling and *needed* her?

"I just said, 'This is what's happening, and I don't really want to get into it, but pretty soon you'll notice anyway, so I'm letting you know.'"

Ivy nodded. That was sort of what she'd said to Kyra and Peyton, too, actually.

"Well, good for you. That you said that." It sounded like she was being sarcastic, but she didn't mean it that way. "Really."

"Dr. Banks helped me figure out what to say."

"That's great." And it *was* great that Will was being so well-adjusted about all this. Ivy couldn't get upset that he was managing without her. That wouldn't be fair.

"Okay, well. I'm gonna go watch the Flyers game," Will said.

He ambled out of the kitchen, bringing the rest of his snack along. Lately, he sometimes reminded Ivy of the baby giraffe they used to love to see at the zoo when they were younger. A little confused about how much space his limbs took up now that he'd gotten so tall all of a sudden, and a little awkward in his movements. Her heart swelled with affection for him.

Mom came in then. "Mmm, popcorn," she said, and Ivy pushed her bowl forward to share. Mom liked to dip hers in mustard, too.

"How's it going, Ives?" she said. "Tell me things."

Tell me things.

Ivy had no idea where to start. She couldn't remember the last time she'd really, *really* talked to Mom.

Mom rubbed one hand over her round, growing belly, and the tiny, tender gesture made Ivy's throat go tight and dry. Ivy thought of all those things Kyra had said at lunch, about what her mom had told her.

Mom had no idea how strained things were with Kyra and Peyton. She had no idea about the emails. She would be so completely confused if she knew Ivy had video chatted with Josh Miller.

Too many feelings broiled inside Ivy's stomach, like butter melting over a too-hot burner, beginning to bubble and turn brown.

She didn't trust herself to start talking to Mom right now when she had no idea what words would come out.

"Not much to tell!" she said. "You can finish the popcorn."

And she tried not to notice how disappointed Mom looked as she left the room.

CHAPTER THIRTEEN

The next morning, Kyra apologized.

"I shouldn't have pushed you like that yester-day," she said. "If you don't want to talk to us about your mom, it's fine. I'm sorry I got so frustrated."

"Oh. It's okay!" Ivy said quickly.

Nana would tell her not to do that. Not to say something was okay when it wasn't—when it felt terrible lately to wonder when she was going to do something Kyra found unbearably exasperating. But that was the default reply when somebody said sorry. And anyway, maybe things *could* be okay. "I appreci-ate you saying that," she added, because that, at least, was a hundred percent true.

And things were better, the whole rest of the week. Maybe Kyra and Peyton hadn't lied about having to see their Mandarin teacher after all. Maybe they'd asked their question quickly and then gone to the bathroom. Maybe their teacher hadn't been in her classroom.

On the way to school on Friday, it occurred to Ivy that it was October, and every October, she and Kyra went to the haunted house at the Eastern State Penitentiary—the giant, castle-like building that used to be a jail but was now just a tourist attraction. She was going to find Kyra and Peyton first thing, she decided, and ask if they wanted to go over the weekend.

But as she walked through the eighth-grade hallway, she got distracted. She kept hearing Sydney DelMonte's name, and her boyfriend Patrick's name, too.

People were saying something about Patrick playing terribly at a big soccer game, letting in a bunch of goals.

"Poor guy," Chloe was saying to her friends, Morgan and Nora. "I heard the coach from Penn was there, too, and he tanked."

"That's so sad," Morgan said.

Chloe nodded. "I can't believe Sydney did that. Ugh, and she always acts like she's so perfect and sweet. What a fake."

Ivy lingered near Chlo-Mo-No, trying to hear more, but then Morgan noticed her watching and elbowed Chloe, who said, "Yes? Did you need something?" And Ivy hustled off.

Had Sydney broken up with Patrick, then? Ivy was busy trying to figure out why that would make Sydney a fake, so she was startled when someone called her name.

"Ivy Campbell, just the person I've been looking for!" Lila Britton was standing in front of Ivy's locker, hugging her sketchbook.

That was a surprise. "Were you hoping I brought baked goods?" Ivy asked.

Lila placed one hand over her heart. "Ivy! How dare you assume that I'm only coming over to talk to you because I want something!" She was chewing bright pink gum, even though gum wasn't allowed at school. "Although technically I'm only coming over to talk to you because I want something."

Ivy laughed. "What's up?"

"What are you doing after school today? Any chance I can tag along?" Lila blew a bubble, which got caught on the tip of her nose and slowly deflated.

"You want to hang out with me?"

"Weeeelll, I sort of told my moms I had plans with a friend because they were all worked up about how I'm not making an effort to get to know anybody here. So now I kinda need a plan, and I thought of you."

Ivy opened her locker and put away the books she didn't need for the morning. "I'm going to my nana's," she said. "We bake every Friday afternoon."

"Perfect!" Lila said. "I love baking and other people's nanas!"

"Um, you do?"

"Well, I love baked goods. And chances are pretty decent that I'll like your grandmother better than I like my own. My grandma's kind of a jerk."

Ivy closed her locker. How was she supposed to respond to that? Who called their own grandma a jerk?

"Come on, Saint Ivy, I'm desperate here." Lila steepled her fingers together, pleading.

"Okay, okay. I'll text my nana to ask."

"Yes! Baking-with-Ivy's-nana high five!" Lila cheered, holding up her hand.

Chlo-Mo-No walked past, and Chloe mumbled, "So odd."

"What, you want a high five, too?" Lila asked Chloe.

And to Ivy's surprise, Chloe cracked up. "You're so *weird*, Lila," she said. Nora told her not to be mean, but Lila didn't seem to care.

"I'd rather be weird than a lot of other things!" Lila called.

"I've noticed!" Chloe yelled back. Her voice wasn't entirely unfriendly when she said it.

Ivy heard the rest of the Sydney-and-Patrick story at lunch from Kyra and Peyton, who had heard it from Nora. They were sort of friends with her now, since she was in the play, too.

"She cheated on him with that guy she used to work with at the fro-yo place," Kyra reported. "You know, the cute one who plays baseball at St. Peter's Prep?"

Damian. That was his name. He had brown skin, buzzed black hair, a big smile, and really muscly arms. He was so good-looking that Kyra had forgotten a spoon the last time she and Ivy had gone for frozen yogurt, and he was nice, too. Sydney had introduced him and Ivy once, and after that he always called Ivy by name.

"That's just a rumor, though," Peyton said. "I feel like we shouldn't spread it."

Kyra leaned in and lowered her voice. "No, I heard

Blake talking about it in study hall. He said Patrick literally walked in on them."

Ivy gasped.

"I know. So dramatic, right?" Kyra said. "Like a movie."

Ivy shook her head. "That doesn't sound like Sydney."

"Because you know Sydney so well?" Kyra's Styrofoam-on-Styrofoam voice was back, so Ivy changed the subject.

"Hey, we should go to the haunted house, don't you think?" she asked. "This weekend?"

"Ooh, that sounds fun," Peyton said.

"Definitely," Kyra agreed. "I don't know if this weekend works. But soon."

"Oh." Ivy swallowed down her disappointment. "Okay. Soon."

After school, Kyra and Peyton headed to rehearsal and Ivy and Lila took the bus together.

Along the way, Ivy pointed out the library, her favorite bagel place, and the penitentiary where the haunted house was.

"Hold up, there's a haunted house at a *jail*?"

Ivy tried to explain that it wasn't an active jail—just a cool, spooky old building.

"This city," Lila said. "So weird."

"Hey, I thought you liked weird stuff," Ivy pointed out, and Lila made her eyes huge.

"There's *interesting* weird, and then there's *hanging-out-at-a-creepy-old-prison* weird," she said, which made Ivy laugh.

The bus passed the frozen yogurt place next, and Ivy leaned toward the window and tried to stare inside the store, as if there might be some evidence of whatever had happened between Sydney and Damian nestled among the self-serve toppings.

When they made it to Nana's and got off the elevator on the twenty-first floor, Nana was standing in the hallway as usual, wearing her bright pink F.A.B. apron.

She gave Ivy a sticky-lipstick cheek kiss, and then she leaned right in to hug Lila, who stiffened for a second but didn't pull away. And in the Nana-est of all Nana-ish things, she held up two purple F.A.B. aprons—one for Ivy and a second one for Lila.

"This is for you," she told Lila. "Your own fab-ulous Friday Afternoon Baking apron!"

"Nana, she's not coming every Friday. It's only one day."

Nana waggled a pink-manicured finger. "Don't be rude, Ivy. That's no way to welcome a guest."

Lila elbowed her. "Yeah, Ivy. Don't be rude."

"I just . . . How did you possibly have time to get a third apron when you've only known Lila was coming for, like, seven hours?"

"Oh, I have tons of these things," Nana replied. "I accidentally ordered twelve instead of two. You can have pink if you prefer, Lila. Or one of each! Entirely up to you."

"Purple's good!" Lila said, shimmying into the apron and spinning around so Ivy could tie the back.

They headed into the kitchen, and Lila paused in front of the big window. Nothing else in the neighborhood was anywhere near as high as Nana's apartment building—not even the trees. Looking out, you could see block after block of restaurants and shops and houses and parks. New-construction homes like Kyra's and Dad and Leo's stuck out, all angular and bright amid the older row houses, but everything looked tiny from this high up.

"Nice view," Lila said.

"The units on the other side of the building have the *really* nice views," Nana replied. Those were the "high-rent" units, according to Nana, and they looked out at the sprawling art museum and the Schuylkill River, with its tree-lined path. "But this isn't bad, either. I was in a house in the suburbs my whole adult life, but I'm done checking my own gutters and shoveling my front walk. I'd rather die in a high-rise where somebody will notice if I don't come out of my apartment."

Sheesh, there she went with the morbidity.

"Nana, don't scare Lila." Ivy pulled Lila away from the window and toward the counter, where Nana had set out the ingredients for today's recipe: a bowl of apples, a bottle of orange juice, vegetable oil, and a tube pan. "Jewish apple cake?" Ivy guessed.

"Got it in one!" Nana said.

Nana had an actual recipe this time, written in her mother's swoopy script on yellowing paper, so Ivy began to copy straight from that, adding Nana's expert advice: how it was important to use a tube pan—which looked kind of like a Bundt cake pan but straighter—because the cake didn't have enough flour to hold its own shape. How the cake was good on the first day, better on the second, and best on the third, so if you were making it for a special occasion, you should bake it ahead of time. And how Nana liked to cover it with foil for half the baking time so the top didn't get too brown.

Lila leaned in to read the original recipe over Ivy's shoulder. "Wait, I know this cake. I . . . Someone in my family used to make this. This same exact recipe. The orange juice and vegetable oil and all of it. Except he called it Dutch apple cake. He said it was a Pennsylvania Dutch thing."

Ivy thought Nana would tell Lila she was mistaken, but instead, Nana said, "Sure. Jewish apple cake, Dutch apple cake, German apple cake—all the same thing."

"Wait, really?" Ivy asked.

Nana nodded. "I don't know who started making it first, but we've all claimed it."

"Huh." Ivy was a little disappointed, honestly. The cake was delicious no matter what it was called, but Ivy liked when Nana's recipes were linked to Jewish traditions.

Nana said it didn't matter that Dad had grown up Presbyterian instead of Jewish, or that Mom wasn't observant and Ivy hadn't gone to Hebrew school and barely ever went to synagogue. Nana said being Jewish was still part of Ivy's identity, and she didn't have to say she was "half this" or "not really that"; she could embrace *all* the parts of herself. That wasn't always easy—especially last year, when there had been bar and bat mitzvahs almost every other weekend and Ivy had felt so conscious about all the things she didn't know and the hard work she hadn't done. But

Ivy liked baking Jewish recipes and lighting Hanukkah candles and eating matzah at Passover. She liked learning about Jewish foods and traditions because she liked being connected to that part of Nana—to that part of her*self*.

"I wonder where the recipe really comes from," Ivy said. "And how it spread so much."

"You should look into it with your mom!" Nana suggested. "That's right up her alley."

Ivy smiled. "Research is her superpower."

Mom had a T-shirt from her grad school days that said that: *Research is my superpower.* Dad had given it to her ages ago, when they first started dating—back when he was finishing medical school, and she was getting her master's degree in history.

"Really," Nana urged. "Your mom would love a project with you."

"Sure, maybe," Ivy said. "Anyway, I'll write that down, too. About all the different names."

Ivy copied down the end of the recipe, and the three of them finished peeling and chopping the apples, which they tossed in sugar and cinnamon. They sifted the dry ingredients, whisked the wet ones, and mixed everything together.

Next, they layered the ingredients into the tube pan: half the batter, half the apples, the rest of the batter, and the second half of the apples, and they put the pan into the oven to bake. Nana excused herself to get changed for her Friday night dinner plans with her neighbors, and Ivy and Lila offered to clean up.

"I'll scrub dishes, you dry?" Ivy suggested, handing Lila a dish towel. They got into a good rhythm, moving quickly through the bowls and spoons. "You okay?" Ivy asked, because Lila had been strangely quiet the whole time they'd been at Nana's.

"Mmm-hmm."

That wasn't particularly convincing, but Ivy didn't want to push. "Well, just warning you, Nana probably won't let us eat any of this cake when it comes out of the oven."

Lila paused halfway through drying a whisk. "Wait, what?"

"You heard her, about how the cake isn't as good the first day. She's going to make us wait a day or two. That's what she did when we made sour cream coffee cake."

Lila's mouth fell open. "But she'll let us take some with us, right? So we'll just eat it after we leave."

"She'll find out and take away your apron," Ivy joked, and Lila laughed.

Sometimes, when something funny caught Lila off guard, her laugh was high and musical, like chimes. Kyra and Peyton hadn't laughed at Ivy's jokes much lately. It was nice that Lila did.

Nice enough that Ivy asked, "Hey. Who's the person who used to make Dutch apple cake?"

Lila's smile disappeared, and she stepped away from the sink, as if she needed to put physical distance between herself and Ivy's question.

"I didn't mean to upset you," Ivy said. "You don't have to—"

"I'm not upset," Lila said. But she kept tucking the longer side of her hair behind her ear, again and again, even though it wouldn't stay.

The timer went off, which meant it was time to take the foil off the top of the cake, and Ivy was glad to have a task. She put on Nana's blue-and-white-checked oven mitts and opened the oven door. Apple-spiced heat whooshed out. She breathed it in as she plucked off the foil and snuck a look at Lila, who was very focused on drying a spoon that was already completely dry.

Ivy went back to the sink, gently took the spoon from Lila's hands, and set it on the drying rack.

"You know what? You're right," she said. "The cake smells way too good to wait two days to eat. We should at least have a little as soon as we leave today."

"Okay, thank goodness!" Lila smiled, and Ivy relaxed. "You promise you won't tell Nana on me?"

"Promise," Ivy confirmed, and she started washing a measuring cup.

A little while later, when the cake finished baking and Ivy took it out of the oven, Nana bustled in, wearing a black sweaterdress with a bright pink scarf.

"Mmm, smells divine, looks even better," she said. "Now, as soon as this cools, we'll pack some up for you to take home. But remember: Wait until at least tomorrow to dig in. Sunday, ideally."

Ivy and Lila exchanged a look.

"Got it, Nana!" Ivy said.

A little while later, Lila went to use the bathroom, and Nana put her hand on Ivy's shoulder. "Your mom really would love to research the history of Jewish apple cake with you, I'll bet."

Ivy's hands clenched into fists. Why was Nana pushing this?

"She's busy with all these grant applications and things for work. And she's tired all the time."

Nana adjusted her scarf and gave Ivy's shoulder a squeeze.

"Your mom will never be too busy or too tired for you, sweet girl. But she might have a harder time than usual figuring out what you need right now, with everything that's going on. So if there's something you want—something that would make things easier—you let her know. Okay?"

Ivy swallowed down a lump in her throat. "I don't need anything. Things aren't hard."

And they weren't. Ivy was so lucky in so many ways. Things were so much harder for so many other people. Like Lila, who'd had to move for eighth grade and had almost cried when Ivy asked her who used to make apple cake.

"Just think about it," Nana said.

And then Lila came back, and Nana patted Ivy's cheek once and then started dividing up the cake.

CHAPTER FOURTEEN

After Ivy and Lila left Nana's apartment, they each scarfed down a piece of apple cake in the lobby of Nana's building, giggling as they ate. They said good-bye and Ivy was about to head home when she realized she didn't have the packet she needed for her history homework. It was only a twenty-minute walk to school, but Mom didn't like her walking that far by herself.

She checked the time. Will's soccer practice was about to end, and Mom would be leaving work to pick him up soon. Ivy was starting to text him to see if he could get the packet from her locker when she noticed Nana's apartment-building shuttle in the circle out front. The shuttle took residents into Center City, and there was a stop right by school. So Ivy texted Mom that she'd meet her and Will there to head home together, and five minutes later, the shuttle driver dropped her off. She passed the bench where Sydney had been crying all those weeks before.

Poor Sydney. Or, poor Patrick. Or both, maybe?

Ivy flashed her ID at the after-school guy at the back door and jogged up the stairs to grab what she needed. Then she went back out and sat on Sydney's bench to wait for Mom and Will.

A familiar car pulled up in the pickup line—Kyra's mom's maroon SUV. And then Kyra and Peyton came out from rehearsal and headed to the car. Together.

Kyra opened the back door and slid in first. Peyton noticed Ivy right before she got in, and she waved. Ivy just sat there, frozen, not picking up her hand to wave back until the car was long gone.

Kyra had said she didn't think this weekend would work for the haunted house at the penitentiary. Ivy had assumed that meant she had family stuff, but it must have meant she only wanted to hang out with Peyton.

Peyton sent a text. **Sorry! My parents are away this weekend so they asked Kyra's parents if I could stay there. Didn't mean to leave you out!**

Right.

But Peyton's parents had gone away one time last year. Peyton had spent the night at *Ivy's* house, and they'd invited Kyra to come, too.

Ivy supposed it was nice that Peyton hadn't *meant* to leave her out . . . but not as nice as if Peyton had done something to make sure Ivy would be included.

After a moment, Ivy heard the click and swing of crutches on pavement, and then Josh Miller sat down next to her.

"You look like you've had a rough afternoon," he said.

Ivy shrugged. "Just a rough last couple of minutes."

"I'm jealous, then." Josh rested his crutches against the bench, in the space between them.

What were the rules for where to look when you were sitting side by side instead of across from somebody? This close, with a light shining above them, Ivy could see that Josh had freckles on his cheeks. Just a sprinkling, with a few that were darker than the rest, like dots somebody had made with a pen amid a bunch of pencil marks. She wasn't sure if she should try to make eye contact or not.

"Rough afternoon for you?" she asked.

"Rough week. Rough *lots* of weeks."

Ivy focused her eyes on the handles of his crutches. "What's going on? I mean, I know your knee, obviously. But . . . is there something else, too?"

Josh counted off on his fingers. "My knee. No soccer. My parents getting divorced. My dad . . . Well, you've seen my dad at soccer games, right? You know what he's like."

Ivy thought back to that game when his dad had screamed at the ref. Josh's little sister had been there, and she'd cried when her dad had left the field, muttering curse words and insults under his breath. He hadn't even said goodbye to her.

"I'm really sorry," Ivy said.

Josh kicked the end of one of his crutches with his good leg. "Whatever. You've been through the divorce thing. It's not like it makes me special or unusual or anything, having my parents split up."

"But you're still allowed to be upset about it."

Ivy's words rang in her ears. She was echoing something both Mom and Dad had said to her multiple times back when they separated. Nana, too.

It's okay to grieve for the family we used to be. Change is hard. Give yourself space to be sad.

But it wasn't like she'd lost Dad the way Mom had lost *her* father when she was little, when he'd left Nana and moved far away. It's not even like the divorce was bitter.

"I'm not upset that he moved out," Josh said. "My parents fought all the time. If anything I'm surprised they stayed together so long. It's more that my dad . . . Ever since the knee thing, he's been . . ."

Josh trailed off and shook his head. Then he straightened his crutches and pushed himself up to standing.

"I gotta go. My mom and sister are here," he said, pointing at the curb. "Anyway. Thanks again for your help with history the other day. Ms. Ramos sent my mom a nice email instead of a mad one, saying she could tell I'd tried."

Ivy felt a little bit sick, since he really *hadn't* tried. But she pressed the toes of her sneakers into the ground, hard. It hadn't been a big deal, what she'd done. It had been worth it.

"Wait, Josh?" she called. "If you want to talk more about . . . what we were just talking about, with your dad. You have my number. And my email."

She studied his face in the semidarkness, waiting to see if he'd react to the mention of email, but his expression didn't change.

"Okay," he said. "Well, see ya. Thanks."

And later that night, the next anonymous message showed up.

To: Ivy Campbell <ivy.campbell@lelandmagnet.org>
From: <downbythebay5@mailme.com>
Subject: Here we go again

You know what's weird? How you can be okay with something . . . like, you can be almost completely functional and think you're doing fine, and then some little thing happens and *bam*. You're not okay at all. One tiny thing throws everything off. But then it takes ten zillion tiny things to claw your way out of the funk. Not fair at all, right?

Have a good weekend, Saint Ivy.

She read the email again and again, but it didn't offer up any more information than Josh had already given her. *Something* had put him in a bad mood today. But how could Ivy help in any meaningful way when she had no idea *what*?

She could tell him something vague and validating, like she had in her other emails. But how many times could she say the same thing?

Josh had been about to talk to her for real before

his mom showed up to get him—Ivy was almost positive he had. So she decided to be brave and give him a little push now.

> **To: <downbythebay5@mailme.com>**
> **From: Ivy Campbell <ivy.campbell@leland**
> **magnet.org>**
> **Subject: Re: Here we go again**
>
> Hi. I will do as many of the ten zillion things as
> I can to help you claw your way out of the funk.
> But it might help if I knew what's actually going
> on with you and what tiny thing made everything
> feel awful.
>   Will you tell me?

The reply was immediate and three words long: **Sorry. I can't.**

Those three words squeezed all the air out of Ivy's lungs. Josh was shutting her down. He wasn't ready. She shouldn't have pushed at all. It was hard for boys, maybe, to talk about stuff like this. She wrote back immediately, apologizing for asking. Saying the nice, nonspecific things she should have said to begin with.

She hit *Refresh* over and over and over, but nothing from downbythebay5 showed up. Not that night, not the whole rest of the weekend.

CHAPTER FIFTEEN

On Sunday, in between obsessively checking her email, Ivy saw Sydney. It was only for a minute, when she and Will were leaving Dad and Leo's and Sydney was coming back from a walk with her dog, Baxter. Sydney wore a big sweatshirt with the hood pulled tight around her face and no makeup. Ivy almost didn't recognize her.

Baxter scampered over to Ivy and Will and they both leaned down to pet him, but Sydney didn't stop to chat the way she usually did.

"Hey, Ivy. Hey, Will. Baxter, come on." She tugged his leash until he followed her up the stairs to the Del-Montes' house.

"You heard about her and Patrick?" Will asked once Sydney and Baxter were inside.

"I heard they broke up," Ivy said. "I heard she cheated on him?"

They walked to the end of the street and turned onto the main road. "That's what Blake said. With that guy Damian from the fro-yo place. He was really mad."

Ivy blinked. "Who was he mad at?"

Will looked at her, blond eyebrows raised, like it should have been obvious. "*Sydney*. For cheating on Patrick."

"But she's his sister."

"That doesn't mean he can't be mad at her," Will pointed out.

As they crossed the street, Ivy thought of all the times she'd seen Patrick at the DelMontes' house. "I guess Blake was close with Patrick, too."

Will nodded. "He said they were supposed to go to the Eagles game today, but now that's not happening. Blake was calling Sydney . . ." He paused, and his face flashed red. "I don't want to say it, what he was calling her. She's always been so nice, you know?"

"She's still nice," Ivy said quickly.

But she thought about what Sydney had told her

that day when she was crying: that maybe she wasn't the same person she used to be.

Had she already cheated on Patrick then—is that why she'd said that? And if she had . . . did that change who she was, at her core?

Ivy thought of Mom's framed print, *Wherever you go, there you are.* Was that not really true, that no matter what happened, people stayed the same deep down?

Did people actually change in all sorts of huge, disappointing ways?

Josh was absent from school on Monday and Tuesday. Ivy was worried something might be really wrong, so she emailed downbythebay5 again on Tuesday night.

To: <downbythebay5@mailme.com>
From: Ivy Campbell <ivy.campbell@leland magnet.org>
Subject: thinking of you

You don't have to tell me anything you don't want to tell me. But can you just let me know if you're okay and if there's anything I can do?

The reply came fast, at least:

To: Ivy Campbell <ivy.campbell@lelandmagnet
.org>
From: <downbythebay5@mailme.com>
Subject: Re: thinking of you

I'm okay. And don't think so. But thanks, Saint Ivy.

And then Josh was back in school on Wednesday and acting normal, flirting with Chlo-Mo-No and joking around with Blake. He barely talked to Ivy at all, but he was coughing in history class, so maybe he'd been sick.

Ivy had student government meetings at lunch every day that week, since they were getting ready for the Thanksgiving food-and-coat drive. She had sat with Elias on Monday and apologized for not going to percussion ensemble the morning he'd invited her. She'd completely forgotten about it, actually. "Oh!" he said, like maybe he'd forgotten he'd told her she should come. "No worries." So Kyra was probably right that he was only doing his part to recruit girls and he didn't actually like her. He'd probably sound more disappointed if he did.

At end of the day on Wednesday, Peyton caught up

with Ivy in the hallway. Peyton always wore a necklace that had been her mom's, with a small round charm in the front, and she twisted the charm one way and then the other.

"Are you upset with me and Kyra?" she asked. "I know you said you have student government and I saw you guys hanging all those posters, but . . . are you avoiding us?"

"Oh! No, I'm not avoiding you," Ivy replied. But the truth was, she'd been grateful for a break from sitting with them in the cafeteria.

"I'm not trying to, like, box you out of being best friends with Kyra," Peyton said. "I miss you. I have no idea what's going on with you. I want to catch up."

Ivy's body relaxed a tiny bit. "I miss you, too."

It was around this time last year that they'd become really good friends, actually—the late fall. They'd known each other a little in sixth grade, but then they'd gotten partnered up on a science project around Halloween, and they'd spent a bunch of time together over Thanksgiving break when Kyra was in Virginia seeing her grandparents.

"What's going on with you?" Ivy asked. "How's the play? How's everything else?"

Peyton bit her bottom lip and twisted the charm on her necklace again. Kyra was such a fast talker and thinker. You asked her a question, you got a response in an instant. But Peyton took her time when she had something important to say. She took a deep breath and opened her mouth . . . and right then, Ivy heard the click, clack, swing of crutches behind her and she couldn't help it—she whipped her head around to look at Josh.

She wanted to know what Peyton was about to say—she really, *really* did—but she also needed to see if Josh would make eye contact with her this time. To see if she could somehow silently communicate to him that she was still here for him.

Josh gave her and Peyton a quick nod before he disappeared around the corner, and whatever Peyton had been about to say disappeared, too.

"Do you like Josh?" Peyton asked.

"What? No!"

"It's okay if you do." Peyton picked at a tiny fleck of leftover blue polish on her thumbnail. "I don't have any claim on him. He barely talks to me this year. But if you like him . . . I want to hear it from you. So I don't have to wonder."

Ivy's cheeks flamed. "I don't like Josh."

"Okay," Peyton said, but her voice was high and tight. "Well, I have to get to rehearsal. I'll see you later."

And then she left and Lila was there, slinging an arm around Ivy's shoulders.

"I've got some bad news," Lila announced. "I've got a violin lesson on Friday, so I can't make it to Friday Afternoon Baking. Do you want to break it to Nana or should I?"

Ivy laughed, loud and surprised. It felt good to laugh.

"I think *somehow* we'll manage without you. But come another Friday, if you want."

"Sure thing," Lila said.

Lila waited while Ivy packed her things and they walked outside together. They weren't for-real friends, but still—Lila's company distracted her from thinking about the way Josh was still mostly ignoring her and Peyton had shut down from what she'd been about to say. So that was something.

CHAPTER SIXTEEN

On Friday, Ms. Ramos assigned a take-home history test. She said she was required to give at least one major test each term, but she wanted to teach critical thinking and genuine research skills, not rote memorization.

So kids could study with other people as much as they wanted, but once they looked at the test, they were on their own. They had to mark their start and end time, and they had two hours to finish. They could type their answers, and they could even look up information. They just needed to show that they could "find, synthesize, and analyze" information independently, within a relatively short time.

Dad and Leo were away at one of Dad's medical

conferences on Saturday and Will was at his best friend Langston's, so Mom helped Ivy study. The two of them ate mustard-dipped popcorn and talked about all the stuff Ivy had been learning, and Ivy felt closer to Mom than she had in a long time, even though they only really talked about history.

She took the test Sunday morning, and then she and Mom went to Will's soccer game. They dropped him off for warm-ups and claimed a spot on the sideline.

Mom was almost at the twenty-week halfway point of pregnancy now, and she was really showing. Not as much with her jacket on, but everyone seemed to know. A few other moms stopped to ask how she was feeling and to say how incredible she was for what she was doing. One made some completely obnoxious comments about how she knew there were celebrities who paid other people to have babies for them, but she'd never heard of any regular people who used surrogates.

Ivy's mouth dropped open. People used surrogates if they wanted biological children and that was the only way they could have them, not because they just didn't want to be pregnant. And Erin and Christopher weren't paying Mom, but even if they had been, so what? Ivy had done a bunch of research last spring, and she'd read about some people who were "compensated surrogates," meaning they got paid. They were just looking for a way to earn money by doing something that made a huge, positive difference for other people.

But Mom plastered a smile on her face, squeezed Ivy's hand, and said how grateful she was that she could do this for her friends. Ivy got the impression it wasn't the first time somebody had said something this rude and clueless to Mom about the pregnancy, and she squeezed Mom's hand back, tight.

Lila wasn't at the game today, and Josh was on the bench by himself. He was paging through a notebook, but the paper kept ruffling in the breeze. He looked back over his shoulder, spotted Ivy, and motioned her over.

Her heart raced as she stood.

"Um . . . I'm just going to . . . I need to talk to Josh Miller for a second," she said to Mom, who was talking to Mrs. DelMonte now, and she hustled off before Mom had a chance to respond.

"Take a seat," Josh said. "How's it going?"

It was probably against some rule to sit on the team's bench when she was definitely not on the team, but she sat anyway.

"Fine," she replied. "How about you?"

"I have a favor to ask," Josh said. He glanced around to make sure no one was listening and lowered his voice. "It's . . . kind of a big thing. It's just . . . the take-home test."

"Oh. I'm so sorry. I wish I could help you study, but I already took it."

Josh stretched his bad leg out in front of him. "That's okay, actually. That you've taken it."

He dug his hands down into the pockets of his team sweatshirt, which wasn't anywhere near warm enough for the weather. He must be cold, and he still had a cough. She wanted to bring him a blanket, maybe some tea.

"I was wondering if there's any way you could share a few of your answers with me," Josh said.

Ivy's mouth fell open. "You want me to show you my answers for the *test*?"

Josh shushed her. "Not all of them. Just, like, for the last three long-answer questions."

The coach called out instructions to the team, and somebody else's parents were chatting with Mom now. Ivy's brain spun and spun and spun.

"I know it's a lot to ask," Josh said.

As if Ivy were hesitating because of the *size* of the request. She would have baked him a hundred more batches of brookies. She would have stayed up all night on video chat with him, letting him vent about his dad and his knee and anything else. But this was cheating. On an actual *test*. That counted for a huge percentage of their grade.

"I don't know what to do." His voice broke, and his eyes looked so tired. "My dad wants me to go to this private high school he and all my uncles went to, and he thought I'd get in because of soccer. But now that I'm hurt and the coach can't see me play, he thinks my grades are too low. And Ms. Ramos keeps giving us more and more work and I can't do it all." He coughed again, then swigged some water.

"That sounds like a lot of pressure," Ivy said.

"Yes! My dad's been MIA since I got hurt, except to nag me about school." He pounded a fist against the metal bench. "He mostly was MIA before, except he'd show up at games when I could still play. But he's supposed to come over tonight, take us to my sister's favorite restaurant for her birthday . . ." *Pound. Pound. Pound.* "But he and my mom got this email from Ms. Ramos about the take-home test and how I have to do well on it. He said he's going to check my answers the second he walks in the door, and if I haven't finished the test and done a good job, then he'll leave."

"He wouldn't take your sister out without you?"

Josh shook his head. "He thinks it'll give me *added accountability*, knowing I'll be letting her down." Extra-loud *pound*.

Ivy thought about when her own dad had moved out. How he'd tried extra hard to be around for everything. All the things he'd done to make it clear how much he loved Ivy and Will. It wasn't Josh's fault he didn't have a nice dad like Ivy did.

But . . . the rules for the test were clear. They weren't even allowed to *talk* about it once they'd seen the questions.

"I won't read your answers." Josh held up one hand like a pledge. "I promise. If you email them to me, I'll literally cut and paste them into my document so my dad thinks I finished the test on my own, and then as soon as we get home from dinner, I'll delete them and do the questions myself. I'll delete your whole email."

On the field, the forwards started taking shots on goal. Blake kicked the ball too high, and it sailed over the net. Lila's brother ran after it.

What Josh wanted to do was still against the rules. Josh was supposed to finish the whole test within two hours. But Ivy couldn't control whether or not he lied about when he started and finished, and maybe she *could* control whether or not Josh's sister got to have dinner with her father for her birthday. Maybe she *could* control whether or not Josh had to be the one to let her down.

"You're sure your dad will read your answers? You couldn't paste in something else to make it seem like it's done, or—"

"He doesn't trust me. He'll at least skim them."

On the field, the ref walked to the center line and called for the captains. Josh was captain, usually, but Blake had taken over.

Ivy had specifically told Josh she'd do anything she could to help him. He was opening up to her, just like she'd wanted him to. Sending him these answers wasn't right, but helping someone who needed help definitely *was*.

"Okay," Ivy finally said. "I'll do it."

Josh's breath whooshed out in a puff.

"I don't know what I'd do without you, Ivy," he said. "Thank you so, so much."

CHAPTER SEVENTEEN

Thursday was the day of Mom's twenty-week ultrasound, and Ivy woke up way before her alarm went off that morning.

She'd looked at that baby development site again last night before bed, so she knew a lot—maybe too much—about what was happening with the baby and what would happen at the ultrasound.

She knew that at twenty weeks, the baby was the size of a sweet potato, which wasn't all that helpful, since sweet potatoes didn't come in one standard size. She knew that the ultrasound technician would check to see that the baby was growing right by measuring the heart, kidneys, brain, lungs, bones, and on and on . . . There were *so* many organs that had to grow at the right rate and develop all the right functions.

The sites she'd looked at said the same things Dad had, about how unlikely it was for anything to be "significantly" wrong at this phase, if all the previous tests had been normal. But what about Mom's hormone levels being off at the beginning?

And a less than one percent chance of things being wrong sounded tiny until you thought about just how many people were pregnant in the world at any given second. One percent of all those people wasn't a tiny number at all.

Ivy knew she wouldn't fall back to sleep, so she tiptoed down to the kitchen and searched the fridge and cupboards.

They had everything she needed for those superfood muffins, so she lined up ingredients and bowls and measuring cups and spoons, and she let the predictable, soothing routine of baking wash over her, relaxing her muscles and slowing her breath. She tried out a new tip she'd learned from Nana: to start the oven at a higher temperature for five minutes and then lower it for the rest of the baking time, because that made the muffins rise higher.

And pretty soon, the muffins were ready. Puffy

and sweet-smelling and perfect. Ivy set them out on the table once they cooled.

When Mom came downstairs, Ivy announced, "I made superfood muffins for your big day!"

Mom's eyes glossed over with tears and she hugged Ivy, which felt a little strange now, since there was this firm, budding round belly between them . . . but *good* strange, actually. Like as long as things were okay today—which they *had* to be—then this pregnancy could bring them together as easily as it could wedge them apart.

"Can I touch your stomach?" Ivy asked.

"Oh! Of course," Mom said.

So Ivy put her hand right above Mom's belly button.

"Can you feel the baby?" she asked. "Kicking and moving around?"

The baby site said most women felt the baby's movement by sixteen or eighteen weeks.

"A little fluttering." Mom wiped away a tear and smiled. "Gosh, it takes me back to when I was pregnant with you. I didn't know what I was feeling when you kicked. Not until I went for that twenty-week ultrasound and saw your tiny legs moving on the screen. It was the most incredible thing. My little sweet pea."

That's what Mom and Dad had called Ivy before

she was born, when they hadn't chosen her name yet. *Sweet pea.* They both still called her that every once in a while.

Mom sat down in her usual chair, and Ivy sat in hers.

"So. How are you doing?" Mom asked as she helped herself to a warm, golden-brown muffin. "With everything?"

"I'm great," Ivy said.

It was a reflex answer, because how Ivy was doing wasn't the point on a day like today.

But right now, it felt true.

At lunch, Ivy saw a new text from Mom to her and Will.

The baby's healthy and growing well! I'm going out for an early dinner with Erin and Christopher to celebrate but will leave money for pizza and tell you more when I get home. Love you both so much!

Ivy smiled as she stood in the cafeteria line to get her food. For the first time, she let herself imagine this baby as an actual, tiny person she'd get to hold and see on holidays they spent with Erin and Christopher and babysit for, maybe. By the time this baby was her age, she'd be twenty-six—finished with college. Kyra had a really young, cool, fun aunt who came to visit sometimes and took her on amazing adventures. Maybe Ivy could be like a cool, fun aunt for Erin and Christopher's kid. She thought again about how happy she'd made Mom that morning when she'd baked those muffins and asked to feel Mom's belly. She should do more things like that for Mom. And maybe now that they were past this milestone and Erin and Christopher were ready to talk about the baby, Ivy wouldn't feel so out of the loop. She and Mom could go back to being as close as they used to be, and once Mom reached the end of her pregnancy, if she was really uncomfortable, Ivy could bring her meals in her room so she could rest in bed, and they could take virtual tours of houses that had gone on the market and do those crossword puzzles Mom liked.

Ivy picked up her food—grilled cheese, her favorite, because everything about this day was perfect so far—and she paused when she passed the table where the soccer guys sat. Josh wasn't there yet even though Ivy had seen him that morning—the seat next to Blake was empty—but Will was on the end with a few other seventh graders.

Will might not have seen Mom's text, and even if

he had . . . Ivy was so full of hope and affection right now, for Mom and the baby and Will and *everyone*. So she leaned down next to Will and said, "Hey. Mom texted, did you see?"

Will paused with his turkey sandwich halfway to his mouth.

"It was a good text. She said everything's great. The baby's doing well."

"Okay. Good. Thanks," Will said. "See you later."

He wanted Ivy to *leave*. His voice was tight and his cheeks were turning red, and *whoosh*. There went all that happy affection Ivy had felt a moment before.

"I thought you'd want to know about this huge thing," she whispered. She meant to whisper, anyway, but her heart was beating so hard now, and the cafeteria was so loud, and it was hard to gauge her own volume. "Sorry if I was wrong."

The redness that had started in Will's cheeks spread to the tips of his ears and all the way down his neck.

"I do want to know." He squeezed his sandwich so tightly that cheese fell out the back. "I'll talk to you about it at home, okay?"

His eyes were pleading. He was desperate for her to leave him alone.

Something broiled in Ivy's stomach. Anger. She

felt angry. But she shouldn't. Will got to decide when he wanted to talk about the surrogacy and when he didn't. That was the deal.

"Okay," she said. "Maybe we can get ice cream after soccer. Like, to celebrate."

"Sure. Maybe."

Ivy pasted a smile back on and headed to the table where Kyra and Peyton sat.

"Hey. What's up?" Kyra asked.

A few minutes ago, when all Ivy was feeling was relieved and excited and happy, she would have told them about the ultrasound. But now she just said, "Nothing. How about with you?"

She listened to them talk for the rest of the lunch period, but she didn't say a word.

After lunch, Ivy headed to math class, copied down the warm-up problem on the board, and got to work.

But then Ms. Ramos knocked on the door and whispered something to Ivy's math teacher. *Uh-oh.* Somebody was about to get bad news, or somebody was in trouble. Ms. Ramos started walking toward Ivy's side of the room. Toward Ivy's desk.

She bent down so close that Ivy could smell coffee and spearmint mingled on her breath.

"Ivy," she whispered. "Come with me."

Ivy's mind flashed to the soccer table at lunch. How Josh had never shown up. But . . . there was no way Ms. Ramos could know about the answers Ivy had shown Josh. He wasn't even going to read them. He'd *promised*.

Ivy felt everyone's eyes on her as she gathered up her things and followed Ms. Ramos out the door and down the hall, into the empty history classroom.

Ms. Ramos took one of the student desks instead of sitting at the teacher desk, and she motioned for Ivy to sit next to her.

"Do you know why you're here?" she asked.

Ivy's mouth had gone as dry as it did at the dentist's office, when the hygienist used the little tube to suck up her saliva. She shook her head.

"Is there something you want to tell me about the take-home test?"

Ivy stared at Ms. Ramos's long, narrow fingers, which tapped against the desk from her thumb up to her pinky as if she were playing a scale on the piano.

Think, Ivy. Ms. Ramos seemed to know about the test. But she *couldn't*. Not if Josh had kept his promise.

So maybe Ivy hadn't done as well as she'd thought? Maybe she'd misunderstood what Ms. Ramos was looking for? Misread the instructions and gotten a really bad grade?

"Were my answers not good?"

Ms. Ramos sighed and twisted her long hair over one shoulder. "Your answers were very good."

Slowly, Ms. Ramos pulled papers out of a manila folder. Ivy's test. Then Josh's. There was his name at the top. And there were his first several answers—really, really short. Only a couple of lines each, even though they were supposed to be a full paragraph. And then she turned the page and there were Josh's last three answers. Long and detailed and *Ivy's*.

"This is a mistake," Ivy said.

Maybe Josh had accidentally given Ms. Ramos the wrong version—the one he had printed out for his dad.

But then she took a closer look and saw that Josh's answers were very, very close to hers, but not identical. He'd added a line break here and there to split her longer paragraphs into shorter ones. He'd cut out a few of her words and added some of his own. These were her ideas, but he'd tried to disguise them.

"A mistake?" Ms. Ramos echoed.

And it *was* a mistake, but not the kind Ivy had meant.

She'd made a terrible mistake, breaking Ms. Ramos's rules and trusting Josh.

"I'm so sorry. I didn't think he was going to copy the answers."

Ms. Ramos's forehead crinkled, and Ivy thought about saying more . . . But what? It wasn't her place to tell about Josh's dad, and she'd done the wrong thing no matter what. She deserved to be in trouble.

"I thought he needed help," she finally said. "I can't really explain more."

"Ivy. This didn't help Josh," Ms. Ramos said. "Even if you hadn't gotten caught, giving Josh your answers wouldn't have helped him. It would have been a Band-Aid at the most, covering up how much he was struggling. It wouldn't have taught him what to do when he gets stuck."

Thoughts whirred around in Ivy's brain like Nana's mixer on the highest setting. She knew that old saying "Two wrongs don't make a right." She knew she shouldn't have broken a rule to make up for what a jerk Josh's dad was being. But she didn't know what she *should* have done.

"I've checked in with your other teachers, so I know you've never been in trouble before." Ms. Ramos tipped her head down a little, looking Ivy in the eye. "The way I see it, this is a learning opportunity. So it's a zero on the take-home test and I'll have to—"

"Wait, a *zero*?" Ivy cut in. "But I answered all the questions. You said my answers were good."

"It's the school policy. That's the consequence for cheating. I'll have to call your parents, too. But I won't recommend any additional punishment."

She kept talking, but Ivy didn't register any more words.

"You have to call my parents? *Today?*"

Ms. Ramos leaned forward in her chair. "Are you afraid of what might happen when your parents find out?"

Ivy shook her head hard.

She wasn't afraid of how her parents would react, because nothing they could do would make her feel any worse than she felt right now.

Today was supposed to be all about the baby and Erin and Christopher and Mom. And instead, it was going to be all about what Ivy had done.

Ivy had ruined this special day Mom and Erin had been looking forward to for months now. She'd ruined the perfect breakfast she and Mom had had this morning. She'd ruined everything.

CHAPTER EIGHTEEN

Somehow, Ivy made it through her last two classes. When the final bell rang, she headed to her locker to pack up her things, and as she passed the principal's office, Josh came out.

He looked right at Ivy, and his face was *mad*.

But why would Josh be angry with her? If anything, shouldn't she be angry with *him*?

He angled his head toward the water fountain in the corner of the hallway, next to a classroom that had emptied out. He crutched over, and Ivy followed.

"You *told* Ms. Ramos?" he said. "Why would you admit to giving me your answers?"

Ivy was too stunned to form words.

"She couldn't have proven anything, if you hadn't told her," he added.

"Josh . . . I . . . She knew," Ivy said.

"She *suspected*," Josh said. "She had no proof until you confessed. And now I'm in extra trouble because I denied it. I'm suspended for two days!"

It was all too much—the slap of these words, the anger in Josh's face, the dread of the conversation she had to have with her parents.

"You weren't even supposed to read my answers!" she squeaked.

"I know! I'm sorry, okay? I got stuck. Those questions were way too hard. It was way too late at night, and I had yours right there and I didn't know what to do. I messed up. I'm a jerk and a screwup and a liar and a cheater, okay? I get it. I suck."

He turned his face toward the corner and Ivy thought he might cry.

"You don't suck," she said softly. "I shouldn't have sent you my answers. I should have . . ." But she trailed off because she still wasn't sure what she should have done. Encouraged him to confront his dad or talk to Ms. Ramos about how much he was struggling? He would have just shut down, the way he had when she'd pushed him before.

"I'm really sorry you're suspended." She took a

deep breath. It was time to say it. "I know, Josh. About the emails. I figured it out."

He looked back at her, his eyebrows closing in together.

"What did you figure out?"

Over his shoulder, Chlo-Mo-No were huddled together, watching them and whispering.

This was really, really far from the ideal time or place to talk about this, but Ivy didn't know what else to do. "I know you're the one sending me the emails. I know you're downbythebay5, and I want to help."

He shook his head in slow motion, as if he were underwater. "What are you talking about? What emails? Who is downbythebay5?"

His face was blank. Baffled. Josh had no idea what she was talking about.

There was so much noise in the hallway and so much noise inside Ivy's brain. She couldn't talk because she couldn't think. She could barely even breathe. She'd been *wrong*?

She'd ruined her history grade and Mom's big day and *everything* all because she wanted to help Josh, since she was so, so sure that he was downbythebay5 and he needed her, but he wasn't. He didn't.

"Look, I have to go," Josh said. "I'm supposed to pack up my stuff and meet my mom back in the principal's office. I'm sorry I got you in trouble. I'll . . . I'll stay away from you now, okay? I'll leave you alone."

As he went, Ivy stared at the cinder-block walls in the hallway—the grooves and dents and shine of the white paint and gray-black smudges. The walls had been repainted over the summer. They'd been pure white when school started. All these chips and smudges were from this school year, which wasn't even a third of the way done. It was hard to believe how much could get messed up in so little time.

And then there were Kyra and Peyton, closing in on her.

"Is it true?" Kyra asked. "Did you help Josh cheat and now he's suspended?"

Ivy had no idea what to say.

"Let's talk in the bathroom." Peyton guided Ivy down the hall to the bathroom. She peeked under the stalls to make sure nobody else was in there. "Okay. Ivy. What happened?" she asked. "Did you really give Josh your answers for the history test?"

The three of them were standing in front of the mirror, and Ivy looked at their reflections. Peyton's confused face, Kyra's exasperated one. They both had high ponytails today, and those shiny hoop earrings, glimmering away.

"Ivy?" Peyton prompted.

I didn't mean to help him cheat. I thought he needed me. I was trying to help.

All those things were true, but none of them would fix anything.

"Whatever. This is a waste of time," Kyra said. "Ivy's not going to talk to us. She never does."

"Wait . . . *What?*" Ivy said.

"You don't talk to us about anything real. You don't actually act like a *friend*." Kyra said the words extra slowly, as if she were explaining a complicated mathematical concept Ivy might not otherwise grasp. "*Friends* don't do weird, secretive things with someone else's crush. *Friends* actually *talk* to each other about things like their mom being pregnant with someone else's baby." Peyton flinched at Kyra's wording, and Kyra sighed. "I just mean . . ."

Peyton took over.

"It's just . . . You want *us* to talk to *you*. But you don't talk to us about what's really going on for you. And whatever you did, with Josh. I'm trying to give you the benefit of the doubt. I keep trying. But you're making it pretty hard."

Kyra gripped Peyton's hand so it was the two of them, connected, and Ivy. Apart. "Friendships are supposed to be equal," Kyra said. "You only want to be *Saint Ivy* and feel like you're better than everybody else. You won't let anyone else even *try* to be there for you."

Anger tightened Ivy's jaw and neck and shoulders and spread down, squeezing her lungs and broiling in her stomach—taking over her whole body like that kids' song about getting eaten by a boa constrictor, but from the top down instead of the bottom up.

"*You're* the ones who don't talk to *me*!" The words burst out, loud and raw. "You're the ones who lie about going to see your Mandarin teacher and have sleepovers without me. You can tell yourself this is my fault if you want, but that won't make it true!"

Peyton's and Kyra's eyes went wide, so now their expressions matched, too. They didn't correct her about going to see their Mandarin teacher. Ivy could feel her emotions whipping up, bigger and scarier and out of control. She knew she should stop, but she didn't know how, so she gave in, letting all her terrible thoughts spill out.

"You say you don't want me to be left out, but you leave me out over and over. All the time!" she told Peyton. Then she turned to Kyra. "And *you've* been a bad friend since you came back from camp. You act like I'm the most annoying person you've ever met. I'm done wondering what I did wrong and how I could make you like me again. You're not good friends, either of you. I'm done with you both!"

The words hung there in the air, sharp and messy. *Mean.* Maybe not even *true*.

Tears spilled out of Kyra's eyes, and Peyton blinked and bit her lip, and then her tears came, too. Ivy rushed out of the bathroom, crashing into the doorframe.

"Ivy?" someone called. Lila. "Are you okay?"

Ivy didn't answer. She ran to her locker, grabbed her things, and bolted toward the bus line. But then her phone buzzed with a text from Mom.

Dad and I are coming to pick you up. Please be outside at the car line waiting.

So Ivy turned around and walked the other way, shame and dread pressing down on her shoulders.

CHAPTER NINETEEN

Dad's gray sedan pulled up with Mom in the passenger seat, and Ivy got in the back seat.

The car still smelled new, even though it was a couple of years old, and it was impossibly clean, as always. No wrappers or wood chips or pennies or crumbs or any of the stuff that covered the mats on the floor of Mom's car now, or the old family car Mom and Dad used to share.

"You talked to Ms. Ramos?" Ivy said.

There was a long pause before Mom confirmed, "We did. Yes."

"I'm so sorry," Ivy said. "I'm so, so sorry."

Dad merged onto the parkway and honked as a car veered in front of him.

"We'll talk as soon as we get home," Mom said. She reached back to squeeze Ivy's hand. "We'll figure everything out. Okay?"

Dad let out an exasperated groan, and Ivy couldn't tell if it was directed at her or the traffic. She looked down at the pristine mat beneath her feet and thought back to the beginning of fifth grade, before Dad had moved out, when all four of them had gone to a Honda dealership in the suburbs to get the car Mom still drove.

Dad had done a bunch of research to choose the best family SUV, and Will and Ivy had gotten to pick the color. After they'd left the dealership, they'd picked up soft pretzels and water ice and stopped at a park, where Will had spotted a skinny brown snake. It had been such a happy, hopeful day. But that had only been a few months before Dad had left. Had he known that he was going to leave? The idea that Dad might have realized he wouldn't actually be driving the new family car squeezed Ivy's rib cage and made it hard to breathe.

Dad found a parking spot on the street near their house, and they all got out. A woman walked by pushing a stroller. She glanced at Mom's belly and smiled, and Ivy realized—this woman thought Mom and Dad were still married, with their own new baby on the way. Tears filled her eyes, and she swiped them away fast.

When they got inside, Mom sat on one end of the living room couch and signaled for Ivy to sit next to her. Dad shifted from one foot to the other until Mom said, "Rob." And he sank down into the cushion on Ivy's other side.

"So. Talk to us, Ivy," Mom said. "What happened with this test?"

"This isn't like you, Ivy," Dad added. "I know there's a lot going on right now. But we expect you to have better judgment than this."

Mom put a soft, warm hand on Ivy's wrist.

"Sweetie," she said. "Please. Help us understand."

Ivy wanted to talk to Mom like she used to. She wanted to tell her all the things Josh had said at the soccer game, all the things the emailer had written, and all the ways she'd mixed things up.

But then Mom touched her belly, and Ivy remembered all over again that this day was supposed to be about the baby, not Ivy and everything she'd ruined. Mom should have been going out to dinner with Erin and Christopher, not leaving work early to deal with *this*.

"I felt bad for Josh because of his knee and because he wasn't doing well in class and his dad was pressuring him," she said. "I know how wrong I was, though. It won't happen again."

"It better not. You got a *zero* on a test, Ivy," Dad said. No trace of his usual jolly self. "We're lucky it's middle school and not high school, so colleges won't see your grade."

"But the grade isn't the most important thing," Mom cut in. "We want to make sure you're okay. We want to help."

"I *am* okay," Ivy insisted. "I'll find a way to get extra credit to make up for the grade. I won't do anything like this ever again. I promise."

Mom's phone started ringing.

"It's not important," she said. "Whoever's calling, I'll call back."

But as soon as her phone stopped ringing, Dad's started. He didn't answer either, but then the house line rang, too.

"Maybe I'd better get that after all," Mom said.

Dad scooted in toward Ivy as Mom walked away. "Mom's right, as always. More than anything else, we want to support you."

He patted Ivy's knee, and Ivy mumbled a *thanks*, but mostly she was straining to hear Mom's end of the phone conversation. Who kept calling?

Mom thanked the person, finally, and came back. "Everyone's okay," she said. "But that was the principal at Leland. Will got in a fight in the locker room with Blake DelMonte. All I know is that neither of them is badly hurt, but they're both suspended. We need to go back to the school and get him."

The rest of the afternoon passed in a blur. When Will, Mom, and Dad got home an hour later, they'd brought pizza from the place by school instead of the neighborhood spot they usually ordered from. It was lukewarm and the crust was soggy, and Ivy struggled to force down a slice. The four of them ate almost the entire meal in silence.

"Why don't you two head upstairs?" Dad suggested when they finished their food. "Mom and I will talk for a bit down here, and we'll come check in with you soon."

Will pushed past Ivy on the way up the stairs and slammed the door to his room behind him. Ivy went back into her room and sat there at her desk, ordering herself to finish her homework so she wouldn't mess up her other grades, too. She couldn't focus, though. She checked her email and saw a new email from downbythebay5 in her inbox. All it said was:

To: Ivy Campbell <ivy.campbell@lelandmagnet
.org>
From: <downbythebay5@mailme.com>
Subject: Are you OK?

Ivy, Are you okay? I'm here if you need
somebody to talk/type to.

Ivy put her head in her hands. Downbythebay5 wasn't Josh. It wasn't Sydney. It was somebody who knew how much she had messed things up today . . . but she wasn't sure that really narrowed things down. *Everybody* probably knew Josh was suspended by now. Everybody probably knew why. And now down-bythebay5 thought *Ivy* needed help instead of the other way around.

These emails only led to embarrassment and disaster. She pounded her fist against the desk, hard, accidentally knocking over her water bottle and spilling it on the ground.

Perfect.

She went to get a towel from the bathroom but froze when she heard Dad's voice from downstairs.

"Just breathe," Dad was telling Mom. "In for the count of four, then hold it. Out for the count of six. Good. Here, let's get you some water."

And then there was Mom's voice, soft and scared. "I'm okay, I think. Just stressed."

"Anybody would be after the day you've had," Dad said. "Seriously, Rach. Go lie down for a little while. We can talk to the kids tomorrow. I'll stay here in case they need anything."

Ivy scurried back to her room as she heard Mom coming upstairs. What was happening? Her fingers shook as she opened a new browser window on her laptop.

Stress and pregnancy, she typed. So, so many results. *Early births. Miscarriage. Complications.*

Most of the complications were things that would affect the baby. But some of them were dangerous for the mom, too.

And Mom was of "advanced maternal age," as the baby development site put it. What if Mom got too stressed because of her job losing funding and Ivy and Will being complete disasters, and the baby came too early to survive? What if the combination of stress and pregnancy put *Mom* in some kind of danger?

Ivy closed her laptop and made herself a promise, right then: She was not going to give her mom one more reason to worry. She'd never forgive herself if Mom or the baby weren't okay because she'd added to Mom's stress.

CHAPTER TWENTY

The next morning, Mom insisted she'd had a great night's sleep and felt fine. Ivy went to school alone, since Will was suspended.

Kyra and Peyton were sitting on the ground in front of Kyra's locker, wearing earbuds and bopping their heads. Peyton pulled her earbuds out right away when she saw Ivy, and then Kyra did, too. They didn't stand up, though, and Ivy didn't know if she should sit down.

"I'm sorry about yesterday," she said, awkwardly towering above them. "I shouldn't have snapped like that. I shouldn't have said those mean things."

Kyra and Peyton locked eyes with each other for a long time before Kyra spoke.

"I'm sorry, too." She messed with her headphone cord, rubbing it between two fingertips. "You were right. That I've been getting annoyed with you all the time. I just . . . I liked being at camp, where nobody knew anything about me yet. When I got back . . . I don't know. I felt trapped."

Ivy struggled to swallow. She wasn't sure what she'd expected Kyra to say, but it wasn't that. "I didn't mean to *trap* you."

"No, I know." Kyra sighed. "And I didn't mean to keep snapping at you, but I kept doing it and then feeling bad about it and then doing it again. I don't know if we make sense anymore. As friends. We're just . . . not the same."

Oh. Ivy couldn't tell if Kyra meant they shouldn't be friends anymore because they weren't the same as each other, or because they weren't the same as they used to be. But it didn't matter much, she guessed. The end result was the same either way.

"I'm sorry I've been mean to you," Kyra said, finally looking up to meet Ivy's eyes. "But also . . . it really is hard to try to be friends with somebody who's so determined to be the nicest person ever. It feels crappy, never getting to be the one to help or listen or whatever. You have to give other people a turn."

"I . . . Okay," Ivy squeaked.

Peyton still hadn't said anything, but Ivy was afraid she might start to cry if she stood there any longer, and she'd done what she wanted to do. She'd apologized. That was the only thing within her control, and there was another conversation she needed to have this morning.

She nodded goodbye to Peyton and Kyra and went to Ms. Ramos's classroom, where Ms. Ramos sat at her desk, eating yogurt.

It felt awkward to barge in on a teacher's breakfast, but Ms. Ramos turned off her music and said, "Ivy. Hey. I've been wondering how you're doing."

Ivy wasn't sure if she should pull a chair over or stand or what, so she settled for perching on the edge of a desk and launching into what she'd planned out on the way to school.

"I'm really sorry about what happened, and I deserve the zero—I get that. But I'm wondering if there's anything I can do? Any extra credit at all, to improve my grade and show I've learned my lesson."

"Hmm." Ms. Ramos took a long sip from her travel coffee mug, which said *#1 Teacher!* in purple cursive, and then set it back down on her desk. Behind her head, the bulletin board was covered with bright yellow paper and rimmed with a cheerful multicolor border.

There was a sign in the middle that said "All authentic research is *you*-search. Begin with what *you* care about and go from there." It had been set up like that all year. "Make me a proposal," Ms. Ramos said finally.

Ivy squirmed, and the desk she'd been leaning against tipped forward, so she stood up straight. "A proposal?"

Ms. Ramos nodded. "I'm not going to tack extra points onto your grade. But if you can come up with a research project you're genuinely interested in, I'll accept an additional piece of work and grade it the way I'd grade any other assignment. So if you do an excellent job, it'll improve your average. If you don't do an excellent job, then it won't." She smiled an encouraging smile. "I'm sure you'll do an excellent job, though."

"You want me to make up my own assignment by myself?"

Ms. Ramos tapped her spoon against the edge of her bowl. "It doesn't have to be all by yourself. Actually, that's an idea. Maybe you should work with a classmate. To get some experience collaborating in positive, appropriate ways. Sound good?"

It didn't, really, but Ivy nodded.

"Whatever you choose, though, it has to be

something you truly, genuinely care about," Ms. Ramos pressed. "Something you wonder about for real."

Something you wonder about for real.

"Does the person have to be in my class? Or is it okay if they're in one of your other sections?"

Ms. Ramos thought for a moment. "Any section would be fine."

Ivy said thank you and left the room. She tried to ignore all the people watching her walk by—probably whispering about her after yesterday—as an idea took shape.

At lunch, more whispers floated over the usual cafeteria din.

Josh. Cheating. Suspended.

Will and Blake. Fight.

Ivy speed-walked past the tables jammed full of eighth graders and found Lila at the end of a table in the back corner.

Lila looked up from her sketch pad when Ivy plunked down her tray. "Oh, hey. How are you?"

The words were harmless, but Lila's tone made Ivy's skin itch. It was the same tone people used to talk to crying little kids.

"I'm fine," Ivy said.

Lila's eyes narrowed. "Really? Because I heard something about Josh Miller and a history test? And your brother pushing Blake DelMonte into a locker?"

Ugh. Leave it to Lila to come right out and *say* something like that.

"The history test thing was kind of a misunderstanding. And I don't even know what happened with Will and Blake and the locker. But—"

"You *don't*? Will didn't tell you?"

Ivy's mouth went dentist-office-dry as she shook her head.

"Huh, I thought you and Will were super close." Lila leaned forward and spoke more quietly. "Harrison said Blake made an obnoxious joke about your mom having someone else's bun in her oven. Harrison said his smug little face looked so shocked when his head smashed against the locker. I wish there were video. Gah, Blake's the worst."

Oh no.

Ivy was the one who'd brought up the pregnancy yesterday in front of Blake and all those guys at lunch, even though she'd known Will didn't want to talk about it. Maybe he *couldn't* talk about it or else he would snap, and he'd been working so, so hard not to snap.

"Sorry," Lila said, wincing. "Did I go too far? Should I not have said that about the smashing and the video?"

"It's . . . it's okay."

"Harrison said everybody thought Blake was being a jerk. I didn't mean to make you feel worse. What your mom's doing is really awesome, by the way. I didn't know before Harrison told me."

"It is. Yeah." Ivy took a deep breath. "There's something I need to talk to you about, actually. Something . . . not related to any of that. A project."

Lila dipped a fish stick in tartar sauce and ate it in two bites. "I'm listening."

"Okay. So you know how you're not doing well in history?" *Oops.* That hadn't come out right. "Sorry. What I mean is, you want to pull up your history grade, yeah? That's what you were supposed to meet with Ms. Ramos about?"

"Well . . . my *mom* would like me to pull up my history grade. And I would like my mom to stop bugging me. So in effect, yes."

"And your mom also wants you to make friends at Leland?" Ivy asked.

"Both moms are united on that one. Big yep."

"Okay. I need to pull up my history grade, too."

"After the Josh–history test situation we will not talk about," Lila chimed in, but Ivy ignored her.

"Ms. Ramos says I can do an extra assignment, if it's something I'm genuinely excited about and I find someone to work with me."

Lila picked up another fish stick. "And you want *me* to do a 'genuinely exciting' extra history project with you?"

"I was thinking—that cake we made together. Jewish apple cake, Dutch apple cake, whatever. We could research the different versions, find out when each culture started making it—that kind of thing. Maybe interview our family members, even?"

Lila put down her fish stick without taking a bite. "I don't think so."

Oh.

Lila hadn't wanted to talk about whoever had made the cake. Of course she wouldn't want to do a project about it. What had Ivy been thinking?

"Look, forget it. It was a bad idea. I'll think of something else."

"No, it's a good idea. But I don't want to do the apple cake." Lila crunched on a carrot.

"But . . . the apple cake was the idea, though," Ivy said.

"Let's find a different recipe. I saw a cooking show one time where the host guy was searching for the perfect Boston cream pie and there was all this stuff about the history of Boston cream pie—like how it isn't actually from Boston and it isn't actually a pie. We could do that instead, or something else."

Ivy raised her eyebrows. "You want to figure out some other dessert and research its history?"

"And bake it, too. Ideally something chocolate. I'm genuinely excited about chocolate."

Ivy smiled. "Who isn't?"

"Okay! Then we have a deal. Chocolate-related research to improve our history grades and convince our parents we have friends."

Ivy winced at the *friend* part, but it was true. She didn't really have any friends anymore.

"Deal," she agreed.

CHAPTER TWENTY-ONE

Ms. Ramos gave Lila and Ivy a little over a month to work on the project. She said as long as they turned it in before winter break, it would count toward their first-semester grades. When Mom and Dad brought up the take-home test again, Ivy told them all about the extra assignment and promised she'd talk to one of them or another adult the next time somebody asked her for help she wasn't comfortable giving, and that seemed to reassure them.

At school, Ivy and Lila started sitting together at lunch most days. Sometimes they brainstormed desserts for their project, sometimes Ivy suggested more Philadelphia museums and parks and restaurants Lila might like, and sometimes Lila complained about everything that annoyed her about Philly and listed all the New York stuff she missed: the bagels, the pizza, the far superior subway system, and on and on and on.

The day before Thanksgiving break, they settled in at what had become their regular table in the corner. The cafeteria was even louder than usual, with everybody revved up for vacation.

"What are you doing for Turkey Day?" Lila asked over all the noise.

"I'm staying here. Going to my dad and Leo's for the big meal. That's his partner, Leo. They live a few blocks away from me."

Lila nibbled the crust of her sandwich. "What's your mom doing?"

"Oh, she'll be there, too. And my nana."

Erin and Christopher would, also, because they always had Thanksgiving with Ivy's family, but that felt too complicated to explain.

"Huh," Lila said. "Everyone all together, huh? Even though . . ."

She trailed off and Ivy grinned. "Didn't you get the 'All families are different and that's okay' talk back in elementary school?" she asked, parroting what Lila had said to her at that soccer game early in the season. "How about you? Are you staying in Philly?"

"Nope. I'm going to New York." Lila speared a tater tot with a fork and dunked it in a pool of ketchup.

"You must be excited then, huh? To go back to Brooklyn, where everything's ten zillion times better?"

Ivy smiled so Lila would know she was kidding around, but Lila didn't smile back.

"We're not staying in Brooklyn. We have to stay with my aunt and uncle outside the city." She speared another tater tot.

"Oh. Well, will you get to see your friends?"

"I don't know. Hey, when's the baby due, by the way?"

Ivy was mostly used to how fast Lila changed the subject when she didn't want to get into something, but the question still startled her. "Oh. Um . . . March. March twenty-second."

Lila nodded. "Cool."

She didn't ask any more questions, though, and Ivy didn't really have anything else to say. They were mostly quiet until the lunch monitor dismissed them. Lila took off toward the arts wing for her next class, and Ivy ended up right behind Peyton on the way out of the cafeteria. Kyra always left a day early to visit her grandparents at Thanksgiving, so Peyton was on her own.

Ivy thought back to Thanksgiving break last year,

when they'd spent so much time together just the two of them. Peyton had told Ivy how she kind of hated Thanksgiving because they spent the day with her stepmom's huge, loud family, and all her cousins were so close with each other but she didn't fit. Ivy wished she could say something that would transport her and Peyton back to how things were at this time last year, when they were first becoming close friends.

A rowdy group of sixth graders pushed past, knocking Ivy into Peyton.

"Sorry!" she said. "I got bumped."

Peyton smiled. "No problem. Have a good Thanksgiving."

"You too," Ivy said. "Or, I mean . . . I hope it's okay. I hope you're okay."

"Yeah. You too. Listen, I've actually been wanting to say—"

But Ivy never got to hear what she'd wanted to say, because Blake and Josh pushed through behind them. Both of them ignored Ivy—Josh had ignored her ever since they got in trouble. But he didn't ignore Peyton.

"The Peyton-ator!" he said as he crutched past.

"Pey-Day!" Blake chimed in. "Hey, that's kinda good. What do you think, Pey-Day? You like it?"

"Um, sure?" Peyton giggled.

Peyton hadn't really been on people's radar yet

last fall when Josh and Blake were in their nickname-giving phase. She was probably happy to get a nick-name from them now.

She fell into step with them, and more people pushed through. She glanced back over her shoulder at Ivy, but there were tons of kids in between them now, so all Ivy could do was give her a little wave and then watch her disappear around the next corner.

That afternoon, the bus was emptier than usual. Will took the early bus with Ivy now that soccer season was over, and he usually sat with other seventh graders. But today he was by himself, so Ivy took the seat across the aisle from him.

He was squeezing something in his right hand, and Ivy's heart squeezed, too, when she saw what it was: a homemade green stress ball—flour, funneled inside a few layers of balloons. She used to help him make them back when he got so frustrated.

"Hey," she said. "You want to come to Nana's with me?"

Ivy and Nana had planned a special Wednesday Afternoon Baking session so Nana could teach Ivy the art of baking an "exceptional" pumpkin pie.

"Nah. I'm gonna go home."

"I bet she'll make you hot cocoa the way you like it. Come on, it'll be fun!"

But Will shook his head. "No thanks," he said, and frustration flared inside Ivy. Why wouldn't he talk to her? Why wouldn't he even *try*?

She curled her hands into fists, her fingernails digging into her palms. Maybe *she* needed a stress ball. Maybe she had just as much anger deep inside as he did.

Sometimes it felt like a door inside her had cracked open this fall—a door to a secret, dark place filled with thoughts she didn't want to think and feelings she didn't want to feel. And that door had swung open for a minute when she'd yelled at Peyton and Kyra. She had to be careful not to let it swing open again, because who knew what would burst out?

CHAPTER TWENTY-TWO

Nana had a lot of opinions about how to make an exceptional pumpkin pie.

The first rule was that you had to chill the dough in the pan and then "pre-bake" it in the oven on its own, weighed down with metal balls called pie weights, before adding the filling. The second thing was, you had to simmer the pumpkin filling on the stove and then strain it to get rid of grittiness and make sure it was smooth.

Nana was so definite about baking. What mattered most, what was worth the extra effort, what you could skip if you had to. Did that kind of certainty come from years and years of experience, or was it something you either had or didn't have, like brown eyes or the ability to curl your tongue? Ivy didn't feel definite about much of anything these days. And even when she did, she often turned out to be wrong.

But it was pretty comforting listening to Nana's rules and trusting that as long as they used all the right ingredients and followed the right steps in the right order, they'd create something beautiful and delicious. The two pumpkin pies they made looked bakery-perfect—smooth, even tops, light golden-brown edges. Ivy couldn't wait to try them.

On Thanksgiving afternoon, Ivy, Mom, and Will saw Blake DelMonte on their way to Dad and Leo's, but he didn't make eye contact as he rushed past them toward his front door holding a pie in one of the green cardboard containers from the grocery store. Ivy could practically feel the anger radiating off Will's body as Blake went by. She wanted to say something sisterly and supportive, but before she came up with anything, Leo opened the door, smiling his enormous Leo smile. He leaned way down to hug each of them one by one and ushered them inside.

Dad and Leo's house was set up with a foyer and bathroom and sitting room on the first floor, the kitchen and living room and dining room on the second, and the bedrooms on the third. Everybody else was upstairs on the second floor, but Erin rushed down to greet them all immediately, looking glamorous in her fitted navy dress with fluttery sleeves, tights, and boots. A rush of shame clobbered Ivy. She was so embarrassed about the day of the twenty-week ultrasound when Mom had had to skip out on the celebratory dinner, even though Mom had promised she hadn't given Erin and Christopher any details about what Ivy had done.

But Erin hugged Ivy tightly and said, "It's so great to see you! Look how grown up you are. It's been way too long. Everything good?" She smelled like flowers and vanilla, just like always, and some of the embarrassment floated away.

Usually, Erin had zillions of questions for Ivy—about friends, school, books, and piano before Ivy had decided to quit, because Erin played, too. Erin was *Mom's* friend, yes, but it always felt like she was Ivy's as well.

Today, though, she didn't ask anything. She practically dragged Mom up the stairs into the kitchen, saying, "So, Rach! I made meatballs! Red meat is supposed to be the best source of iron!"

Mom didn't usually eat red meat, but she took a meatball with a toothpick. "Oh. Okay. Thanks!"

"I read that the type of iron in red meat is easier for your body to absorb than the type that's in leafy greens," Erin went on. "And this is Christopher's family recipe. So I thought I'd make a batch to share."

A lump formed in Ivy's throat and she looked at Mom. "Wait. Why do you need iron?"

Mom locked eyes with Erin as she finished the meatball and patted her mouth with a napkin. "The last batch of blood tests showed that my iron levels are a little low," she told Ivy. "But that's very common in pregnancy. It's nothing to worry about."

Ivy glanced at Leo, who had followed them into the kitchen to open a bottle of wine. He didn't react at all. Did that mean he already knew?

"Sorry, Ivy," Erin chimed in. "This is my nervous energy coming out. I do silly things like stress-cooking meatballs sometimes, to feel like I have some control."

She said it in an offhanded, almost jokey way, but Ivy could tell she didn't *feel* offhanded or jokey. Ivy looked at Erin's flat stomach under her fitted dress, and then at Mom's rounded one. That had to be hard: not being the one actually eating all those pregnancy superfoods that supposedly nourished the fetus. Not being the one who felt the baby flutter inside, or had strangers smile and ask when the baby was due.

"Well, the meatballs smell great," Ivy said. "So that seems like a pretty good deal for everyone, if it made you feel better to cook them."

Erin laughed and put her arm around Ivy's shoulders. "You're so sweet, Ives. I hope some of your mom's sweetness rubs off on this baby, just like it rubbed off on you."

Mom shot Ivy a grateful smile, and Ivy felt warm and cozy and happy all through appetizers and dinner. Will was extra quiet, as usual these days, but everyone else was having a good time. Everything was going so well. Until Nana brought out the two pumpkin pies, and it all fell apart.

At first, everybody *oohed* and *ahhed* about how great the pies looked, and Erin and Christopher wanted to know all about Nana's exceptional pie rules and all the other things Ivy had learned at Friday Afternoon Baking lessons. And then Mom suggested that Ivy tell everybody about the project she was doing with Lila, and Christopher got excited, because he was an education professor at UPenn, and he always got excited when Ivy and Will were doing interesting things at school.

"Now *that's* the kind of genuine research schools should be teaching," he said. "I'm impressed your history curriculum is so progressive!"

Will let out a harsh, one-note laugh and shoveled a huge bite of pie into his mouth.

Ivy cleared her throat. "Uh, yeah. My teacher's really into authentic research."

Now Will rolled his eyes.

"What?" Ivy asked.

Will shrugged. "The whole class doesn't have this super-amazing project. So it isn't actually part of the history curriculum."

Christopher tilted his head to the side, perplexed.

What was Will doing? He'd barely spoken throughout the entire meal. Why did he have to chime in now?

"Will. That's enough," Dad warned.

Ivy took a deep breath. "That's true, I guess. It's sort of extra credit."

"And why do you need extra credit?" Will's tone was at least as sharp as the giant knife Dad had used to carve the turkey.

"Will. That's enough," Mom said.

But Will wasn't finished. He set down his fork, which clanged against his dessert plate. "If Ivy's going to brag about how great this project is, she should tell everybody why she needs extra credit instead of acting like she never does anything wrong!"

His voice was so mean, and Erin's and Christopher's

faces were so confused, and so many feelings swirled fast and huge in Ivy's chest, and then, suddenly, she heard her own voice, as loud and mean and mad as Will's.

"Why don't *you* tell everybody why you were suspended from school? Or how you really feel about this baby no one's allowed to bring up around you?"

Everything went silent. All the background sounds of silverware against china and ice cubes in glasses stopped. Will's face turned as purplish-red as the cranberry sauce, and Ivy felt sick.

She'd let anger take over again. She'd turned into someone she didn't recognize. Someone terrible.

She braced herself for Will to yell back, but he didn't. He looked at Dad. "Can I be excused?"

Dad nodded. "Go upstairs and cool down. We'll talk after we finish eating."

Tears spilled out the corners of Ivy's eyes as Will's footsteps pounded on the stairs and her terrible words echoed in her head.

Erin and Christopher stared down at their plates. Mom reached out to take Ivy's hand, but Ivy pulled away.

What was happening? Who even *was* she?

What if Mom's stress peaked right now, the way it had the day of the twenty-week ultrasound? What if her blood pressure spiked too high and it was too much strain on the baby, who was already deprived of iron, apparently?

"I'm so sorry." Ivy stared down at Leo's grandmother's fancy dessert plate: white china with blue flowers and a shiny silver rim, her slice of exceptional pumpkin pie sitting in the middle. "I didn't mean to say any of that. I'll apologize. I'll get Will to come back down."

"Sweetheart," Mom said. "Let's give him space."

"You shouldn't have said what you said," Dad added. "And Will shouldn't have said what he said. But there are a lot of emotions swirling around right now."

"For all of us," Mom said.

Christopher nodded. "We all lose our tempers sometimes."

Then Mom gasped.

"What is it?" Ivy asked. "Are you okay? Is the baby okay?"

Erin stood up too fast, her chair crashing to the ground.

"I'm fine. I'm good!" Mom said. Then she laughed. "The baby kicked so hard. Ooh. There's another jab. Come feel!"

Ivy reached out and felt it twice—something small

and hard, hitting Mom's side. A foot? And then Erin was there and *duh. Erin* was the one who should get to feel this baby moving. Erin and Christopher. It was their kid, not Ivy's. The least Ivy could do was get out of the way.

"Oh my gosh! I feel it! Chris! I feel it!" Erin said.

And Christopher felt, too, and they were crying and laughing and hugging, and Ivy backed away from the table, where her perfect piece of pie sat on the special-occasion china, still untouched.

After dinner, Mom and Dad went upstairs to talk to Will, and when they came back down, Mom said, "Will's going to stay here tonight and you can talk to him in the morning. You ready to go home?"

Ivy didn't trust herself to speak, so she just nodded. She hated that she couldn't make things right with Will tonight, and she hated that she was relieved that she didn't have to try yet.

She took the leftover pie Nana forced on her, said her goodbyes, and followed Mom out the door. The night was clear and crisp, in that way that usually emptied her mind and refreshed her. She breathed in the air, grateful that, for a moment at least, the coldness was the only thing she could focus on.

"Hey," Mom said, linking arms with her as they walked. "How are you, sweet pea? You okay?"

Ivy bit down on the inside of her cheek. "I'm so sorry. That was terrible. *I* was terrible."

"Hey." Mom hugged Ivy right there on the sidewalk. "Ivy. Honey. Everybody has moments they're not proud of. We all say things we don't mean and hurt other people. It's awful, but it's part of being human."

Ivy hugged Mom back and tried to cheer up so Mom wouldn't worry. But the problem was, Ivy was afraid that maybe, deep down, she *did* mean the hurtful things she'd said to Will and Kyra and Peyton. Maybe, deep down, she wasn't a very kind person at all. After all, she'd thought she was really smart until she started middle school and so many people were smarter. She'd thought she was a great piano player until she noticed how much better Elias was. Maybe this was the same kind of thing all over again: She'd thought she was a good person, but she wasn't. Not really.

Mom and Ivy started walking again, and when they turned onto the main street, Ivy spotted Sydney DelMonte walking Baxter the dog and coming their way.

Ivy waved and called out, "Happy Thanksgiving!"

"Hey. Happy Thanksgiving," Sydney called back. But her voice sounded hoarse, and when she passed under a streetlamp, Ivy could see that her face was blotchy and wet. She was crying.

"I'm going to stop and talk to Sydney for a minute, okay?" Ivy said to Mom. "I'll see you at home."

Mom hesitated. "It's cold, honey, and it's getting late."

"It'll only be a minute," Ivy promised.

Mom raised her eyebrows.

"*Please*," Ivy said, and Mom sighed.

"Just a minute," Mom said. "I'll see you at home very soon."

"Definitely." Mom waved to Sydney and then crossed the street. Baxter scampered toward Ivy and jumped up on her legs, so she reached down to scratch the fur behind his ears.

"Uh . . . hi," Sydney said. "Are you not going with your mom?"

"I just wanted to see if you're okay," Ivy said. "Has it been a rough Thanksgiving?"

Sydney wiped her tears with the sleeve of her pretty gray wool coat. "You could say that."

Ivy didn't want to pry, so she tried to lighten the mood.

"I saw Blake carrying a pie from the grocery store, so I'm guessing your dessert was disappointing."

Sydney let out a surprised laugh. "It really was. The crust was somehow both dry *and* mushy. And he chose cherry even though I told him to get pumpkin."

Ivy wrinkled her nose. "It's not Thanksgiving without pumpkin. Or at least apple."

Baxter scampered around Sydney, and she had to untangle her legs from his leash. "We were supposed to go to Patrick's house for Thanksgiving. They have this huge party, and they invite all their friends who don't live near family. But I assume you heard? Patrick and I broke up, I destroyed his life and the soccer team's whole season, et cetera, et cetera."

Ivy hesitated. "I . . . heard you're not together anymore. I'm sorry about that. And I'm sorry about your Thanksgiving."

Sydney shrugged. "At least I get a break from having people at school whisper about me behind my back and call me terrible names to my face." She said it fake-cheerfully, as if this wasn't a big deal, and Ivy thought of Erin, being offhanded and jokey, making fun of herself for cooking those meatballs and wanting to take care of Mom.

"That's awful," Ivy said.

Baxter circled Sydney again, panting.

"Okay, buddy. We're going," she told him. "Anyway, nice to see you, Ivy. Hope your Thanksgiving was way better than mine."

"Wait!" Ivy held the leftover pie out toward Sydney. "This is pumpkin pie, if you're interested. I made it with my grandmother."

It was probably a silly thing to offer. It wasn't as if pie would fix everything that Sydney was dealing with—even *exceptional* pie. But Sydney smiled.

"I feel bad taking your pie."

"I already ate plenty," Ivy insisted, even though she hadn't. "I want you to have it."

Baxter pulled the leash again. "Okay, then. Thank you."

Ivy handed over the container. "You're welcome. I hope you like it."

It was a small thing, giving away her leftover pie, but Ivy hoped it made Sydney feel a little better. It had definitely made *her* feel better.

As she walked home, she wondered about that day when she'd knocked on Sydney's door and Sydney had claimed that she and Patrick were good, even though they must not have been. Was she cheating on him then? Had she lied to Ivy and said Patrick was coming over when really *Damian* was?

Or had she been trying to talk herself into believing she and Patrick were okay so she wouldn't have to break his heart, but then she ended up breaking it anyway? When she insisted everything was okay, was she only lying to Ivy, or was she lying to herself, too?

Ivy froze.

If Sydney *had* lied when she'd said everything was okay, was it possible that she'd also lied when she said she hadn't sent the emails?

Was it possible that Ivy had been right in the first place and Sydney *was* downbythebay5?

CHAPTER TWENTY-THREE

Will knocked on the door to Ivy's bedroom the next afternoon.

"Come in," she called, but he stayed there in the doorway, leaning against the frame.

"I'm sorry about what happened yesterday. I should have kept my mouth shut about your project." He said it fast, looking down at his sneakers and bouncing on his toes. Ready to get this apology over with and take off.

"I'm sorry, too. I'm really sorry about all those things I said. I just . . . I feel like we've grown apart so much. I feel like you don't need me. I wish we could talk about stuff." Ivy was trying—really trying—to be honest right now, and Will looked up from his shoes at least.

"Do you want to talk to *me* about stuff? Or do you only want me to talk to you?"

It felt like a trick question. "Both, I guess? Everything feels so different now."

Will jutted out his chin, the way he used to do when a grown-up was about to scold him and he didn't think he'd done anything wrong. "*I'm* different now. I can deal with stuff better. I know when I'm getting frustrated and I know how to handle it. Usually."

"That's great. That's . . . that's really great."

"But?" Will prompted.

"No but!" Ivy insisted.

But I miss you.

But I don't understand why that means you have to push me away.

Those were the things she wanted to say. Those words were there, scratching at her tongue, but maybe they were too needy. Too vulnerable.

"Okay, then," Will said. "I picked Mexican food for dinner. Mom wants to know if you want the usual."

"Yep. The usual's good," Ivy said. And Will went back downstairs, conversation over.

• • •

Back at school on Monday morning, Ivy was reading on a bench in the hallway before first period, and Blake DelMonte slammed something down next to her. The loud clang of glass on wood made her jump.

"This is your container," he said. "My sister said to give it back to you. She said thanks for the pie."

"Oh," Ivy said. "Um, you can tell her I said 'You're welcome.'"

"Gee, *can* I?" Blake said, clapping his hands together. "Thanks so much. Lucky me."

He walked off, shaking his head and muttering to himself. *Weird* was the only word Ivy caught.

"*That* seemed unnecessarily hostile," someone said. Lila, sitting down next to Ivy. "How was your Thanksgiving? And also: Why did you give Blake's sister pie?"

Ivy sighed. "It's complicated."

Lila stuck out her tongue. "Uggggggh. I hate it when people say that."

"When people say what? 'It's complicated'?"

Lila nodded. "It's such a cop-out. It doesn't mean anything. *Everything* is complicated. It's just something people say when they don't want to answer a question but they aren't brave enough to come out and say that. No offense."

Ivy's jaw tightened. "*Not* everything is complicated. And *I* hate it when people say 'No offense' as if that gives them permission to be rude."

And to Ivy's surprise, Lila laughed.

"You're right, it's completely obnoxious. Sorry about that."

Ivy's frustration fizzled. "Oh. Um, that's okay."

"Anyway! Is Blake's sister as awful as he is?"

"What? No," Ivy said. "She's nothing like him at all. Why, have you heard stuff about her? She's really nice. People are being awful to her and she doesn't deserve it, even if she did something bad."

Ivy thought of Mom saying we all make mistakes and hurt each other. Funny how much easier that was to believe when it was somebody else doing the hurting.

"Plus, she has Blake as a brother," Lila cut in. "That's gotta be rough. But . . . you tried to make her feel better by giving her baked goods?"

It sounded sort of pathetic when Lila said it like that. "It was just leftover pie. And maybe baked goods can't fix *everything*, but they definitely can't hurt."

"I guess, yeah. Even if it's pie." Lila wrinkled her nose.

"Wait. You don't like pie?" Ivy asked.

"I mean . . . when cake exists, what's the point?"

Ivy shook her head. "I feel like you've never had really excellent pie, if that's what you think."

"*I* feel like cake is just better. Period. The end," Lila said.

Peyton and Kyra came around the corner together. Kyra was in Turbo Mode, telling some story that involved a lot of dramatic hand gestures, so she didn't notice Ivy. Peyton did, though, and she gave Ivy a quick smile, so Ivy smiled back. She kept walking past with Kyra, though. She didn't stop to talk. Not that Ivy had been expecting her to, but still.

Anyway. "Did you have pie at Thanksgiving?" Ivy asked Lila.

"Yes. Apple, and it was underwhelming, but there was lots of ice cream."

"Was it good to go back to New York?" Ivy asked. "Even if it wasn't Brooklyn?"

"It was . . ." Lila stopped and smacked herself in the face. "Ack! I was totally about to say *it's complicated.*"

Ivy laughed. "So you don't want to talk about it, then?"

"Bingo."

"I don't really want to talk about my Thanksgiving, either," Ivy admitted.

"Yeah, I figured."

"You did?"

"I mean, I asked you how your Thanksgiving was and you didn't answer." The bell rang for first period, and Lila stood up. "See you at lunch, Saint Ivy!"

"Yeah. See you then," Ivy said.

She had sort of dreaded lunch for most of the year, even when she still sat with Kyra and Peyton. But now she was actually looking forward to it.

The next weekend, Ivy went over to Lila's house to work on their project.

Lila's house wasn't far away from Ivy's—a little bit northwest, where there wasn't as much new construction. The row houses were old, like on Ivy's block, but bigger and not as well maintained. Most of them had tall, wooden front doors that were painted bright colors, and Lila's was a purplish-blue.

One of Lila's moms opened the door—Becky, with the highlighted hair and big, colorful jewelry.

"Welcome to our half-empty home!" she said.

It really *was* half-empty. Mom would have loved

the shiny hardwood floors and tall ceilings, but half of the enormous living room was bare.

"We didn't have this much space in Brooklyn," Becky explained. "So it's a work in progress."

"I like the paint colors," Ivy said, looking for something to compliment.

The kitchen was painted a sunny yellow, the dining room walls were smoky blue, and the mostly empty living room was bright green.

Lila showed up at the bottom of the stairway. "Oh, we hate them. We just haven't gotten a chance to repaint."

"*Lila*," her mom scolded.

"It's true!"

Lila's other mom joined them from the kitchen. "I'm Maya," she said. "And *hate* is a strong word. I would say we're . . . looking forward to making this place our own."

"Oh yeah. Can't wait." Lila twirled one finger in the air. "Woo-hoo."

Maya shook her head at Lila, but she was smiling. "We're happy to have you, Ivy. It's nice to see Lila making friends."

"*Especially* when the friends encourage Lila to take an interest in schoolwork," Becky added.

"Aaand that's our cue to go," Lila said, pulling Ivy up the stairs.

"Nice to meet you!" Ivy called. "Thanks for having me!"

"Nice to meet you! Thanks for having me!" Lila said in a high-pitched voice. "Do you ever get tired of being so nice all the time?"

"Do *you* ever get tired of being so negative all the time?" Ivy asked.

"Nope!"

Lila's bedroom was at the end of the hall. The walls were Pepto-Bismol pink, and somebody had painted the ceiling sky blue with fluffy clouds and a sun. The built-in bookshelves that covered an entire wall were bare, except for one shelf of framed photos. A stack of books and art supplies sat at the corner of the desk, and a couple of boxes were piled against one wall. Ivy would have guessed that Lila's family had moved in a couple of days ago if she hadn't known they'd been here for months.

Lila plopped down on her bed. "Sorry about my parents."

Ivy sat on Lila's desk chair. "They seem really nice."

Lila raised her eyebrows.

"They do!"

Lila sat up. "Oh, come on. You heard what my mom said, right? '*Especially* when the friends encourage Lila to take an interest in schoolwork.' She's always like that."

Ivy thought of that second email from downbythebay5—*My room is not a fun place to be at the moment . . . My parents do not get me!* She imagined Lila typing those words in this very room, with the aggressively pink walls and sponged-on ceiling clouds, and her heart sped up. For one bold second, she considered asking if Lila was downbythebay5, but she didn't have the guts. And anyway, she was pretty sure it wasn't Lila. Lila hadn't even *liked* Ivy when the first email showed up.

"That . . . sounds hard," Ivy said, but Lila shrugged.

"It is what it is. She's disappointed that her own flesh and blood doesn't follow along in her over-achieving genius footsteps, but at least she's got Harrison, who actually likes school."

Ivy's mind caught on that phrase, *flesh and blood.*

"Is Harrison . . . Are he and Becky not biologically related?"

Ivy was worried she might have overstepped, but Lila didn't seem offended. "Right. He's Maya's biological kid, I'm Becky's. We both have the same dad."

She walked over to the bookshelf and picked up

a framed photo of her and Harrison with a tall white guy who had light brown hair and glasses.

"His name's Tom. He's an engineer. We're supposed to be super math-y because of him—I'm pretty sure that was the plan. But it only worked with Harrison."

"What's he like?" Ivy asked. "Do you see him a lot?"

"Yeah. He lives in Chicago, but he visits every summer. He's great. Quiet, funny. It's kind of weird when he comes, since he's not here all the time. He doesn't know us super well in some ways, but he also, like, gave us half our genes. But it's not *bad* weird."

Lila put the photo back, and Ivy looked at the other framed pictures on the shelf. There was one of Lila with her arms around two other girls, and there was one of Lila, Harrison, their parents, and an older man with white hair and an enormous smile.

"Is that your grandfather?" Ivy asked, pointing.

She thought she was asking a completely harmless question, but Lila stiffened. "Not my grandfather. No."

"Oh. Who is he?" Ivy asked.

Lila turned the photo over. *Yikes.*

"I'm sorry. I didn't mean to make you uncomfortable," Ivy said.

Lila sat back down on the bed. "Not your fault. I should have put the photo away if I didn't want to talk about it." She flashed a quick, unconvincing smile. "Or I should have just said, 'It's complicated.' Anyway, we should figure out our project."

Right.

"Okay. Well, I think German chocolate cake has the most stuff to research, so that's my vote," Ivy said.

"And it's chocolate. So obviously I'm in," Lila agreed.

And just like that, Lila was back to her usual self. The only hint that something had upset her was that framed photo, still facedown on the mostly empty shelf.

CHAPTER TWENTY-FOUR

The first interesting thing about German chocolate cake was that it wasn't from Germany.

It was named after a guy named Samuel German, who decided to add sugar to baking chocolate to make it sweeter. The second interesting thing was that he did that back in the 1850s, but nobody really made the cake until almost a century later. It started out as a regional dessert in Texas, but then it spread all over the place after a Dallas newspaper ran the recipe in 1957. The third interesting thing—and Ivy's favorite—was that the newspaper got the recipe *wrong*. It said to use eight ounces of chocolate instead of four, and a correction was printed a few days later. But even so, the recipe basically went viral.

Lila pointed out that the wrong version just had extra chocolate, which couldn't be a bad thing, but Ivy wasn't so sure. You had to melt the chocolate in water, and if double the chocolate was diluted by the same amount of water, that might change the texture, not just the taste.

They decided to write a newspaper article about the cake's history instead of a regular essay, since the newspaper was part of its story. Over the next couple of weeks, they drafted it and revised it and then Nana helped them bake their own German chocolate cake, too. On the Friday before winter break, they turned in their article and brought the cake to Ms. Ramos during recess. They had to carry it past a whole cluster of eighth graders—including Josh, Blake, Chlo-Mo-No, Kyra, and Peyton—and Blake called out, "Aw shucks, my birthday's not until March."

"If we have extra, can I smash it in his face?" Lila whispered to Ivy as they walked by.

Ms. Ramos gave them an A and promised to email their parents right away to tell them what a great job they'd done, which was pretty much exactly what Ivy had wanted. She should have been happy. But at lunch, as she waited for Lila to show up at their usual table, she was nervous and a little bit sad. Maybe she and Lila wouldn't have anything to talk about without the project. Maybe they wouldn't sit together anymore, even.

Five minutes passed, and most of the seats around Ivy filled up, but Lila still didn't arrive. Finally, somebody tapped her on the shoulder, and she nearly choked on her bite of pierogi because it was Josh, not Lila, with Blake right behind him.

"Any chance you've got any more of that cake you brought to Ms. Ramos, Opi?" Josh asked.

As if they were *friends.*

Ivy opened her mouth, closed it, and opened it again, completely at a loss. And then Lila was there, sliding into her usual seat and saying, "Not for you we don't."

Blake snort-laughed and mimicked her in a high-pitched voice. *"Not for you!* Oh well. Worth a try. Let's go, Miller."

He walked away, and Josh followed on his crutches.

"Sorry I'm late," Lila said. "I had to stop in to see Dr. Nathanson."

Dr. Nathanson was the guidance counselor. "Is everything okay?"

Lila shrugged. "No less okay than usual."

Over Lila's shoulder, Ivy noticed that Josh was no longer following Blake. He was headed back their way.

Lila turned her head and saw him, too. "Ugh," she said. "Can we help you?"

He ignored Lila and addressed only Ivy. "I wanted to say sorry again. I . . . When I asked you to send me your answers, I really wasn't going to use them. And then I panicked. And I know that doesn't change anything. But I'm sorry."

Lila rolled her eyes, but Ivy said, "Okay. Thanks for saying that."

Josh exhaled in a loud whoosh. "Also. What were the emails you were talking about? Somebody was emailing you, and you thought it was me?"

Ivy wanted to crawl under the table.

"It was a mix-up," she said. "It doesn't matter. It wasn't important."

"Miller," Blake yelled from the middle of the cafeteria. "Dude, we're not getting cake. Why are you still talking to them?"

"Right. Okay. See ya, Ivy," Josh said, and then he was gone.

But now Lila was looking at Ivy way, way too intently. As if she were trying to count her eyelashes or something. "What was he talking about? You thought he was emailing you?"

Ivy waved off the question. "I was getting these

random emails. I thought they were from Josh. I was wrong. It was probably a prank or something."

The thought flashed in her mind again that the emails could have been from Lila, but Lila's face gave nothing away.

"Huh. Weird," she said.

And Lila wouldn't have thought it was weird that Ivy had gotten emails if she'd been the one sending them. Right?

"Hey." Nyeema Jackson, the star of the soccer team, leaned across the empty seat between her and Lila. Nyeema and Ivy were in the same homeroom, and Nyeema was always friendly. "Did Josh and Blake try to mooch food off you and then insult you?"

"Pretty much," Lila said.

Nyeema groaned and shook her head hard, which made her long braids fly back and forth. "I am *so* ready to start high school next year and watch them be scrawny freshmen nobody cares about."

Lila cackled. "Yes! I thought everybody around here worshipped those guys."

Then Nyeema's friend Ana Lopez complimented Lila's T-shirt, which said *I'd rather be traveling to distant galaxies.* Apparently it was a reference to a sci-fi show Lila, Nyeema, and Ana loved and Ivy had never heard of.

Ivy mostly checked out of the conversation at that point. The three of them watched all the same shows and read all the same books. Plus, Ana was almost as artistic as Lila. Ivy liked Nyeema and Ana, but she had nothing to add to the discussion at all. If Lila wanted to make actual friends in Philadelphia, maybe Nyeema and Ana were better choices.

When the day was over, Ivy was surprised to see Peyton waiting at her locker.

"Hey," Peyton said.

"Hey. How's it going?"

Before Peyton could answer, Blake and Josh walked by.

"See ya this weekend, Pey-Day!" Josh called.

"See you," Peyton said. Once they were gone, she told Ivy, "There's a bat mitzvah for a girl we both know. She goes to my synagogue and her parents are friends with Josh's." She shrugged and messed with the cuff of her sweater sleeve. "Um, so my family's having a New Year's Day party again. You should come. If you want."

"Oh! Um, thanks!" Ivy had gone last year, and it

had been really fun. It was mostly for Peyton's relatives and her parents' friends, and Ivy had felt sort of special to be included. She definitely hadn't expected to be invited again.

"Monica told me to make sure to ask you," Peyton added. "Kyra will still be at her grandparents', but I think some other people will be there. So, yeah. You should come. If you want to."

Ivy's heart deflated.

It was Peyton's stepmom's idea, not hers.

"I think I might have some family stuff," she said. "But I'll let you know if I can make it."

"Okay," Peyton said. "Well . . . text me. Or whatever."

Ivy wanted to ask how things were between Peyton and Monica lately. She missed Peyton. More than she missed Kyra, even though Kyra was the one she'd known forever. Maybe it was inevitable that Ivy and Kyra had grown apart—maybe Ivy couldn't have stopped that from happening. But it felt like she and Peyton really *could* still be good friends, if everything had gone a little bit differently.

"Okay. Well, I hope you have a good break," Ivy said.

"Yeah. You too."

And then Peyton headed to the auditorium for

rehearsal, and Ivy went out to the bus line. She was bored and a little bit sad, and she was wondering about the emails again for the first time in a while, now that Josh had brought them up. So she opened her email and searched for downbythebay5's last message—the one from the day of the twenty-week ultrasound, when everything had gone so wrong.

Even though weeks and weeks had passed, she decided to write back now.

> **To: <downbythebay5@mailme.com>**
> **From: Ivy Campbell <ivy.campbell@lelandmagnet .org>**
> **Subject: Re: Are you OK?**
>
> Hey. Sorry I didn't reply. I guess I wasn't all that okay that day you sent this, but I am now. Mostly.
> How about you?

CHAPTER TWENTY-FIVE

On Christmas Day, Mom didn't go with Ivy and Will to Dad and Leo's house.

She said a quiet morning alone sounded like a dream. She said she had more work to do because she was in charge of a big, important fundraiser party for the historical society in February, and they really needed it to be a success. She said she might take a nap, too, even though she'd gone to bed early the night before, and the baby development site had said this was the time of pregnancy when people had the most energy.

"But everything's okay?" Ivy asked. "With your hormones and iron?"

"Everything's good," Mom promised. But Ivy didn't completely believe her. She wasn't sure Mom would tell her if something was wrong.

While Will finished wrapping presents, Ivy made a list of all the things that worried her: Mom being over forty, pregnancy-induced anemia, hormone imbalance, fatigue in the second trimester. She went online and searched for each thing.

Some of the stuff that came up was reassuring. Being anemic was super common, like Mom had said, and it could make a person tired. But if iron got *too* low and then a person lost a lot of blood when the baby came, that could be dangerous.

And being over forty meant Mom was at a higher risk for things like gestational diabetes and pre-eclampsia. Gestational diabetes could lead to all sorts of risks, like getting regular diabetes after the baby was born. And preeclampsia was even scarier. It meant doctors might have to take the baby out immediately, even if it was way too early for the baby to survive, or else the mom could die.

"What are you reading?"

Will stood in the doorway with his coat on, ready to go, and Ivy slammed her laptop shut.

"Nothing," she said. "I'll get my stuff."

They stopped to say goodbye to Mom, who noticed Ivy was freaking out and asked what was wrong.

Ivy wanted so, so much to do what she would have done before this year. To spill every scary thing she'd just read so Mom would stroke her hair and rub her back and reassure her about each of them, one by one. But this time it was *Mom* she was worried about.

So Ivy insisted nothing was wrong and tried her best to enjoy Christmas brunch at Dad and Leo's and to *ooh* and *ahh* over her presents.

After they ate, Will and Dad set up Will's new FIFA video game, Leo set up his new tabletop basil plant, and Ivy tried to settle in on the couch with her new book, but she couldn't concentrate. She pulled out her phone, wanting to search for pregnancy risks again and see what she'd missed before, and that's when she saw the new email. From downbythebay5, finally. After all this time.

To: Ivy Campbell <ivy.campbell@lelandmagnet
.org>
From: <downbythebay5@mailme.com>
Subject: Re: Re: Are you OK?

Hey. So. I'm sorry you weren't okay that day but I'm glad you mostly are now.

Me too, I think. Mostly.

I wasn't ready to *actually* talk about what was going on before. I guess I wanted to . . . vague-vent? Is that a thing? I wanted someone to know things sucked. Someone like you, who would care that they sucked. But I didn't want anyone to know exactly *how* they sucked because that would involve putting into words some things I didn't want to put into words.

I still don't *want* to say it all, but I think I should. Not over email, but . . . maybe soon? We can talk? For real, in person?

See you soon, Saint Ivy. Happy December 25th.

See. For real. In person.

Her heart pounded as she read the email again.

And then she glanced out the window and saw someone sitting outside under the twinkly white lights that hung above the communal picnic table in the courtyard between the townhouses. It was cold and gross out, but there was Sydney DelMonte, all by herself.

Ivy grabbed her coat.

"Be right back," she called. "I need to . . ." She didn't know quite *what* she needed to do. She didn't know why she felt so totally sure she should go out there to check on Sydney—she only knew she did. "I need to do something," she finished.

"Now?" Dad asked, but Ivy didn't stop to answer.

When she went outside, Sydney looked up and waved. A casual wave, as if she wasn't surprised to see Ivy. As if she'd been expecting her.

Ivy's heartbeat echoed in her ears. In movies, there was music in the background in dramatic moments, prompting the audience to realize something big was about to happen. Ivy felt like her heartbeat was the soundtrack, preparing her.

"Hey," Sydney said. "Merry Christmas."

"Merry Christmas." Misty rain fell sideways into Ivy's face, so she tightened the hood of her coat. "Is it okay if I join you? Do you want to talk?"

"Sure. I'd rather talk than think." Sydney let out half a laugh. "I guess this is our thing, huh? Meeting up when I'm freaking out on major holidays. First Thanksgiving, now Christmas."

Ivy half laughed, too, as she sat down on the other side of the cold, wet picnic table. The backs of her jeans were instantly soaked. "How come you're freaking out?"

Sydney blew out a big, slow puff of cold air. "My whole extended family's inside my house right now, and if one more person asks me about my sweet, handsome boyfriend, Patrick, I'm going to lose it."

Ivy winced. "Yikes. They don't know you broke up?"

"Nope. Apparently no one got the memo that I broke his heart and he got back at me by spreading a rumor that I cheated on him and making half the school hate me."

She said it so matter-of-factly—almost *cheerfully*—that it took Ivy a second to process the words.

"Wait, rumor? As in, you didn't cheat on him?"

"Nope!"

"Wait," Ivy said again. "He made that up?"

Sydney tipped her head back to look at the gray sky. Small black birds circled overhead. Ivy counted one bird, then a second, a third, and a fourth before Sydney answered.

"He didn't completely make it up. I liked Damian. I tried not to have feelings for him, and then I tried to end things with Patrick. Because I couldn't be with Patrick when I couldn't stop thinking about Damian. But then Patrick was so upset when I tried to break up with him, and our lives were just so intertwined. So I switched shifts at work and tried to avoid Damian, but that didn't work, either."

Ivy was putting every ounce of her attention into keeping up with all these revelations, but she was still confused. "Um, it didn't work?"

Sydney sighed. "Somebody called in sick, we ended up working together. We talked about everything—how we felt, why we couldn't do anything about it. And then Patrick showed up to visit me. He could tell something was going on, I confessed everything, and we broke up."

A helicopter whirred by above the birds, its propeller cut-cut-cutting through the pitter-patter sound of the rain.

"And then he told everybody you cheated on him?" Ivy asked.

"He was really upset. And embarrassed, especially after he played so badly in that game. I don't know how many people he told. Things spread."

It almost sounded like Sydney was defending him.

"But he didn't stop things from spreading?"

Sydney shook her head. "No. Not even when people wrote really, really awful comments on this photo of the two of us that he had on Instagram. He didn't take the comments down. Or when people said stuff to me at school—stuff I know he heard. His friends found Damian online and said awful stuff to him, too. Patrick let it all happen."

"That's awful," Ivy said. "That isn't okay."

"No. You're right. It's not." Sydney smiled a small, sad smile.

"Have you tried to tell people what really happened?" Ivy asked.

"A few. It didn't really take. The whole thing's . . . I don't know. It's a mess." She sighed again. "I shouldn't be unloading this on you. Saint Ivy. That's what your friends call you, right? Even for Saint Ivy, this is a little much."

Saint Ivy. Sydney knew about the nickname. That was one thing Ivy hadn't been sure about before, when she'd thought Sydney was the emailer—whether Sydney would have overheard it. But she knew.

"It isn't too much." Ivy's heart was beating even faster and louder now, her own, increasingly insistent soundtrack. Telling her, *Pay attention. This is big. This is it.*

Sydney pushed herself up off the wet bench. "I've been hiding out long enough. I should go back in and face Christmas."

"One thing," Ivy blurted. This was her chance to ask. She had to know for sure this time. "That day I saw you? Outside the middle school . . ."

Sydney nodded, as if she'd expected the question. "That was the day I was determined to break up with

Patrick. The night before, Damian and I had almost kissed. We didn't, but I knew I had to end things. I just wasn't brave enough to do it."

"And then . . . the day I knocked on your door?" Ivy prompted. "The next weekend?"

"That was after I couldn't go through with it. I was trying to convince myself I could make things work. I'm sorry I didn't tell you the truth about everything," Sydney said. "I couldn't deal."

Okay.

That was it, right? That was the admission Ivy had been waiting for.

Sydney was downbythebay5. She hadn't been ready to admit what was happening, so she'd pretended she hadn't sent the emails, but she had.

Ivy got up, too, and hugged Sydney. "I'm glad you told me."

"Oh! Um . . . me too." Sydney froze for a second before hugging Ivy back. She sounded a little flustered. But Ivy was a little flustered, too.

She was also drenched and freezing, so when she went back to the townhouse, she brushed off Dad's questions about what she'd been doing outside, took a shower, and got dressed in some sweats she'd left here a while ago. They were a little short in the arms and legs, but warm.

And then she emailed downbythebay5, because there should be *some* moment of connection or appreciation or *something* after this conversation she'd been waiting to have for weeks.

> To: <downbythebay5@mailme.com>
> From: Ivy Campbell <ivy.campbell@leland magnet.org>
> Subject: Thanks for talking
>
> I'm really glad you emailed me back today and really glad we talked. I'm so, so sorry about everything you've been going through. I'm here anytime. And for what it's worth, I'm happy you're the one who's been emailing. I was sort of hoping it was you. Xoxo

Then she added her number at the bottom, in case Sydney wanted to call or text instead of emailing.

Will knocked on the door. "Is everything okay?" he asked. "Why were you out there in the rain so long with Sydney?"

"Everything's okay," she said. "But it's sort of private, between me and Sydney. So I can't talk about it."

"Oookaaay," Will muttered as his face flashed red. Even though he should have understood that Ivy didn't want to talk about something, since she was supposed to accept that he didn't want to talk about *anything*.

CHAPTER TWENTY-SIX

Ivy didn't get a response to that email, and she started to worry that she'd misread things yet again.

She almost sent another message saying, "We did talk the other day, right? Am I confused?" But she didn't want to be pushy. And anyway, if somehow she'd been wrong and downbythebay5 was someone she hadn't talked to yet, they would have corrected her. They would have said they had no idea what she was talking about, she was almost positive.

She tried not to obsess over the emails, but she didn't have much of anything going on. Dad and Leo were visiting Leo's family in Vermont. Nana had gone to Florida for the entire month of January to visit her friends who had retired there because, as she put it, who knew how long they'd still be around to invite her, so she'd better take the opportunity when she got it. Will was busy with his friends and his video games, and Mom was busy with the fundraiser for work.

Ivy texted Lila to see if she wanted to hang out, but Lila just responded, **Can't. In NYC.** And that was it. No "See you soon," no "How are you," nothing.

Ivy couldn't bring herself to go to Peyton's family's New Year's Day party when probably only Monica wanted her there, so she spent that morning baking dark chocolate raspberry scones. She'd never made scones before, and they turned out great: buttery, crumbly, and perfectly puffed up. But when Mom came downstairs to the sweet-smelling kitchen, everything got weird and tense.

Mom gushed about how wonderful the scones smelled and what a treat they were, but then she served herself the tiniest piece imaginable. She cut off the corner of one scone, and that was all she ate.

"Oh, Ivy, this is incredible!" she said. "It tastes even better than it looks."

But if it tasted so great, why wasn't she eating a normal-sized portion? She didn't have any more at all. Not the rest of that day, not the next day. Every time Ivy checked the tin, she saw the remaining three-quarters of Mom's scone, untouched. Unwanted.

Why didn't Mom want to eat Ivy's scones?

And why did she keep going to her room and shutting the door every time anyone called? She always went upstairs for work calls, but now she was doing it when she talked to Erin and Nana, too.

When Dad called and asked to talk to Mom after he'd caught up with Ivy and Will and Mom took *that* call upstairs, Ivy was about to snap.

"Maybe you should go out and do something," Will said as Ivy paced around the kitchen. "No offense, but . . . have you left the house at all this week?"

Ivy flinched at the *no offense*—she really did hate that. But Will was actually right. She needed to do something. Something meaningful that would make her feel more like herself. And she needed to stop fixating on those scones. So she packaged up the rest and took them to Sydney's house.

Sydney liked Ivy's baking, after all. Sydney deserved to have someone do extra-nice things for her, to counteract the awful things other people had done.

Nobody answered the door when Ivy knocked, so she left the scones on the front step with a note. And that night, Sydney texted her to say how yummy they were.

Texted.

And Ivy had only given Sydney her phone number in that last email to downbythebay5.

My pleasure! Ivy wrote back. **Text again anytime! I'm here.**

Three dots appeared, showing Ivy that Sydney was replying, and then they disappeared and no message ever showed up. But that was okay. Ivy knew that Sydney was the emailer, and Sydney knew Ivy was there for her. That was plenty.

First thing in the morning on the first day back at school after winter break, Ivy spotted Peyton and Kyra coming out of the music room.

Kyra wore boots with chunky heels and a deep blue sweater Ivy hadn't seen before, and her hair was a couple of inches shorter than it was before break. She looked older—like a sophomore in high school.

Peyton wore an oversized sweatshirt instead of one of her cute, fitted shirts, and her hair was pulled into a messy low ponytail even though there had been an across-the-board ponytail shift this year, and now everyone wore their ponytails high and bouncy.

"Hey, Ivy," Kyra said, friendly but not *friend*-y. This is how she'd been since their fight. Not mean, not annoyed. Pleasant, in a distant way that sometimes made Ivy miss the mean stuff, because then Kyra had at least cared. "How was your break?"

"Pretty good," Ivy replied. "How about yours?"

"Great!"

Peyton didn't say anything, though. And then Josh Miller walked by—finally off crutches now—with a couple other soccer guys.

"It's the Gingerbread Girl!" one of them called.

"Run, run, as fast as you can!" another chimed in.

Peyton was gnawing on her bottom lip, close to tears, and then the boys were gone and Kyra dragged Peyton off toward the bathroom.

What had just happened? Those boys were calling Peyton the Gingerbread Girl? As in that rhyme about a gingerbread man? *Run run, as fast as you can, you can't catch me, I'm the Gingerbread Man?* What did that have to do with Peyton, and why had it made her so upset?

Ivy continued toward her locker, glancing back over her shoulder at the bathroom door Peyton and Kyra had disappeared behind. She was so distracted that she almost didn't notice Lila, who sat on the bench near the math rooms, wearing a vintage-looking Brooklyn Bowling shirt and scowling at a page of her sketchbook.

"Oh. Hey," she said, after she'd nearly tripped over Lila's maroon lace-up boot. "Did you have a nice break?"

"Eh, not really," Lila responded without looking up from her drawing.

Ivy sighed. "Sorry. Me neither."

"Huh." Lila closed her sketchbook. "Why was your break not nice?"

Ivy perched on the other side of the bench, but before she could decide how to answer, Blake Del-Monte stopped in front of them. He shoved the glass container from the scones into Ivy's lap.

"I'm supposed to give this back to you."

"Oh," Ivy said. "Um, thanks for—"

"Sydney doesn't need you dropping off baked goods. You're not friends," Blake said.

Ivy's whole body went hot, from the top of her head down to her toes. Her sweater suddenly felt too tight in the arms and unbearably itchy.

She liked to bake. She liked creating things from scratch that could give people joy. She hadn't done anything wrong, had she?

"Baking isn't a normal way to try to make other people like you, just so you know," Blake added. "It's kind of pathetic."

Thoughts swirled and flashed in Ivy's mind, but

she couldn't grab hold of them. She couldn't come up with anything to say.

"Wow," Lila jumped in. "It must be hard to be so insecure that the only way you can make yourself feel bigger is by making everybody else feel small."

Insecure.

As soon as Lila said the word, Ivy knew it was true, even though it had never occurred to her. Josh was Blake's best friend, and Josh was cuter and funnier and better at soccer. Every teacher who'd had Sydney when she was in middle school raved about how wonderful she had been and seemed disappointed when Blake was nothing like her. Blake was always trying to get under people's skin and make them feel bad, and that was probably because *he* felt bad.

Blake just stood there, his eyes bulging and his face red.

"Whatever," he finally said. "Nice *bowling* shirt." And then he took off.

Lila threw her head back and cackled.

"Oh man! Did you see the look on his face? That was the most fun I've had in weeks, shutting him up." Then she looked at Ivy. "Oh, come on. Please don't tell me you feel sorry for Blake DelMonte."

Ivy shrugged. "Everybody's got their own stuff they're dealing with."

"Nuh-uh. Not an excuse to be terrible to everyone. But P.S. Did you really bake for his sister again? Because you can't save everybody who's having a hard time. You know that, right? Not everybody wants your help."

Ivy bristled. "Sydney does, though."

Lila raised one eyebrow. "And she told you that?"

"Yes!"

"Directly? She said those exact words? That she wants help from you?"

"Basically!" Ivy said. "Yes!"

Ms. Ramos hurried by, saying, "My star research team! Welcome back!"

And then the assistant principal told everybody to hurry up and get to homeroom, so the topic fizzled for the time being.

Later, at lunch, Lila brought up the subject again. "What exactly did Sydney say that made you think she wants your help?"

Ivy looked her straight in the eye and said, "It's complicated, Lila," which made them both crack up.

"Seriously, though," Lila started. But then Nyeema and Ana sat down and started talking to Lila about more shows and books Ivy didn't know anything about.

Ivy zoned out and watched Peyton and Kyra

across the cafeteria, sitting just the two of them. Best friends. Completely in sync. She wondered what Sydney was doing right now. Whether maybe Sydney was in the high school cafeteria, sitting at the end of a table filled with other people, feeling alone.

The next weekend, Dad and Leo were still away, so instead of going to their house for brunch, Ivy went to Kepners'. She'd just sat down at a table with her bagel and whitefish when she noticed Sofia Rodriguez throwing away her trash. Sofia was Sydney's best friend—or she used to be, anyway. And she was dating one of Patrick's best friends. Here she was at the bagel place right by Sydney's house, with two other girls but no Sydney, laughing and chatting as if everything was wonderful and Sydney didn't exist.

It didn't really take.

That's what Sydney had said when Ivy had asked if she'd told people she didn't cheat on Patrick. She'd probably tried to tell Sofia, but Sofia hadn't listened.

Ivy stood up. She couldn't just sit here. She was going to tell Sofia how wrong she was, not sticking by her friend.

But then she froze because there was Lila, holding a tray with a paper-wrapped bagel on a plate.

Ivy was so flustered, she somehow stumbled over the leg of a chair, and Lila burst out into loud, delighted laugher.

"Sorry!" Lila said. "I don't mean to laugh at you. I can't help it. People falling is funny!"

"I'm glad I could entertain you."

Lila held up her hands. "Seriously. It's a thing. It's called incongruity—look it up. When people randomly fall, it's unexpected, so our brains don't know what to do and we end up laughing."

Sofia and her friends were at the door now, leaving. So there went that. Ivy sighed.

"I see you took my bagel recommendation?"

Lila shrugged. "Don't be too flattered. It's not like I have other options." She gestured to the table where Ivy had been sitting. "Can I join you?"

"Of course. I want to be close by so you can tell me how right I was and thank me."

"Hang on, now. Let's wait and see." Lila sanitized her hands, unwrapped her bagel, and poked the top with one fingertip. "Crispy outside, doughy middle. And they didn't offer to toast it, which is a good sign."

"I told you this place is the best."

"Let's not get ahead of ourselves." Lila finished her inspection and took a small bite. "Decent."

Ivy laughed. "That's a huge compliment, coming from you."

"I mean, it's not a New York bagel. But it's not as bad as the other bagels I've had here. Which is something."

"Oh come on, admit it," Ivy said. "It's great."

"It's *decent*," Lila repeated. But when she had to leave a few minutes later, she bought a dozen more to go. She'd *definitely* liked the bagels. And Ivy was almost as happy as she would have been if she'd made them herself.

CHAPTER TWENTY-SEVEN

Nana was finally back from Florida, so the next Friday was the first Friday Afternoon Baking session Ivy and Nana had had in ages. They were making molasses cookies—Mom's favorite.

When Ivy arrived, Nana had all the ingredients lined up as usual, and she pulled out a recipe card with a pastel flower border and even, swoopy cursive.

Chewy Molasses Spice Cookies, the top line read. *From the kitchen of Deborah Berger.*

Deborah Berger. The name was familiar, but it took Ivy a second to place it.

"My mother-in-law," Nana said. "Your great-grandmother."

"She gave you this?"

Nana nodded. "She threw me a bridal shower before I married your grandfather. All the guests brought recipes, and this is the one she gave me."

Whoa. Ivy didn't usually think of Mom's father as her grandfather, since she'd never met him. He'd left Nana when Mom was three and moved to California, where he was from. Mom had barely known him. He'd died young, when Ivy and Will were really little, and only Mom had gone to San Francisco for the funeral. Ivy wasn't sure if Mom had known her grandmother on that side of the family at all. She ran her fingertips over the cursive on the recipe card, wondering if Deborah Berger was still alive and what she would think about Nana and Ivy making her cookies.

"Is it kind of sad for you?" Ivy asked. "Baking these cookies that came from your ex-husband's family?"

Nana adjusted the top of her apron. "Oh, honey. He and I were married a very long time ago." She smiled. "And these are very good cookies."

"Well, was it sad a long time ago?"

Nana patted Ivy's cheek. "Yes. It was sad a long time ago. Now, these cookies aren't going to bake themselves. Let's get to work, shall we?"

Once the cookies were in the oven, Ivy relaxed and breathed in their spicy-sweet scent.

Then she looked back at the recipe card and thought of Mom. Mom had always called them "Nana's molasses cookies." Did she not know where the recipe had come from? Did she not really want to think about it?

Ivy had known for as long as she could remember that Mom's father hadn't been around for most of her life. She'd overheard Mom telling Erin that she would never, ever stand in the way of Ivy and Will spending time with Dad and Leo because she didn't want them to lose their dad like she'd lost hers. It wasn't new information that Mom hadn't had a dad in the way Ivy did. But for the first time, Ivy tried to imagine what that must have been like for Mom, knowing her dad had chosen not only to leave, but to *disappear.* Her heart ached for little-girl Mom and much-younger Nana, and her heart ached because she missed Mom so, so much right now, even though they saw each other every single day and slept in the same house every single night. Mom was so tired and so busy getting ready for this fundraiser next weekend, and she'd basically stopped asking Ivy to tell her things because Ivy hadn't in so long.

There was something about the delicious, familiar scent of those cookies and the careful, swoopy cursive on the recipe card that made Ivy a hundred percent determined to forget about all the things that had worried her and hurt her feelings and made her shut down from Mom. Ivy wanted to take the shuttle into Center City and show up at Mom's office with a tin of the cookies.

Or better yet . . . Nana had gotten this recipe at a bridal shower. People had baby showers, too, right?

"Do you think we should throw a baby shower for Mom and Erin?" Ivy asked.

Nana arched her eyebrows so high they nearly reached her hairline.

"Nothing big. Just a little party? We could make cute baby-themed desserts."

The timer went off for the cookies and Nana took the first two batches out of the oven, but she didn't put the next two cookie sheets in, even though they were loaded up and ready to go.

Nana loved parties. Ivy thought she would be excited, but she frowned.

"You know, Jews don't usually have baby showers. It's seen as bad luck, to make a big fuss before the baby comes. I'm not sure your mom would want something like that, especially with everything Erin and Christopher have been through."

"Oh. I didn't know that," Ivy said. She felt a little bit ashamed that she'd had no idea.

Nana took off her oven mitts, wiped her hands on her apron, and patted Ivy's cheek. "Maybe after the baby comes, we can do something. When your mom can enjoy sweets again."

Ivy paused, waiting for those words to make sense. "What do you mean, when she can enjoy sweets again?"

Nana's mouth fell open. "Oh. *Oh*. I thought . . ." Now she put the oven mitts back on and busied herself with the second round of baking sheets. "Look at me, forgetting to put these in!"

She'd thought Ivy knew something. And Ivy didn't. Of course. Because Mom hadn't told her.

"What is it?" Ivy squeaked out, over the thudding of her heart. "I need to know."

"We should call your mom."

"She's in meetings all afternoon. Tell me. Please!"

Nana sighed. "Everything's okay. Your mom has gestational diabetes. It means she has to be careful about things like sugar intake for now. She'll be completely fine once she delivers the baby. Everything will go back to normal once the baby comes."

But Ivy had already researched gestational

diabetes. It usually went away, but not always. It put people at a greater risk of getting type 2 diabetes, and type 2 diabetes put people at risk for all sorts of things.

What if Mom *wasn't* completely fine once the baby came? What if everything *didn't* go back to normal? Because really, it might not. Maybe too many things in Ivy's family had changed and stretched and begun to fray, and they wouldn't magically snap back into place.

I wish Mom had never agreed to do this. I wish the IVF hadn't worked. I wish she weren't carrying this baby.

Those thoughts flashed in Ivy's brain and sent shock waves through her body. Those were terrible things to wish for.

"I shouldn't have said anything," Nana said. "Me and my big mouth."

Nana hadn't set a timer for this new batch of cookies. They were probably going to burn, and their scent was too thick and sweet. Nana had her hand on Ivy's arm, and Ivy wanted her to let go. She needed space.

"You could call her," Nana said. "Even if she's in meetings, she'd step out and talk to you, if you need her. Or you could call your dad?"

Ivy didn't want to call either of them, but she wanted to leave Nana's apartment so she could be alone, and this was her chance.

"Okay. Yeah, I'll call . . . one of them. I'm going to go, actually. I'll call from home. But thanks, Nana. Love you. See you soon. I'm fine!"

She kissed Nana's cheek and hurried out. She took the elevator downstairs and rushed past all the old people in the lobby instead of smiling at everyone the way she usually did. As soon as she was outside, breathing in ice-cold air, she looked up gestational diabetes on her phone.

The baby could come early or grow too big. A C-section might be necessary.

They were getting closer to the due date, at least. Seven weeks to go now.

She searched for *babies born at 33 weeks*. Babies almost always survived, it seemed. But lots of things could go wrong with their lungs and hearts and other organs. They often had to stay in the hospital for a long time.

Ivy remembered those terrible thoughts that had flashed in her head at Nana's. Those awful things she'd wished.

They weren't true, she told herself. She was glad the

baby was coming. She wanted the baby to be all right. She needed the baby to be all right.

She walked past the construction on the next block, where somebody had bought a house she and Mom used to love, and now they were tearing it down to build something sleek and modern and boring that would look exactly like all the other new construction.

She wanted to scream at the construction workers hauling enormous beams into place, even though it wasn't their fault and it hadn't been *her* house. She'd never even been inside it.

"Hey. Ivy, right? Are you okay? Do you need anything?" a deep voice asked.

Ivy looked up to see Damian from the frozen yogurt place. The guy everyone thought Sydney had cheated on Patrick with, even though she hadn't. Ivy wanted to scream at him, too, even though that made no sense at all.

Her cheeks flamed as she mumbled that she was fine and took off toward home. And as she was walking inside her house, she saw a text from Mom.

Just talked to Nana. So sorry to worry you. I'm finishing up this meeting as fast as possible. I'll come home ASAP

so we can talk. Please don't worry. Love
you so much.

Don't worry, Mom was telling her, as if worrying
was something she could just decide to stop doing,
like running or clapping her hands.

Then don't keep secrets from me! she wanted to
write back.

But then a text came in from Lila. **My moms and
I are getting cheesesteaks because they've
decided it's our duty as Philly residents
to discover good ones. Where should we
go? Wanna come? We can pick you up.**

Ivy smiled. That sounded fun, actually. For the first
time in several minutes, she didn't want to scream
at anyone.

**Actually, is it okay if I go out to
dinner with Lila and her family and we
talk later?** she wrote to Mom.

Mom called back instead of texting again. When
Ivy picked up, she said, "Hey. Are you okay? You really
want to go with Lila?"

"I'm fine," Ivy promised.

Fine was a word like *complicated*, though—it
didn't mean much of anything. It just stopped a
conversation.

Someone in the background called Mom's name, and she said she'd be right there.

"You should go back to your meeting. I'm really fine. I want to go with Lila. I'll see you when I get back."

Mom sighed. "Okay. Have fun then, sweets."

She sounded disappointed.

But this was for the best. Ivy wasn't ready to talk to her. It was better to disappoint her a little than scream at her or say something terrible.

CHAPTER TWENTY-EIGHT

Lila and her parents picked Ivy up, and they went to the place she suggested in Old City. Harrison was at a friend's house, so it was just the four of them, and they ordered all the sandwiches Ivy recommended and asked the server to have them cut into quarters so they could each try everything.

They got one regular cheesesteak with the gooey cheese and grilled onions, one barbecue, one chicken cheesesteak, and one grilled chicken hoagie with smoked provolone and broccoli rabe. As they ate, they asked for other Philadelphia recommendations, too, so Ivy told them about where to get the best soft pretzels and water ice, even though Lila got all huffy about how the name water ice made no sense, and what Ivy was really talking about was Italian ice.

"How about Reading Terminal Market?" Becky asked. "I've heard we should check it out."

"Oh yeah, it's great," Ivy said. "There are tons of restaurants and dessert places and cheese shops and stuff. It's always super crowded, but you should definitely go."

"And there's Pennsylvania Dutch food?" Becky asked.

Ivy remembered the thing with the apple cake—how Lila had shut down—and checked her face for a reaction, but she was looking at her food, picking off onions. "There are some Amish stands, yeah."

Becky turned to Maya. "I bet they have Pennsylvania Dutch filling."

"That's the stuff that's like a cross between mashed potatoes and stuffing, right? They do. We've gotten it before," Ivy said.

Now Lila was rolling a greasy onion bit between her fingers, then flicking it off her plate.

"Maybe we should go to Reading Terminal next weekend," Maya suggested. "Saturday?"

Becky smiled and put one of her hands on top of one of Lila's. "That sounds like a really good thing for next Saturday. What do you think, Lila?"

"Sure! That's fine!" Lila's voice came out too loud for how close together they were sitting. "I saw brownies up there at the counter. Anybody want dessert?"

Becky and Maya exchanged a look, but then Maya said, "Sure. We could share some brownies."

"You want one?" Lila asked Ivy.

"Oh. That's okay," Ivy said. "This isn't really a dessert place. I don't know if they'll be any good."

"It's a place, and they have dessert," Lila said, pointing. "Right there."

"Well, yeah. But those are individually wrapped in plastic."

Lila quirked an eyebrow. "So this is an environmental objection?"

"No. Well, that, too. But when stuff's wrapped in plastic, that usually means it wasn't made in-house." That's what Nana always said.

Lila shrugged and stood up. "Brownies are brownies, Miss Dessert Snob. I'm getting one."

"Fine. But one of the best ice cream places in the city is right over there, so we could get really good ice cream instead of a mediocre brownie. I mean, if that's okay." She looked at Becky and Maya, who nodded.

"Works for me!" Lila said, slipping her arms into her coat.

Becky and Maya stayed at the cheesesteak place to finish their food while Ivy and Lila went across the street to the ice cream shop that was always packed in the summer but mostly empty now, at the beginning of February.

"*Wow* that's good," Lila said as they claimed a table by the windows and she took a bite of her double-chocolate fudge. "You can make all my dessert-related decisions from now on."

Ivy smiled. "In that case, you need to get pie at Reading Terminal! At one of the Amish stands. They have great pie—even Nana thinks so. Oh, and go to the candy shop. I can't remember what it's called, but it's near the bathrooms, and they have *everything*."

Lila scooped up another bite. "You should come. You can show me."

"Oh. Okay, I'll see if I can."

"You *have* to," Lila said. "Especially if we go next Saturday. I'm going to need a buffer."

Ivy calculated out the days between now and then. February 9. She knew it was Will's half-birthday because when he was little, he used to bring half-birthday treats to school, since his real birthday was in the summer. But it wasn't a significant day aside from that, as far as she knew. "Is Saturday a special day for some reason?"

Lila sighed. "Only in my family." Then her phone dinged. "Speaking of, they're ready to go. You done?"

Ivy was pretty sure Lila wouldn't want her to ask why next Saturday was important for her family, so she finished the end of her mint chocolate chip and put on her coat. Just as she and Lila were leaving, a bunch of high school kids came in. One guy was wearing a Fillmore Central Soccer sweatshirt, which made Ivy think of Sydney's ex-boyfriend, Patrick.

And once she was thinking of Patrick, she remembered that February 9 wasn't just Will's half-birthday, it was Sydney's birthday, too. Last year, Ivy and Will had been at Dad and Leo's for dinner, and Sydney had had a bunch of people over. The walls were thin enough that Ivy and her family could hear everybody singing her happy birthday next door, and Will had joked that he should get cake, too—at least half a piece. And then when they were heading home, Sydney had invited them to come in and have some.

She'd held Patrick's hand and made a big thing about how sweet he'd been to get her favorite kind of cake: cookies and cream.

She obviously wouldn't be celebrating with Patrick this year, though. Ivy wondered if she'd get to celebrate with friends at all.

Back at home, Mom sat at the kitchen table with a mug of tea. She was on the phone, but she said good-bye when Ivy came in and sat down next to her.

"Hey, sweet pea," she said. "You have fun?"

Ivy nodded, and Mom tapped her fingertips against the side of her mug. It was the one Ivy had painted when she was in fifth grade.

"Everything set for the fundraiser next weekend?" Ivy asked.

Mom sighed. "I sure hope so." Then she smiled. "I'm glad you and Lila are hanging out. Sounds like things with Kyra and Peyton have been hard."

Sounds like? Ivy's muscles tensed. "What do you mean?"

"Well, you haven't spent time with them for a while. And I saw Kyra's mom the other day. She said you and Kyra had had a falling-out around Thanksgiving." Mom took a tiny sip of tea and set the cup back down so gently it didn't make a sound.

Ivy looked at the lopsided, ugly flower on the front of the mug. Kyra had been with her when she'd decorated it three years ago. Dad had taken Ivy, Kyra, and Will to the pottery-painting place near Kyra's church. Kyra had painted a ceramic picture frame with stars and hearts. She'd still had it the last time Ivy was at her house, with an old photo of the two of them inside. Had she gotten rid of it or replaced the photo? Or left it as a memento of a friendship that used to be important to her but wasn't anymore? Ivy couldn't decide which option was sadder.

Will had decorated a plate to look like a soccer ball, with uneven black and white hexagons. Ivy had wanted to make something for Mom because it was right after Erin and Christopher had lost their baby. Mom was spending a lot of time with them, and she seemed so, so sad.

So Ivy had painted the mug with Mom's favorite colors: blue on the inside and pale yellow on the outside. She'd tried to paint a pink flower on the front, but she kept messing up the shape and then making the petals bigger to cover up her mistakes.

Ivy had still thought Mom and Dad were happily married back then, but Dad moved out a couple of months later.

Ivy had thought Mom needed cheering up because she was so sad about Erin and Christopher losing their baby. But maybe she'd been sad about splitting up with Dad, too. How long had Mom and Dad acted like they were happy when they weren't?

"You know you can always talk to me. About

anything, no matter what," Mom said. "I wish you'd told me about whatever fight you had with Kyra and Peyton. That must have been hard."

And I wish you'd told me about anything, Ivy thought.

Maybe Mom never really had, though. Maybe she'd only acted like she was confiding in Ivy when she was actually keeping all the big stuff from her.

Mom yawned.

"We can talk tomorrow if you're tired," Ivy said.

"I'd like to talk now." Mom leaned in toward Ivy, tipping her forehead down to make eye contact, but Ivy looked at the smooth, honey-colored wood of their small, round kitchen table—an antique Mom and Dad had picked out at a flea market when they were first married. So different from the big, new, rectangular table Dad and Leo had now.

"I don't want you to worry about what Nana told you," Mom said. "Gestational diabetes is pretty common. The doctors are monitoring me carefully. We're doing everything we need to do, okay? We have it under control."

We. We. We.

"Do you have any questions for me?"

But Ivy didn't have any idea where to start.

She wanted to know how long Mom and Dad had known they were going to get a divorce. She wanted to know if other things were going wrong with this pregnancy, too, but nobody had blurted them out in front of her yet. But she also *didn't* want to know either of those things.

"I don't have any questions," she lied. "I'm okay."

She willed herself to hug Mom or put her hand on Mom's belly the way she had the morning of the twenty-week ultrasound—that had made Mom so, so happy. But she couldn't force herself to do it.

It doesn't cost anything to be kind.

That's what Mom used to say to Ivy and Will when they were little and she wanted them to be polite to a grown-up or include another kid.

But it felt like it *would* cost something to be kind to Mom right now.

It felt like it would cost an awful lot.

CHAPTER TWENTY-NINE

That Sunday morning, Ivy and Will walked past Sydney on the way to Dad and Leo's for brunch. She was outside the coffee shop, holding a drink and talking to a woman dressed in workout clothes.

Sydney caught Ivy's eye and mouthed, *Save me!*

So Ivy told Will she'd catch up and jogged over.

"Hey, there you are!" Sydney said. "Kathleen, this is Ivy. She lives in the neighborhood. I'm . . . tutoring her. So we'd better go. It was so nice to see you!"

"You too, sweetheart," Kathleen said, squeezing Sydney into a hug.

Once Ivy and Sydney turned the corner, Sydney said, "Sorry about that. That's Patrick's mom. I hadn't seen her in a long time. That was . . . a little much."

Ahh. "Was she mean to you?"

"No, she was super nice, which was almost worse. She said they all miss me. She has a birthday present for me that she wants to drop off next weekend." Sydney shook her head. "I don't know why that was so intense for me, seeing her."

"It seems like the whole situation has been pretty intense," Ivy said.

"Yeah. Things have been way better lately, though. People seem to have forgotten how much they hate me. They've moved on." Sydney shrugged, and they turned onto the side street where Dad, Leo, and the DelMontes lived. Blake was out in the street on his skateboard. His wheels whirred along the ground, until he saw Ivy walking with Sydney and kicked the front of the board down to stop.

"You've gotta be kidding me," he muttered as he stormed inside.

"Sorry about him," Sydney said. "He's having a rough time, but he's also being a little punk. Thanks again for saving me."

"Anytime," Ivy said. "I'm glad things are better. And hey, happy birthday, if I don't see you. It's next Saturday, right? The ninth?"

Sydney looked startled. *Oops.*

"I remember from last year, because you shared

your cake with us," Ivy explained. "It's Will's half-birthday, too, so the date stuck. You have any plans?"

"Not really. My friends and I used to have this birthday breakfast tradition. We'd go to the diner and put candles in the pancakes. But I'm not really part of that group anymore, since Patrick is. So I'm not sure what I'll do."

Sydney didn't sound upset about that, but she must have been, deep down.

"I could bake you a cake!" Ivy blurted.

Sydney raised her eyebrows.

"Or not. But actual cake is better than pancakes, in my opinion, and I bake something every Friday anyway. So just—if you want me to make you a cake, I can."

Sydney's phone chimed.

"I'm sure any cake you make would be better than pancakes," she said.

Ivy grinned. "Then I'll make you one! It's no problem. I can bring it over on Saturday, if you want me to."

Sydney's phone chimed again, and she checked the screen. "Okay, thanks, Ivy. That's sweet. I'll see you soon!"

She ran up the stairs and into her house. Blake would be awful about the cake, obviously, but Ivy didn't care. She felt the opposite of how she'd felt the night before with Mom. Then, being kind would have cost more than she had left inside her. Now she was filled back up to the brim.

The Wizard of Oz was happening the next weekend, so there were posters all around the school on Monday. Ivy hadn't realized it was already time for the show, even though it felt like ages ago when she'd helped Peyton and Kyra prepare their audition songs.

At assembly on Wednesday morning, Peyton, Kyra, and the rest of the cast got up onstage to remind everybody when the performances were: one Friday evening, one Saturday evening, and one Sunday afternoon.

Then they performed a few scenes to get people excited to go. Kyra spun around in circles, swept up in a pretend tornado, and then Peyton, wearing her blue-and-white-checked Dorothy dress and ruby-red shoes, belted out "Somewhere Over the Rainbow." Her voice bounced off the walls and filled the whole enormous space. She sounded even better than usual.

But then Ivy heard whispering behind her. It was Blake, one row back, whispering to Josh. They were all supposed to be sitting in their assigned homeroom rows, but Blake had snuck into the wrong one.

"Peyton looks good, huh? Wearing all that makeup?" Blake said. "I wouldn't mind being her Toto."

Which didn't even make sense, since Toto was a stuffed dog Peyton was carrying in a tiny basket, but sounded gross and inappropriate, the way he said it.

"Yeah. She looks cute in pigtails," Josh agreed.

Ivy's stomach turned. That was a compliment, sort of, but it was the wrong kind of compliment. Peyton was putting everything she had into this song in front of all these people, and they were acting like she was just on display for them to look at.

"You gonna try again with her?" Blake asked. "Or you think she'd run away like before?"

Run away?

Whatever Josh said back was too quiet for Ivy to hear.

Ivy had no idea what they were talking about. She had no idea what that Gingerbread Girl thing had meant. But it had upset Peyton, whatever it was, and they were being so obnoxious right now. So she whipped her head around and glared at them.

Josh looked down, but Blake glared right back. "*What?*"

"Be quiet!" she whispered. "You're being jerks."

"*You're* being annoying. Like always," Blake said.

Josh put his hand up to his forehead as if he were blocking out this whole thing, but he didn't say a word.

"She's not being annoying," somebody hissed. Nyeema, two seats over from Ivy.

"And you *are* being jerks." That was Elias, sitting on Josh's other side.

A teacher shushed all of them and then walked over and said something to Blake, who got up and moved back to the right row.

Ivy cheered extra loud when the song ended and decided she was going to the show this weekend. She hadn't really planned to, and maybe Peyton and Kyra wouldn't care at all if she went. But maybe they would. And either way, she wanted to be there.

She ended up next to Elias in the crowd of people leaving assembly.

"Hey. Thanks for saying that in there. To Blake and Josh," she said.

"No problem. It was true."

Elias had gotten tall this year. She had to look up at him, which was new. His shirt was a tiny bit too big, and she wondered if he liked it that way or even noticed it was baggy. Maybe one of his parents had gotten it big on purpose, since he was growing so fast all of a sudden.

"Are you going to the show?" he asked.

"I think I am, yeah."

"Nice. I'll be there Sunday. Maybe I'll see you?"

They went through the door and into the hallway, where there was more room and the crowd began to disperse. One of Elias's friends, a girl named Leah, ended up on his other side.

"I'll look for you," Ivy said. "If that's when I go."

"Good." Elias smiled. He had a nice smile. Friendly and easy and warm. "I'll look for you, too."

She wasn't sure Elias liked her, and she wasn't sure she liked him. But it was possible that she *could*. And it was kind of fun to wonder.

At the end of the day, Peyton was packing up her things at her locker by herself when Ivy passed. Ivy had plenty of time before she needed to get to the bus, so she stopped.

"Hey. You sounded great today. I'm excited to come see the show."

Peyton's face lit up. "You'll be there? Thank you!"

Some other people from the play called out to Peyton, asking if she was coming to rehearsal yet. "In just a minute," she called back. She closed her locker and turned to Ivy. "Listen. I've thought a lot about what you said, about how I told you I didn't want to leave you out but I kept leaving you out anyway."

"Oh. I was upset," Ivy said. "I didn't—"

"No, you were right." She played with the charm on her necklace. "You remember last year when we could only choose one friend to sit with on the bus to Cape May and I was by myself?"

Ivy nodded. They'd gone for a science field trip, and Ivy and Kyra had sat together because they'd always been partners for that kind of thing. They were already friends with Peyton, but not super close yet, and Peyton had ended up with somebody random because she didn't have a partner. Ivy had felt bad when she noticed, but it was too late to do anything about it.

"That kind of thing's happened to me so many times. At my old school, too. I liked that Kyra was choosing *me* this year. I wanted to stay friends with you. But I also wanted to be best friends with Kyra."

Ivy nodded slowly. That hurt to hear, but it made sense, too. Peyton had gone along with things that excluded Ivy because she didn't want to be excluded.

"I know it doesn't fix anything," Peyton added. "I'm sorry."

But maybe it sort of *did* fix some things. Peyton and Kyra were best friends now, and it seemed like

Kyra was a good friend to Peyton, the way she used to be a good friend to Ivy. There wasn't really any bitterness between Ivy and Kyra anymore. If Ivy could accept how close Kyra and Peyton were, then maybe she and Peyton could have their own, new kind of friendship.

"Thank you. For telling me that," Ivy said. "And I'm sorry about everything with Josh and how I acted when I knew you liked him."

Peyton's face scrunched up.

"I take it you don't like him anymore?"

"Uh, no."

Ivy smiled. "I feel like there's a story there. But you don't have to tell me if you don't want to."

Peyton glanced at the time on her phone. "The short version is, he heard I liked him and tried to kiss me at that bat mitzvah we both went to over winter break. He asked me to dance, and literally the first thing he said was 'So, I heard you're into me and I think you're cute,' and then the next thing I knew, his mouth was coming straight at mine. Our *parents* were there. It was so awkward! So I ran and hid in the bathroom."

"Ugh!" Ivy said.

"I know!"

"So, that Gingerbread Girl thing . . ."

"Run, run, as fast as you can. You can't catch me, I'm the Gingerbread Man. Or . . . Girl, in this case. One of his friends made it up. I think he was embarrassed."

"Ew," Ivy said. "I'm sorry that happened."

"Thanks. I'm okay now." Peyton checked the time again. "I should go. But I'm glad we talked. Maybe next time you can tell me about what's happening with you, too."

Ivy nodded. "Yeah. I'd like that."

Peyton smiled. "I would, too."

CHAPTER THIRTY

Ivy had assumed that Nana would help her bake Sydney's birthday cake that Friday afternoon, but Nana was hosting Shabbat dinner instead of going to her neighbors' apartment, and she wanted to teach Ivy to braid and bake the challah. So Ivy was on her own for the cake.

But she had fun looking up all sorts of recipes and making a plan. She decided to go with cookies and cream, since that was Sydney's favorite, and she took bits of a few different recipes she found online to come up with her own super-recipe. The cake would have alternating layers of chocolate and vanilla, with Oreo cookies crumbled into vanilla buttercream frosting and thick, dark chocolate ganache to spread on top of the frosting. She made a list of ingredients she needed to buy, and her plan was to get the ingredients Thursday after school, bake the cake Friday after she got home from Nana's, drop it off for Sydney sometime before lunch on Saturday, and then head to Reading Terminal to meet Lila. No problem.

But then on Thursday at lunch, Lila plopped her tray down on the table and said, "Hey, so, wanna go on a super-touristy food tour of Reading Terminal instead of just getting the food we want like regular people?"

Ivy finished a bite of her grilled cheese. "Um . . . I guess?"

"My parents booked us tickets for a food tour that meets at eleven. They're absurdly excited." Lila tucked her hair behind her ears. She'd gotten it cut recently, and the two sides were pretty much even now. "I know it's dorky and you could probably *give* a tour of Reading Terminal."

11:00. That was earlier than she'd thought they were going, but she could drop off Sydney's cake around 10:00.

"It's fine!" Ivy said. "It sounds fun, honestly."

"I don't know about fun," Lila said. "Anyway, you should sleep over tomorrow night, so you don't have to come over too early on Saturday. After Friday

Afternoon Baking, if you're free. Maya's cooking, so the food will be good."

Lila said it super casually, as if she didn't care at all either way, but Ivy was beginning to realize she did.

"I'd really like to . . ." she started.

"But you can't," Lila finished for her. "It's fine. No big deal. You have plans?"

"Just something I said I'd do. But I'll be done in plenty of time to meet you by eleven. And a tour will be fun! Seriously."

Lila raised one eyebrow. "You have something you said you'd do? That's mysterious."

Lila obviously wanted her to elaborate, but she knew Lila wouldn't understand.

"Yep! That's me. A woman of mystery."

"You're not going to tell me."

It was a statement, not a question. And Lila sounded annoyed, or maybe hurt.

"Lila, it's not a big deal."

"Then tell me."

Ivy's jaw tightened. *Why don't you tell me what's important about Saturday?* she wanted to ask. *Or who used to make Dutch apple cake, or what it was like when you went back to New York over Thanksgiving and Christmas, or who that old man is in the photo you flipped over?*

"I'm sorry, but I don't want to talk about it." She

said instead, calmly and clearly. She was owning that—not lashing back or changing the subject or saying "It's complicated" as a cop-out.

"Fine," Lila said. "We won't talk about it." She definitely sounded hurt.

Nyeema and Ana sat down, and Ivy was relieved when the three of them started talking about the most recent episode of a show she'd never seen.

On Friday night, Nana convinced Ivy to stay for dinner, so Ivy got home later than she'd planned. She hurried to set out all the cake ingredients and get started.

Will was spending the night at Langston's, and Mom was going to bed extra early, since the fundraiser was the next night. Mom wanted to know what she was baking, and when Ivy said it was a birthday cake, Mom assumed it was for Lila, since she knew Ivy was seeing her the next day.

Ivy didn't contradict her. She told herself that wasn't lying—it was just simplifying things, so Mom could go straight to bed like she wanted, and Ivy could get straight to work.

She sent a quick text to Sydney, wishing her a happy birthday eve and telling her she planned to drop off the cake sometime around 10:00 tomorrow morning. Then she started on the chocolate cake batter, melting and mixing and stirring.

The first problem was that she only had two cake pans and she was baking four cake layers. She would have to wait until the chocolate layers cooled before she could get the vanilla ones into the oven. Plus, each round of cake layers took at least thirty minutes to bake.

It was after 10:00 p.m. when she took the chocolate cake out of the oven and a text came in from Lila.

I just thought of something. Tomorrow morning. The thing you have to do: Does it have to do with Blake's sister?

Ugh. Why wouldn't Lila let this go? Why did Lila *care*?

Ivy didn't reply. She didn't have time. She gave the vanilla cake batter one more stir, set the chocolate cakes aside to cool, and started crushing Oreos with her rolling pin so she could mix cookie bits into the icing. Then her phone rang. Lila.

She sighed and picked up. "Hey. I'm in the middle of something. Is everything okay?"

"The thing tomorrow morning that you're being all weird about," Lila said. "Can you just tell me: Is it for Blake's sister?"

Ivy flinched. "Her name is Sydney."

"Wait, so it is, then?" Lila asked. "Please, tell me you haven't convinced yourself she needs you and only you to help her through some crisis. Have you?"

Ivy whacked the next few cookies with the rolling pin instead of rolling them, and chocolate pieces went flying.

"I told you I don't want to talk about this. I don't push you when *you* don't want to talk about things."

There was a pause, and then Lila said, "I know. But this is different."

"Why?"

Ivy touched the top of one of the chocolate cakes with her fingertip. They were supposed to cool for another ten minutes, but they weren't *that* hot, and the pans were nonstick. Maybe nonstick pans meant she didn't have to wait so long?

Lila sighed into the phone, and the sound crackled in Ivy's ear.

Ivy went for it, flipping the first cake pan over to ease out the cake, but a corner got stuck. Part of the cake clung to the pan, and when Ivy stabilized the rest of the cake so it wouldn't crumble even more, she burned her fingers.

"No!" she shouted. "Ouch!"

"Everything okay?" Lila asked.

"I . . . I have to focus on what I'm doing, okay? I'll be there tomorrow for the food tour. But tonight, please just . . . leave me alone."

There was a pause, and then Lila said, "I think you really want to listen to me right now, Ivy."

Right. Because *Lila* knew exactly what Ivy wanted— way better than Ivy could possibly know for herself.

"Honey?" Mom called from upstairs. "What's going on down there? You all right?"

And now she'd woken up Mom. Perfect.

"I really *don't* want to listen to you." Ivy's words came out too harsh, but it was so late and she was tired, and she needed to end this conversation so she could tell Mom everything was okay and fix this cake.

"Whatever. Fine," Lila said. "Do what you want. I tried. I'm done."

Lila ended the call, and Ivy stared at her phone for a moment, trying to understand why Lila had sounded so mad. But then Mom's footsteps were padding across the hallway upstairs, and Mom was calling, "Ivy?"

So Ivy put down her phone and rushed up to reassure her.

Almost an hour later, Ivy took the vanilla cakes out of the oven. She had made the buttercream frosting and used a little bit of it to glue that broken choco-late cake layer back together, but she was way, way too tired to make the ganache and assemble the lay-ers. So she put everything away for the night and set her alarm.

Early the next morning, she got back to work, tak-ing out the four cake layers and spreading icing on top of the cobbled-together bottom one. She melted dark chocolate and simmered heavy cream on the stove for the ganache. When she mixed the melted chocolate into the pan with the simmering cream, it began to thicken.

Just like magic, Nana would have said.

Ivy smiled, watching the ganache congeal into the perfect consistency. This was working. She was going to pull off the most ambitious recipe she'd ever attempted—a recipe nobody but her had ever made in quite this way.

She spooned ganache on top of the buttercream icing that already covered the bottom layer of the cake, and then she set a vanilla cake layer on top of that. She got into a satisfying rhythm: cake, butter-cream, ganache.

But by the time she put the last layer on, the ganache was beginning to set, getting sticky and thick. She had to hurry up and finish.

As she spread the buttercream icing over the top of the cake, Mom came downstairs, freshly showered. "Looks delicious. Lucky Lila!"

Ivy forced a smile. "How are you feeling? You excited for the fundraiser tonight?"

"I'm excited for it to be over, that's for sure," Mom said.

She edged past Ivy to put on the teakettle, which was a little strange, since she usually had coffee in the morning. Then she toasted a slice of multigrain bread and began to eat it dry.

Ivy gave the ganache another stir and scooped some up.

"Do you want me to drive you over to Lila's with the cake?" Mom offered.

"Oh. No, that's okay. We're meeting at Reading Terminal, actually."

Ivy tried to spread the glop of ganache . . . but it was too thick to spread. She scooped it off, but the damage was done. Now the icing on the top looked messy, and she'd already used the last of the buttercream. How was she going to touch it up?

"The cake is pretty big," Mom pointed out. "You're not going to bring it to Reading Terminal, are you?"

Ivy went over to the stove. Could she thin out the

ganache if she simmered it the tiniest bit? She turned the burner on low. "The cake isn't for Lila, actually." She didn't see a way around admitting that.

"Who is it for, then?"

Instead of answering Mom's question, Ivy attempted to stir the gloppy ganache remains. *Ack.* She was pretty sure heating the pan again wasn't doing the trick. Ganache was half dark chocolate and half cream, and Ivy didn't have any more of either of those things. Maybe she could pour in a little regular milk instead?

"Ivy," Mom said. "Who is the cake for?"

Ivy grabbed the milk from the fridge. "Sydney Del-Monte," she said.

She opened the milk and tried to add a tiny splash, but way too much poured out. *Shoot.*

Mom came up behind Ivy and touched her shoulder. And then Ivy smelled something burning. The ganache was bubbling around the edges, with a pond of milk in the middle. She turned off the burner, but it was too late. The bottom of the ganache was crusty and burnt.

"Ivy?" Mom pulled on Ivy's arm a little to make her turn around, but Ivy didn't *want* to turn around, and she didn't want Mom touching her, and she didn't want to talk to Mom about anything at all.

"Honey," Mom said in that too-gentle voice people used when little kids were getting worked up over nothing. "I'm confused. You're making this cake for Sydney?"

Mom was still holding on to Ivy's arm, and Ivy yanked away, hard, pulling free. Mom stumbled back but kept her balance. She winced and rubbed one hand in a circle over her belly. "What's going on, Ivy?" She sounded exhausted. Exasperated. "Please, explain to me why you're making this very elaborate cake for Sydney DelMonte." She said it as if that were a ridiculous thing to do.

"*Why?*" Ivy snapped. "Why should I tell you that when you don't tell me *anything*! You've shut me out of *everything*!"

Ivy picked up the heavy pan with the ruined ganache and slammed it into the sink.

The little door inside her chest that used to contain all her terrible feelings and thoughts had swung all the way open now. It had broken off its hinges.

"I haven't shut you out," Mom said. "I never meant to shut you out of anything."

"You *have*! You don't let me help. You talk to Dad and Nana and everybody else but you don't tell me anything at all."

Mom shook her head. "Ivy. You're thirteen years old. I *can't* tell you everything."

"You can, but you *won't*!"

"I'm . . . so sorry . . . you're feeling hurt." Mom was kind of out of breath. She winced again, and for one terrible second Ivy was terrified she might have hurt Mom when she pulled her arm away and Mom stumbled backward. But then the moment passed, and Mom's face relaxed.

Mom's phone rang and she looked at the screen. "It's Mark," she said. Her boss. "We need to go over a few last things for tonight. I'll come back down as soon as I can, okay? Please don't go anywhere before we finish this conversation."

Mom went back upstairs.

Ivy's heart pounded as she went over to the sink, and her fingers shook as she scraped burnt, milky ganache out of the pan. She switched on the water and the garbage disposal, and the whole ruined mixture glug-glug-glugged down the drain. She left the pan soaking in the sink and tried one last time to re-spread the top layer of icing.

She made it a little better, anyway. This was as good as it was going to get. She stuck toothpicks in the top and covered the cake with aluminum foil.

Mom was still on the phone, and Ivy had to go now

if she had any shot at meeting Lila on time. This was already later than she'd planned to leave.

She checked bus times on her phone. There should be one at 23rd Street at 10:32. She could make that one if she hurried. The next one, at 10:42, would be cutting it too close for the tour.

She shoved her feet into her warm boots, slipped on her jacket, and left.

CHAPTER THIRTY-ONE

It wasn't until Ivy was outside, balancing the heavy cake in her cold, bare hands, that she realized Sydney hadn't replied to her text from the night before.

Was it possible she hadn't seen it? Could she still be asleep?

But Ivy didn't have time to rethink the plan now, and her arms ached too much from the weight of the cake to slow down. The aluminum foil blew off in the wind, and the cake was so absurdly tall. It was starting to tilt.

She hustled to the DelMontes' house and rang the doorbell with her elbow, since she didn't have a free hand.

Please don't let Blake come to the door, she thought.

Mrs. DelMonte was the one who opened it. Not as good as if Sydney had answered, but not a disaster.

"Ivy!" she said. Cheerful, but confused. "I didn't know you were coming over." She paused. "Or bringing cake!"

"Hi," Ivy said. "Uh, it's for Sydney."

"You made Sydney a birthday cake? That's . . . very sweet. She's at the diner now, but you can leave it here."

Wait. Sydney was *out*?

"For birthday pancakes with her friends?" Ivy asked. "I thought she said that wasn't happening."

Mrs. DelMonte raised her eyebrows. "It's just Syd and her friend Sofia, I think. And they should be home soon. Do you want to wait? I was just icing the cake I made for her, actually. But you can never have too much cake!"

Ivy's fingers were so cold and her arms were so tired and now her mind was swirling.

That was *nice*, that Sydney was out with Sofia. Ivy should be happy about that. But it was hard to feel happy when she was standing here holding this heavy, lopsided cake she'd spent hours making, and there was another cake for Sydney inside, and Sydney wasn't alone and sad on her birthday after all.

"I think I'll just leave it at my dad's. I can bring it back later. If Sydney wants. But it seems like she doesn't need it, so . . . thanks anyway! Bye!"

Ivy rushed back down the DelMontes' front steps and up Dad and Leo's. They were at their Saturday spinning class, but Ivy let herself into their house. She walked up the stairs to the kitchen, set the giant, humiliating cake down on the counter, and left a note telling them she'd come back for it later.

The clock on the microwave said 10:31. She wasn't going to make the 10:32 bus unless it was late. She peeked out the front window to see if it was already coming down 23rd Street. No bus, but there was a guy carrying a large bouquet of yellow and pink flowers. *Damian.*

Oh no. He was heading toward the DelMontes'. *Now*, when Sydney's life was finally getting easier—when she and Sofia were eating pancakes together and the rumors had died down. What was he doing here?

What if Sofia saw Damian and thought Sydney had cheated on Patrick after all? And Patrick's *mother* wanted to bring Sydney a present, too. *She* could show up and see him.

Ivy sprinted down the stairs and out the door, and then she froze. What was she even doing? Was she going to try to make him *leave* somehow? She heard the tap-tap-tap of boots on pavement, and there was Sydney, walking next to Sofia, looking straight at Damian, and . . . beaming. Why was she smiling like that?

"Hey there, birthday girl!" Damian called.

And . . . oh. *Oh.*

The realization hit, sudden and definite. Sydney and Damian were together.

Sydney launched herself into his arms, and he spun her around.

When he put her down, Sydney noticed Ivy and smacked her forehead. "Ivy! Oh no. You texted me. You made a cake! My phone died last night, and then this morning I've gotten so many birthday texts I got behind. I meant to reply. I'm so sorry."

Sydney had gotten behind on birthday texts?

She'd made it seem like she was lonely and sad and bullied, but here she was, with a cute boyfriend holding a bouquet of flowers and a best friend who clearly knew they were together and more birthday messages than she could stay on top of.

"I didn't know you two were dating," Ivy said. "I . . . I wish you'd told me that."

Sydney glanced at Damian, then at Sofia. "I'll come inside in a minute," she told them. They both gave Ivy a confused, pitying look before they started to head up the DelMontes' front steps, and Sydney put one hand on Ivy's elbow.

"Ivy. I didn't realize I hadn't mentioned that Damian and I are dating. But I didn't *have* to tell you that. I don't tell you every detail of my life. That would be kind of strange if I did."

"But . . . you *did*, though," Ivy stammered. "Maybe not every detail, but you told me a lot. And you sent those emails."

"Emails?" Sydney narrowed her pretty amber-colored eyes. "I already told you, I didn't send you emails."

"But then you told me you did!" Hadn't she? "You told me you'd lied before because you hadn't been ready to tell the truth. And you knew my phone number because I wrote it in an email."

"No, I knew your number because I asked Blake," Sydney said slowly. "I have no idea what emails you're talking about."

Ivy's heart pounded against her ribs, which were so cold now they were practically frozen. She pictured them cracking like icicles, one by one. She shook her head, over and over, and her hands began to shake, too.

Blake had her phone number from last year when they'd been in a lab group together. Why hadn't she thought of that? Why hadn't that even occurred to her, that Sydney could have gotten it from him?

Sydney tightened her pale green scarf. "I'm sorry, Ivy. I should have told you not to bake me a cake. I didn't want to hurt your feelings, but . . . You're a really sweet girl, Ivy. I understand why you thought I needed help—you saw me at a lot of low moments. But I'm okay, truly."

Ivy cleared her throat and opened her mouth, but nothing made any sense. She couldn't find any words.

"I won't lie—it's been a rough year," Sydney went on. "But I have people I can turn to. And you're in *eighth grade*. You should focus on . . . I don't know. Whatever stuff you do at school. Sports, music, art, whatever your thing is."

But Ivy didn't *have* a thing.

Everybody around her did, but she didn't. Nothing she was actually any good at. Nothing that counted.

Sydney leaned in to give Ivy a hug, and her soft, warm scarf rubbed Ivy's cold cheek. And then Sydney walked back inside and Ivy just stood there, still and numb. She heard a bus rumble down the road a few blocks away. It must be way past 10:32 by now. That had to be the 10:42, and she was going to miss that, too. She sprinted toward 23rd Street, but the bus was already pulling away.

She'd promised Lila she'd be there for the tour, and she wouldn't be. She was trying so hard to do the right thing, but somehow she kept doing every single thing wrong.

CHAPTER THIRTY-TWO

Ivy took out her phone to send an apology text to Lila, and she gasped when she saw the screen.

In the past fifteen minutes, she'd missed calls from Mom, Nana, and Dad. There were two texts from Dad, too.

Ivy, where are you?

Mom's water broke and the baby's coming. She's going to the hospital. Please call me. I love you!

Mom was going to the hospital? The baby wasn't supposed to come yet. The baby wasn't supposed to come for another six weeks.

And Ivy had *yelled* at Mom this morning and made her stumble and wince. She'd left the house even though Mom said not to. Extreme stress could cause early labor. What if Ivy had made this happen? What if the baby wasn't okay? What if *Mom* wasn't?

Ivy's frozen fingers punched out a very different text to Lila than what she'd planned to say a moment before.

My mom's at the hospital having the baby I think. I'm not going to make it today. I'm so sorry.

Lila's response came right away. **OMG I hope everything's okay. Don't worry about the tour!**

Ivy's heart lurched. She was getting a free pass she didn't deserve. Lila had no idea Ivy would have let her down anyway.

She considered texting the truth, but then there was Dad, coming toward her, wearing a parka and athletic shorts from spinning class. He was crossing the street, waving to get Ivy's attention.

But she couldn't do this. She couldn't handle *any* of this. She took off.

She had no idea where she was going—she just ran. One block north and another and another. *She* was the Gingerbread Girl—running, running, determined not to be caught. She veered off toward the fenced-in playground she and Will had loved when they were little kids. They'd called it the teeny playground because everything in it was toddler-sized: sandbox, tiny slides, miniature cars, and miniature house. She unlatched the gate and let herself in. It was empty.

So much had changed since the days when she and Will had come to this playground every week. Her family was different. The whole neighborhood was different. But this playground was the same.

Ivy sat down on the bench where Mom and Dad used to read and sip coffee while she and Will played.

Her mind spun through the things she'd said to Mom today. The way Mom had winced and clutched her side, that terrible thought Ivy had had last week, when she'd wished the IVF had never worked.

The fear that had buzzed in the corners of her brain grew big and loud and inescapable.

She was *not* an exceptionally good person.

She'd been working so, so hard to be kind and generous and good, but she wasn't—not really. Not deep down. She should just accept that. She should stop trying to be someone better than she was.

The gate to the playground opened.

"You're fast, Ives," Dad said, panting. "I didn't know you could sprint like that."

He sat down on the bench next to Ivy, putting

his arm around her, and she let herself crumple against him.

"I'm sorry," she said. "I'm so sorry."

"Hey." Dad pulled his face back and tipped his forehead down to meet her eyes. "It's okay. You're okay. Everything's okay."

Ivy shook her head. "Nothing's okay. I yelled at Mom, and she stumbled, and I left, and she was already so stressed about the fundraiser. It was awful. I was awful. The baby wasn't supposed to come yet."

"Ivy." Dad touched her chin, easing her face up so she had to look at him.

"You don't think you caused Mom to go into labor, do you? Because you definitely didn't."

"But stress can cause early labor. Right?"

"*Extreme* stress," he said. "Sweetie. Mom said she felt sick to her stomach as soon as she woke up this morning. That's a sign of early labor. She was having more and more Braxton Hicks contractions lately—the practice kind, getting her body ready. This was underway, Ives. This was going to happen today no matter what."

"But it's so early."

Dad nodded. "It's early. I would have loved to see that baby stay in there a few weeks longer. But Mom's at a great hospital. She has the best possible care.

Lots and lots of babies are born this early. Earlier, even. And they're okay."

"Okay." Ivy said it once, then again. "Okay." Her heart slowed down, just a little. "I didn't know that. About how she felt sick to her stomach this morning. Or the contractions."

"Nothing is your fault, Ivy," Dad said. "In case you need to hear that again, I'm going to say it. As many times as you need. Nothing in this situation is your fault."

And finally, Ivy let herself cry. Warm tears streamed down her ice-cold cheeks, and Dad hugged her tightly.

"This has been hard on you, huh?" he asked.

Ivy almost pushed away his concern. It had become a reflex, insisting she was fine even if she wasn't. But instead, she nodded and told the truth. "I hate not knowing what's happening."

Dad sighed. "I get that. That's such a tough part of being a kid—sensing that things are happening, but not having all the details. I know Mom's struggled to figure out how much is too much to tell you and Will. Maybe you needed to know more."

"*You've* kept stuff from us, too," Ivy said. "Not only Mom."

She hadn't known she was going to say that until the words had tumbled out.

"Before you moved out, I mean," she explained. "Will and I had no idea you weren't happy until you left. You didn't tell us about Leo until way after you met him."

Next to her, Dad stiffened and drew in a sharp breath.

"I'm sorry," she said. "I know that's not the point right now."

"No. That's true," Dad said. "There was a lot I didn't tell you until after the fact. Honey, I love you and Will more than anything else in the world, and I'm trying as hard as I can—Mom is, too. But I'm sure we haven't gotten everything right."

Ivy shrugged. "I didn't ask you stuff, either, though. You or Mom. Back then when you moved out, or this year."

Weeks ago, Nana had told Ivy to ask Mom for what she needed. Dad used to tell her that, too, all the time—he'd ask over and over whether there was anything she wanted to talk about, anything she wanted to know.

But Ivy hadn't asked for what she needed. She hadn't even tried to figure out what she needed. She'd told herself her own needs weren't important, but that hadn't made them go away. Those thoughts she didn't want to think, those feelings she didn't want to feel—the more she'd tried to ignore them, the more powerful they'd grown.

What had Nana said back in September? *That heart of yours is like a sponge.*

Sponges didn't last all that long. Once they absorbed too much dirt and grime, they couldn't do their job.

Ivy glanced at Dad's bare legs, which were covered in goose bumps.

"Your legs must be frozen."

"A little chilly," Dad admitted. He opened up his gym bag and pulled on his warm-up pants. "That's better."

"Good," Ivy said. "Can I ask you something random?"

"Anything."

"Did you hate our house when you lived there?"

Dad blinked. "Our *house*?"

"It's just . . . Your place with Leo. It's so different. And your car. They're so new and fancy and convenient. Did you ever like living in our creaky old house with all the things that don't work that well?"

Dad tipped his head back, looking at the clear blue

sky. The air was cold and windy, but way up high, the sun was shining bright, trying its best to warm everything up.

"The house is more Mom's taste than mine. I don't think I ever loved the creaks and old radiators and tiny closets. But I did love living there."

"You couldn't have loved it that much. Since you left."

The words came out small and squeaky, but Ivy had said them, after swallowing them down and willing them away so many times.

"Oh, Ives." Dad's voice was thick with emotion.

"I know you love us," Ivy said quickly. "And I know you made sure to live as close to us as you could, and that we're still important to you and—"

"Honey," Dad said. "I know you know all those things. It's still okay to be sad. It's okay to have questions."

He'd said those things already, three years ago. Mom had, too. And so had the therapist Ivy had seen a few times. She should have kept going to therapy like Will had. Maybe then she would have dealt with this already, when it had actually happened.

"This was all so long ago," she said.

"It wasn't *that* long ago." Dad smiled. "We're not talking about a jar of mustard with a use-by date. It takes time to process big changes. We all go at our own pace."

Ivy smiled, too. "That's good, the mustard jar analogy. Did you use that on your Doctors Dish channel? Telling parents to be patient with their kids' emotions?"

Dad laughed. "Nope. I just made it up right now. But I'll keep it in my back pocket." His face turned more serious. "Hey. I want you to know something. I love Leo, and I do love our house and our car. But not a day goes by when I don't miss living on Olive Street with you and Will."

"Really?"

Dad squeezed her shoulder. "I don't miss the lack of central air or the way the basement floods every time it rains. But being there every night when you and Will go to bed and every morning when you wake up? Being there in the middle of the night when one of you has a stomach bug? I miss those things. Every single day."

Ivy wrinkled her nose. "You miss middle-of-the-night throw-up?"

Dad laughed again. "I really do. When Mom and I separated . . . it was something we needed to do. It saved us both, I think, in a lot of ways. But it was also the most devastating decision either of us has ever made."

He was smiling still, but his eyes glistened with tears. He was happy and sad. Thankful to have moved on *and* grieving what he'd lost.

For such a long time, Ivy had tried so hard to be positive and grateful and happy. To push away the grief and confusion and jealousy and worry she'd felt when Dad had left and when she'd found out Mom was carrying this baby, because she didn't think she had a right to feel those things. Not when she was so lucky in so many ways. Not when she wanted to be a kind person, a good daughter, a supportive sister.

But maybe when you shut the door to the bad stuff, a lot of good stuff couldn't get past, either. Everything was all mixed together. Sadness and happiness, jealousy and love, grief and joy. Like ingredients in a recipe, balancing each other out and changing each other when they came together to make something new.

"I love you, Ives," Dad said. "And Mom does, too. So, so much."

"I know. I love you, too."

"Anything else you want to say? I'll sit here as long as you need. Especially now that I'm wearing pants."

Ivy took a deep breath, feeling the cold air tingle in her nostrils before she let it out. She focused on the deepest, ugliest wisps of feelings inside her heart, and she gave them time to curl together into thoughts. Then she forced herself to say those thoughts out loud.

"I'm less afraid that I made Mom go into early labor by yelling at her, since you told me it was already going to happen, but I'm still a little bit afraid of that. And I feel so distant from Mom and Will, and I'm afraid things will never go back to how they were. And I'm afraid I'll always sort of . . . blame this baby for that, and I won't really love the baby. And that'll mean I'm not a very nice person. And also . . . if I'm not a really nice person, then I don't have anything that makes me special. I don't have a *thing* the way everybody else does."

There. That was pretty much everything.

It hurt to think those words and say them, but the sharpest part of the hurt was over quickly, like a flu shot. She could see the fears more clearly now, and they weren't quite as enormous and overwhelming. It was a little bit like math class, when everything got jumbled if she tried to make calculations in her head, but as soon as she wrote the numbers out on paper, she could take control.

"Oh, Ivy. You're funny and caring and thoughtful. You're interested in history and soccer and baking and student government and architecture. You have so *many* things, and you have time to find so many more. It's not a race, to find the things you care about the most," Dad said. "And you're allowed to think unkind thoughts some of the time. Everyone does. I promise."

Ivy took a deep breath and wiped away a tear.

Wherever you go, there you are, that framed print in Mom's room said.

She felt like she'd lost track of herself for a while, maybe, but here she was again now.

CHAPTER THIRTY-THREE

Leo had picked Will up at Langston's house, and the two of them sat on the tall stools at the kitchen counter next to Ivy's cake.

"Hey, you're here!" Leo hopped up and gave Ivy a big hug while Dad hugged Will, and then Ivy and Will hugged each other, too. It was their first real hug in ages. Will was so tall now—the top of her head didn't even reach his chin. And he was crying. He wiped his tears on the sleeve of his Leland Soccer sweatshirt.

"So Will and I were wondering," Leo said. "Is this cake up for grabs? Because it looks pretty incredible."

The embarrassment from this morning rushed

back. "It doesn't look *that* incredible. The top's supposed to have ganache, but I messed it up. I tried to combine different recipes, and I made too much cake. It's way too tall."

"Is there really such a thing as too much cake, though?" Leo asked.

Ivy laughed. "Maybe not. But it's almost tipping over. I should have made half as much cake and cut the layers in half horizontally so I could still alternate chocolate and vanilla."

"Chocolate *and* vanilla cake?" Leo cut in. "And that looks like buttercream frosting. Please tell me that's buttercream frosting, Ivy."

"It's vanilla buttercream with crushed-up Oreos," Ivy confirmed, and Leo clapped his hands like an excited kid.

Ivy could tell he was trying to make her feel good about this cake monstrosity—but she was okay with that. She was grateful for sweet, thoughtful Leo, who always seemed to know when to step back and not take up too much space if Ivy and Will just needed Dad-time and when somebody needed extra attention.

"It was supposed to be for Sydney's birthday because . . . I don't even know. I misunderstood stuff and made a fool out of myself. But we could decide it's for Will's half-birthday."

She almost said, *And the baby's birthday, too*, but that felt like jinxing things when the baby wasn't here yet, as far as they knew.

"Works for me," Will said.

"How about we make some lunch," Dad said, "and then we'll dig in."

Dad and Leo started making sandwiches in the kitchen, and Will turned to Ivy.

"At least you didn't shove Sydney into a locker," he said quietly.

Ivy let out a startled laugh. "*What?*"

"If you were going to do something embarrassing involving a DelMonte sibling, better to bake a cake than start a fight."

"I heard Blake started the fight," Ivy said.

Will looked down at his hands, which he was squeezing into fists, then flexing open, then squeezing closed again. "He was being Blake, but he didn't touch me. I snapped and went after him."

"I didn't realize . . . I didn't know you were embarrassed about it."

Will's eyes went wide. "Everyone knew what I did, Ivy. Everyone in the entire school. I've spent all this time working with Dr. Banks so I *won't* do something like that. And then Blake was a jerk, and I did exactly the thing I'd been trying so hard not to."

Oh. Right.

That seemed so obvious now, how terrible that would feel for Will. But Ivy had been so preoccupied with her own mistakes that she hadn't really stopped to imagine how Will's felt.

"You were doing the best you could," Ivy said. "You really are doing well managing stuff."

Dad and Leo came back with lunch. The four of them ate their sandwiches, and then Dad grabbed a cake knife and dessert plates.

The cake kind of fell apart when Ivy tried to cut it, but it was delicious. The rich, slightly bitter ganache balanced out the sweet buttercream, and the vanilla and chocolate layers were moist and airy. Ivy thought of what Nana had said ages ago, when they'd made that rugelach. That the filling would ooze out and make a big, beautiful mess. It was funny to think of a mess being beautiful, but that's what this cake was: Ivy's own big, beautiful mess.

"Well done, kid," Dad said.

"Mmm," Will agreed, his mouth full.

And then Ivy, Will, and Dad all got a text at the exact same time. From Mom.

A picture came through first: a tiny, red-faced

baby wearing a hat with pink and blue stripes cradled in Erin's arms, with Christopher leaning over Erin's shoulder.

And then Mom's message popped up. She said she and the baby were both doing well, and the baby was almost five pounds, which Dad said was good for being born at thirty-four weeks. It was a girl, and Erin and Christopher had named her Rachel, after Mom. Rachel Hope Billingham. Tears spilled out of Ivy's eyes when she read that.

Then Mom sent another text, saying they could come to the hospital if they wanted.

"Do you want to go?" Dad asked Ivy and Will. "Does that sound good?"

Ivy took a deep breath. "Good" was ice cream and rugelach and sunny skies and grilled cheese in the cafeteria. Visiting Mom in the hospital, meeting this baby Mom had carried inside her body for all these months—this baby Erin and Christopher had been hoping to meet for all these *years*—that was in a different universe than "good." It was scary and exciting and overwhelming and important. And other things, too, that Ivy couldn't find words for.

"I want to go. Yeah," Ivy said.

Will nodded. "Me too."

They finished their cake, and Will had a second

piece. "To celebrate Baby Rachel's birthday, too," he claimed.

And then the three of them—Ivy, Dad, and Will—headed to Dad's shiny, clean car. Will usually rushed to the front seat, but today he got in the back, and Ivy did, too. It felt right, sitting in the back seat with Will—like they had when they were little kids.

As Dad drove west toward the hospital, Will pulled his green homemade stress ball out of his jacket pocket, and then he pulled out a second one and offered it to Ivy. It was yellow, her favorite color, and he'd written her name on it in black marker.

"You made this for me? Thank you."

Will shrugged. "A while ago. Just in case you wanted it," he said, and Ivy's heart swelled with affection and regret and hope, all churned up together.

How long had he been carrying that around for her? And why hadn't she given him a chance to be there for *her* instead of always fixating on how he wouldn't let her be there for him?

She was still squeezing the flour-filled balloon when Dad parked in the hospital garage and turned off the car.

He guided them along through the lobby and into the elevators, one hand on Ivy's back and one on Will's. Mom was recovering on the postpartum floor, but the baby was two floors up from that one, in Neo-natal Intensive Care, and Erin and Christopher were up there with her.

When they got to Mom's room, she was sitting up in the hospital bed. She wore a hospital gown with a sheet pulled up over her middle, and Nana was there, too.

Dad kissed the top of Mom's head and whispered something to her. Nana hugged Ivy and Will tightly and then said, "What do you say, Rob? Shall we head to the cafeteria for some mediocre coffee?"

So Dad and Nana went off together, leaving Mom, Ivy, and Will. Just the three of them.

"Come on over, if you want," Mom said. "You can sit."

Will grabbed Ivy's hand the way he used to when they were little kids, and they walked over to the bed together.

"It's so good to see you both," Mom said.

They each bent down to hug her—Will first, then Ivy. Mom smelled like her usual citrus shampoo, same as she had when she came down to the kitchen that morning, even though this morning felt like a zillion years ago. Ivy perched on the bed below the safety rail, by Mom's knees. Will went around to the other side and sat down, too.

"Are you doing okay?" Ivy asked. "Are you in pain?"

Mom shook her head. "Not too much. I'm exhausted and emotional. But very relieved, and very, very happy the baby's here. And that you're both here, too."

"I guess you're missing the fundraiser tonight, huh?" Ivy said.

Mom laughed. "It seems that way, yeah."

"Well, you did so much work. I'm sure it'll go well," Ivy said.

"I hope so," Mom said. "But I think, even if we raise the money we need and we don't have to cut staff positions, I need to start looking into other options pretty soon. It's been a long time of being unhappy at work. Too long."

Ivy remembered how much better Mom had liked her job when the historical society did more educational programs for teachers and kids. She thought of Ms. Ramos, who'd been a lawyer before she decided to teach instead.

"I still think you'd be a really good history teacher," Ivy said. She'd told Mom that a long time ago, and Mom had said it was too late for her to change careers, but maybe it didn't have to be.

Mom smiled. "I'll think about that. Now, how are you doing?"

Ivy closed her eyes, squeezed that yellow stress balloon, and said, "I'm so sorry about this morning."

"Oh, sweetie. You got upset. I did, too. It happens. We see each other in our best moments and our worst ones. That's what being a family means." Mom looked directly in Ivy's eyes and then Will's to make sure they were both really listening. "I love you so much. Both of you. Always. No matter what."

Ivy let those words fill up her heart. "I love you, too."

Will cleared his throat. "Me too."

Ivy thought about what she'd said to Dad at the teeny playground—how she felt distant from Mom and Will and was afraid things wouldn't go back to the way they were before.

She didn't feel distant from Mom or Will right now. And she didn't think things *could* go back to the way they'd been before. Not exactly. But that didn't have to be a bad thing. There didn't need to be enormous changes, like when somebody bought an old house, tore it down, and started over. It could be more like when they'd renovated their kitchen a few years ago: Most things stayed in place, but some things that hadn't worked so well got fixed up a little.

Dad and Nana came back with coffee, and Ivy noticed Nana was dressed up. She'd probably gone to

Shabbat services this morning before Mom had gone into labor. Ivy decided she'd go to services with Nana next time Nana invited her. She always felt a little out of the loop when she went with Nana to things at the synagogue—like she hadn't done the homework and everyone else had. But she was interested in learning more about Judaism because she wanted to understand that part of Nana, and Mom, and herself. She wanted to give herself a chance to find her way *into* the loop.

And maybe she'd get Will to start kicking the soccer ball around with her at the park again, too. She really did like soccer. She'd never be as good as Will or Josh or Nyeema, but that didn't mean she shouldn't try at all. Maybe she'd try percussion ensemble, too. It would be fun to play music again . . . and fun to hang out with Elias. She should get to know him better and just see what happens.

After a little while, they went up to the NICU floor to meet the baby—Mom in a wheelchair so she wouldn't strain her body and everybody else walking alongside her. Erin and Christopher were there, happy-crying and whispering to each other as they watched the baby sleep in a plastic incubator that kept her warm. There was a wire wound around her toe to keep track of her pulse, and she was so tiny and fragile. But there were so many doctors and nurses taking care of her, and she was surrounded by so much love.

"Is it okay to go closer?" Ivy asked after she'd hugged Erin and Christopher.

"Of course," Erin said.

So Ivy stood right next to the incubator. Next to Erin and Christopher's daughter, who had grown inside Mom's body, from something microscopic into this actual *person*.

"Hey there, little Rachel," Ivy whispered. "I'm really happy you're here. I love you."

And that was a hundred percent true. She was. She did.

CHAPTER THIRTY-FOUR

Mom had to stay at the hospital overnight and she was exhausted, so Dad, Ivy, and Will left to give her a chance to rest.

They ended up behind a city bus on the drive home—the same bus line Ivy was supposed to take that morning to meet Lila. As it rumbled ahead of them, something occurred to Ivy.

It was like the time she couldn't open Nana's bottle of vanilla extract because the top was stuck, and she tried so many things—banging the top against a hard surface, running it under hot water, using a tea towel to get a better grip—and then suddenly, unexpectedly, the cap had given way, twisting off in one easy spin.

All the pieces clicked into place inside Ivy's brain.

Lila had tried to stop Ivy from making a fool out of herself with Sydney.

Lila was secretive and sarcastic and vulnerable.

Lila.

The emails had been from Lila all along. How had she not realized?

"What should we do now?" Dad asked from the driver's seat. "It's almost dinner time. You want to go out to eat? Get takeout and watch a movie?"

"We could go to the Italian place," Will suggested.

That had been their go-to special-occasion place back when it was still the four of them. They hadn't been there in ages.

"Wow. Okay." Dad nodded. "A blast from the past. What do you think, Ivy? That okay with you?"

But Ivy wouldn't be able to eat anything—she wouldn't be able to do anything at all—until she talked to Lila.

"Can you get me takeout for later, actually? I really need to go to Lila's for a little while if it's okay. Since I was supposed to meet up with her today and had to bail. Could you drop me off there?"

Dad looked at Ivy in the rearview mirror.

"I want to hang out with you guys tonight," she told him. "I really do. And Italian food sounds great. But this is important."

Dad considered that. "How about we give you a half an hour or so with Lila while we pick up the food and then come back to get you?"

"Deal," Ivy agreed. "Thanks, Dad."

Her heart thudded against her ribs as they pulled up to Lila's house and she got out, but she was as ready as she was going to be.

The front door had been repainted since the last time Ivy had been there. Now it was a shiny dark blue. Harrison let Ivy in, and she saw that the inside walls had been repainted, too—pale gray, mostly, and neutral green. There were a couple more pieces of furniture in the living room now, also, and some art on the walls.

Upstairs, Ivy knocked on Lila's door. Her bedroom walls were green now, too, but the ceiling still had the same blue sky and white clouds, with a sun in the middle.

Actually, no. It *wasn't* the same. The sky part was a softer blue, and the clouds weren't so puffy. The sun was smaller and less cartoonish, and there were birds flying in a flock, and a wisp of translucent moon peeked out near the far wall. Had Lila done that herself?

Lila lay facedown on the end of her bed, reading, and she looked up when Ivy stepped in.

"Whoa. Hey. What are you doing here?" she said, scrambling to sit up.

Ivy smiled. "Thanks for the warm welcome."

"No, I just mean . . ."

"You weren't expecting me. I know," Ivy said. "Your room looks nice. I love the sky. And it actually looks like someone lives here now."

She gestured toward the built-in bookshelves, which were filled with actual books. The picture from last time was still there, front and center: Lila and her parents and brother with the man who apparently wasn't her grandfather. There was another photo of that same man now, with a young Lila, whose hair was long and almost blond.

"Thanks," Lila said. "It was time. How's your mom? And the baby?"

"They're both doing really well." Ivy took a deep breath. "So. Speaking of time, I think it's time for me to tell you some stuff."

She explained all of it. She started with the baby coming today, and then she went back to the beginning. How she'd *thought* she should feel about the pregnancy, and how she'd really felt. Why she'd thought the emails were coming from Sydney, then Josh, then Sydney again. All the different pieces of "proof" that hadn't proved anything at all.

"It was you, though, right?" she asked. "You're downbythebay5."

Lila hesitated for long enough that Ivy almost doubted herself yet again, but then, finally, she nodded.

"Does it mean something? The email address?"

There were a lot of other things Ivy wanted to know more than she wanted to understand the email address, but that felt like an easy place to start.

Lila shrugged. "Five was our apartment number in Brooklyn. But other than that, I wanted something random and the little kids next door were blaring that song in their backyard. 'Down by the bay, where the watermelons grow.' You remember that song? But it's all, like, 'Back to my home I dare not go.' And I was all sad about not being able to go home—not feeling at home here. So I went with it."

Ivy sat down on the edge of the bed next to Lila. "I did wonder a few times if it could be you. But I didn't think you liked me very much back when I got that first email. I really didn't think you'd go out of your way to write to me."

"Yeah, I didn't like you that much," Lila agreed. "Don't feel bad, though. I didn't like *anyone* very much when I sent you that first email. I was *in* it."

"But things are better now?"

Lila looked up at that sky ceiling she'd painted over, making it her own. "A lot of things are better. A lot of the time." Then she looked back at Ivy. "I'm not as exciting as Josh Miller or Sydney DelMonte, huh? Sorry if you were disappointed."

"Lila, no! I'm not disappointed."

But now she remembered what she'd written in that email on Christmas Day, when she thought she was writing to Sydney—*I'm happy it's you.* Ack, no wonder Lila hadn't corrected her.

"It made me feel special, thinking it was Sydney. This person I'd looked up to. Because I was feeling kind of *not* special. But she and I were never going to be friends for real. And you and I are, I think. So I'm happy it's *you.*"

"In that case..." Lila walked to the bookshelves and picked up that framed photo with the white-haired man in it. The one she'd flipped over before. She brought it back over to the bed. "Okay. This is George. He was Becky's uncle—but he was more like her dad. They were super close. He got sick when I was in second grade, and she wanted to be there for him and his own kids were far away. So we lived with him in Brooklyn, and we stayed, even after he got better. But then he got sick again, and it

326

was all really fast, and he died. And he left his apartment to his kids, who wanted to sell it. So we had to leave."

Ivy scooted a little bit closer to Lila. "I'm so sorry."

"That first day I wrote to you, that was his birthday. And it was a year ago today that he died."

Ivy let out a big breath. She wished she'd known that before—she wished she'd been able to be there for Lila when she was hurting today. But at least she was here now. "So that's why your parents wanted you to do something special today. How was it at Reading Terminal?"

Lila ran a fingertip over the edge of the frame. "It was okay, mostly. The food tour was goofy, but we stuck around after. And we actually talked about him, which we don't do a lot."

"I'm glad," Ivy said. "I assume he's the one who used to make the Dutch apple cake and filling?"

Lila nodded. "We got a lot of his favorite foods. Becky has all his recipes, actually. So maybe we can try making them sometime."

"I'd like that a lot," Ivy said.

Pretty soon, Becky called up to say dinner was ready and Dad texted that he and Will were on the way to pick up Ivy.

They got up and walked out of Lila's bedroom and into the newly painted hallway.

"Do you want to go to *The Wizard of Oz* with me tomorrow?" Ivy asked. "I promised Peyton. And . . . I said I'd maybe find Elias there."

"Elias, huh?" Lila raised her eyebrows, and Ivy felt herself blush.

She shrugged. "He's nice. And he said he'd look for me there."

Lila grinned. "Intriguing. Eh, why not. There's no place like the school auditorium, right? I'll come."

"You can't make fun of the show, though," Ivy warned, and Lila groaned.

"Ugh, fine. I'll try to be as kind as you."

"How's this: If Blake's there, you have my permission to be unkind to him."

Lila paused at the top of the stairs. "Or *you* can be unkind to him. Not even unkind, actually. Just . . . honest. Like, tell him what you really think of the way he treats people. Tell him how he makes you feel if he says something obnoxious. All that good, emotionally healthy stuff. You can do it."

"Yeah," Ivy agreed. "Maybe I can."

"I believe in you," Lila said.

"I do, too, actually."

At least for that moment, she did. Ivy believed in

herself, and Lila, and complicated families, and baking, and kindness—even imperfect, not-every-second kindness like hers.

"See you tomorrow, Saint Ivy," Lila said when they got to the front door.

"Just regular Ivy, I think," Ivy told her, and Lila nodded.

"See you tomorrow, Regular Ivy."

"Can't wait," Ivy said.

Right now, there were a whole lot of things that Ivy couldn't wait to do.

ACKNOWLEDGMENTS

Dear Saint Ivy, We did it! Your story was not an easy one for me to figure out how to tell. I've lost track of how many times I got stuck and started over. But I'm very glad you popped into my mind back in 2017 and stayed with me all this time. This book has taught me a lot about myself as a writer and as a person. It would have meant a lot to middle-school me, and it means a lot to grown-up me. I hope it means a lot to readers, too.

I'm very grateful to everyone who has helped me realize my vision for this story. Thank you to my agent, Sara Crowe, for your unwavering enthusiasm and support. I feel so lucky to have you in my corner. And thank you to my editor, Maggie Lehrman, for all of your insights that strengthened this book immeasurably, and especially for the big suggestion that identified exactly what wasn't working in the second half of the novel and helped me find a path to something better. It's such a joy to get to work on novels with you.

So many thank yous to the whole wonderful team at Abrams, including Andrew Smith, Emily Daluga, Jenny Choy, Brooke Shearouse, Marcie Lawrence, Marie Oishi, Patricia McNamara O'Neill, Nicole Schaefer, Kim Lauber, Hallie Patterson, Elisa Gonzalez, and Jenn Jimenez. I appreciate the care, thought, and passion you put into every step of the bookmaking process, and I'm so grateful for all you do to get my stories into readers' hands. A special thank you, also, to Jason Ford for such a fun, adorable cover.

Jenn Barnes, thank you for your astute feedback on early pages, which helped me discover Ivy's love of baking. Melissa Sarno, thank you for your wise feedback on a close-to-finished version. You helped me appreciate what was working and see where I could pull back, trim, and refine. And Cordelia Jensen, thank you for your sensitive, perceptive, and kind feedback at every single stage of the process. You are an amazing writer, teacher, and friend.

Melissa Baumgart and Fred Kogan, thank you for reading Ivy's story and sharing such thoughtful, generous insights. Your ideas enriched Ivy's character and family. Laura Sibson, thank you for always commiserating with me when writing is hard and celebrating with me when it's wonderful.

Thank you to all my friends and family who so lovingly champion me and my books. Sara Matthews and Ray Fabius, some of my biggest breakthroughs for this novel happened while Cora and Sam were enjoying special time with you. Myles and Clint, I gravitate toward writing characters with brothers because I have two of the best brothers imaginable. I admire you both so much.

To my mom, Elizabeth Morrison: I need a much, much bigger phrase than "thank you" to express how much you give to me, Mike, Cora, and Sam every day and how deeply we appreciate your love and help. I am so, so grateful for all the time you spend with the kids while I write and all the ways you help me carve out space to be my full self. This book would not exist in this form without you.

Mike, thank you for listening and cheering me on every single time I thought I'd figured out the plot of this book . . . and then sympathizing when it turned out I hadn't. Thank you for your patience, kindness, humor, and pride in my work. And Cora and Sam, thank you for inspiring me every day with your imagination, laughter, and love. I can't wait to hear all the stories you'll have to tell.

Read on for a sneak peek
at Laurie's new story

COMING
UP
SH⚾RT

Laurie Morrison
Author of *Up for Air*

CHAPTER
1

I pound my fist into the worn pocket of my glove and crouch into fielding position.

This—right now—is what I live for. It's the softball league semifinals, and we're up 5–4 with one out in the last inning. The other team's center fielder just slapped a perfect bunt down the third base line, so she's the tying run, standing on first base and ready to take off. But there's no way she's crossing home plate. There's no way we're giving up this lead.

"One down, Falcons!" I shout. "Play's to first or second!"

The *cack-cack* cheer starts up on our bench and spreads through the bleachers. *Cack! Cack! Cack!* Faster and faster, louder and louder, with more and more people joining in.

That's the sound actual falcons make when they're protecting their nests, so it's a Butler Middle School thing, to yell *Cack! Cack!* when our teams are protecting a lead. I've never heard the chant get anywhere near this loud at a softball game, though, and I freaking *love* it.

Adrenaline courses through my body. All these people are watching us. Parents. Teachers. The whole baseball team. Even Tyson Carter, who hates me because I got him in trouble for not doing any work on our science project, and his friends who groan when I talk too much in class. They're all here, cheering for my teammates and me.

I glance at Emilia, who's playing second base, and wiggle two fingers in the air. She nods and flashes two fingers back.

A double play ends the game right here. If there's any way Emilia and I can turn two, we will.

"Let's go, Falcons!" Coach Yang yells. "Stay focused now. Play smart!"

The other team's batter gets into her stance, bending her knees and wiggling the bat over her back shoulder.

Right here, I will her. *Hit the ball to me.*

There are two kinds of fielders—that's what Dad says. The ones who want to make the play with the game on the line, and the ones who hope the ball goes somewhere else because they're scared of messing up.

I never play scared. I always want to make the play.

Our pitcher, Monique, whips the ball over the inside

corner of the plate, jamming the batter. The ball pops off the skinny part of the bat and bounces past Monique's outstretched glove, toward me.

Yes.

I charge.

"First! First!" Coach yells.

That's the safe play: tossing the ball to first base to get one out. But the other team's best hitter is in the on-deck circle, up next, and Emilia's ready at second base. I pull my arm back and throw as hard as I can.

Smack.

The ball hits the webbing of Emilia's glove and beats the lead runner by a full step. Emilia pivots and launches the ball to first base, just in time.

"*Out! Out!*" the umpire shouts, pointing to second base and then to first, and I leap into the air and scream my lungs out.

"*Yes!*"

Emilia runs over to do our double play handshake, bumping shoulders and then hips and slapping our gloves together.

"You've got *guts*, Bea," she yells over all the noise. "I can't believe you threw to second on a dribbler!"

"It wasn't a *dribbler*," I protest, even though it kind of was.

Emilia whacks my arm with the outside of her glove. "It was definitely a dribbler. Not that I'm complaining!"

Behind home plate, Coach Yang is talking to the umpire. *Try to turn two if the ball is hit hard, go straight to first if it's not.* That's her rule, and I broke it.

But Dad's the one whose voice I hear in my head when I play softball. And *Dad's* rule is to trust your gut and never second-guess yourself. That's when errors happen, when you let doubt in. I believed I could make that throw, and I did.

My best friend, Jessi, sprints in from center field. "That was *clutch,* Beasy!" she yells. "We're going to the finals!"

On the sideline, everyone is chanting, "Falcons! Falcons!"

Xander Berg-Thomas is there in the front. I spotted him during warm-ups because I basically have Xander Radar, so I *always* spot him. I didn't let myself look back at him the whole game so I wouldn't lose my focus, but I look now, and my already-full heart swells.

The rest of our teammates pile on top of Emilia, Jessi, and me. I end up at the bottom of a mass of sweaty softball players and somebody spikes my toes, but I don't even care. There's nowhere else I'd rather be.

"Great game, Falcons!" Coach Yang calls. "Let's line up and show our opponents some respect."

The other team's waiting, tears streaming down their faces because their season is over. We head over to tell them all good game, and then I scan the crowd for my parents, but I don't see them.

They were here in the bottom of the fifth inning. I saw them cheering after I scored a run. But now, I see everybody else's families except mine, which makes zero sense. My parents wouldn't miss this for the world. *Literally.*

There's a hand on my shoulder—Coach Yang, leading me away from the rest of my team. "That was a risky play, Bea."

And, okay. There. I see Mom's reddish-brown hair and big sunglasses and Dad's red Falcons hat, white shirt, and softball tie. They're standing way far away, closer to the other team's fans than ours. They've folded up their chairs and packed up all their stuff as if they're in a hurry to take off, which is bizarre, but they're here, waving at me. Dad pulls on his earlobe three times.

One. Two. Three.

I. Love. You.

I do it back fast and then focus on Coach.

"I need you to play smart," she's telling me.

I nod, but I'm not going to say sorry. That's a Mom thing: not saying you're sorry when you haven't done anything wrong. Mom says apologies should be reserved for "expressing remorse when you've done something you regret," but girls are conditioned to apologize whenever anyone else is the tiniest bit unhappy and it strips away our power, apologizing so much.

"I know the safe play was throwing to first," I say. "But I didn't want to give their best hitter a chance to beat us."

Coach Yang shakes her head. "If *one* thing had gone wrong, though. If your throw had been a few inches off, or if Emilia hadn't been ready for the ball, we would have given away an out. That could have cost us the game."

I take a breath before I speak so I won't sound like I'm talking back. "I did check that Emilia was ready. I wouldn't have thrown to second if she wasn't."

Coach sighs and finally cracks a smile. "It was an impressive play, Bea. Most high school varsity shortstops can't make a throw like that, and you're in seventh grade."

I grin back. "Thanks, Coach." I'm practically bursting with pride as I follow her back to the bench, where she congratulates the whole team.

"We've got a championship game in two short days," she tells us. "But we'll talk more about that at practice tomorrow. For now, get your stuff and grab your people. Let's head to Luigi's!"

We all erupt in cheers, because Luigi's is where we go to celebrate our biggest wins. We sit together at the long tables in front and recap the best moments of the game while we stuff our faces with extra-cheese pizza. And Coach names a player of the day, who gets the game ball as a souvenir and a Nutella-filled dessert calzone.

Everybody heads off to find their families, and Jessi adjusts the clips that hold back the front pieces of her long black hair. "You think I can get a ride with you? My parents are probably going to want to take the goofballs home."

She points to the sideline, where her five-year-old brothers, Jack and Justin, are picking dandelions and shrieking as they rub the yellow part on each other's cheeks.

"Of course. Meet you in the parking lot?"

"Yep!" She bounds over to her parents, and I swap my spikes for sandals, sling my softball bag over my shoulder, and start walking over to the spot where I last saw Mom and Dad.

But when I pass the bleachers, Xander jogs over to me. My skin heats up, my pulse skyrockets, and my stomach goes wobbly—because that's what happens whenever Xander Berg-Thomas is nearby.

It's been like this since March. One day after spring break, he was wearing a new yellow shirt, and Tyson kept calling him "Sunshine" and singing that "You are my sunshine" song. When I looked over, Xander made his eyes wide and shrugged at me, like, "Tyson's the worst, but what can you do?" and *bam*. Wobbly stomach. Too-fast heart. Giant crush on Xander. Maybe it had always been there under the surface, waiting to activate. I have no clue. Jessi's had a bunch of crushes already, but this is new for me and it's *weird*.

Xander's a little out of breath when he catches up to me. "Bea! Hey, great game! You made some sick plays. You've got a cannon for an arm." He reaches out as if he's going to touch my right bicep, but his fingers freeze before they make contact and he blinks at his hand, as if it moved without his permission. His freckly white cheeks turn so pink they clash with his red Falcons T-shirt, and he stuffs his fists into his shorts pockets.

He's nervous. I make Xander nervous.

Jessi keeps saying he's into me, and I think she might be right.

"Thanks for coming," I say.

He shrugs. "I wanted to. I wanted to see you play."

You.

He could mean "all of you." As in, the whole softball team. But now his cheeks are even pinker, so I don't think he does. He's standing so close that I can hear his breath go in and out, in and out. I can see the gold glints in his brown eyes and the one tiny tuft of dark brown hair at the back that always stands straight up instead of cooperating with his part.

I love that uncooperative tuft of hair. I want to reach up and touch it.

Somebody calls Xander's name, and when I look over to see who it is, I notice: Dad's car is gone. It was right there in the front of the parking lot, and now it's not.

Dad would never leave a softball game without me, especially not a game as big as this, but the car is definitely gone. He's been super stressed about work, but he always, always says I'm more important than any client. I can't think of any reason why he'd just *go*.

"One minute!" Xander calls to his friends, and then he turns back to me. "I saw you at the batting cages last weekend, with your dad. I don't think you saw me. You were in the zone. But I think you love softball as much as I love baseball. I like that." He winces. "That came out so dorky. I don't even know why I said that."

Past Xander's left shoulder, Mom's pacing. Two steps one way, turn, two steps the other.

I split into two Beas. One Bea is thinking Xander is really, really cute when he's nervous, and I *did* see him at the batting cages last weekend, because hello: Xander Radar. And I like that he loves baseball so much, too, and I like *him*. A lot.

But the other Bea needs to know where Dad is and why Mom is pacing and what the heck is going on.

Worried Bea wins.

"It didn't sound dorky. I actually . . . I wish I could keep talking to you. Seriously. But I have to go."

"Oh!" he says. "Um, okay?"

I take off toward Mom, who stops pacing when I get close.

"Bea! What a game, honey!"

Her smile spreads wide. Anybody who doesn't know her would think she's fine, but this isn't her real smile. It's the fake one she glues on when somebody says something rude about an article she's written or when people comment about how different she is from Dad's first wife, who grew up here in Butler and died a long time ago. Mom's fake smile stretches wider than the actual one, but it doesn't crinkle the corners of her eyes.

She pulls me in for a hug, and I can feel her heartbeat, hard and fast.

"Dad had to head home, and we need to go, too. I'll get us a ride, okay?" She punches at the car share app on her phone. "A car should be here in a few minutes."

A car?

She says this as if it's a normal thing, but we've only ever used that app to get a ride to the airport or to go from a museum to a restaurant or something when we take a day trip into Manhattan. There is nothing normal about somebody else's car taking us to our own house.

"What about Luigi's?" I ask. "Everybody's going. I told Jessi we'd give her a ride."

Mom sighs and smooths the top of my hair. "I wish we could go to Luigi's. You deserve to celebrate with your team, but . . . something's come up. We need to get home now. Somebody else will give Jessi a ride."

She loops her arm through my elbow, and we take off toward the parking lot. I don't have my softball bag positioned right, so the knob of my bat smacks my tailbone with every step, but Mom is walking so fast I don't have time to adjust it.

"Bye, Bea! See you at Luigi's!" somebody calls.

I pretend I don't hear because what am I going to say? *I can't come because my dad left for some mysterious and urgent reason, and now Mom and I have to go, too, but I have no clue why?*

Maybe Gran needed Dad for something. That's all I can think of. Except why wouldn't Mom tell me that?

"Here we go." Mom points at a gray sedan that's pulling into the lot.

She greets the driver and opens the back door, motioning for me to climb in. We end up all jammed together with my softball bag on my lap and my school bag between us. As the car pulls away from the field, Mom pushes her sunglasses up on her head to look me straight in the eye.

"Dad will explain what's going on as soon as we get home. Everything will be okay. I promise." She reaches over my stuff to squeeze my hand. "We're the better-than-a-dream team. Right?"

That's what Mom and Dad call us: the better-than-a-dream team. They say the three of us are the family they didn't even dare to *dream* of, back when their worlds fell apart.

"Right," I echo.

The driver wants to know whether he should take this turn or the next one, and Mom pushes her sunglasses back down and tells him this one's fine. I stare out the window as we go through the center of town, past Dad's law office, past Gramps's old dental office, and past the tiny park in the middle of the town square with four benches facing each other. "The Bartlett Benches," they're called, in honor of Dad's grandpa—my great-grandfather, Benjamin Bartlett, who served nine terms in Congress and always had time to sit down on a bench for a coffee and a chat with any of his constituents whenever he was in town. If we turned right and crossed under the train tracks, we'd get to Luigi's, but we keep going straight instead.

I take my phone out to text Jessi and see her message from eight minutes ago. *Beasy! I can't find the car. Where are you?*

A new text comes in now, from Xander. *Are u OK?*

And then a new text from Jessi pops up, too.

OMG Bea. I'm so sorry. Emilia's mom is taking me to Luigi's so don't worry about that. We'll miss you and we love you no matter what!!

Then there's a whole line of hearts. I read the words a second time and blink at the screen. *No matter what.*

What?

"Bea." Mom's voice is urgent. "Put your phone away, please."

"I . . . why? What's going on?"

She squeezes my hand again. "Dad and I will explain as soon as we get inside."

The car pulls onto our street and then into our driveway. Mom thanks the driver and nudges me to open my door.

I grab my things and stumble out, and Mom puts her arm around my shoulders and guides me up our front steps.

For the first time in my entire life, I'm terrified to walk inside my own house.

The story continues in COMING UP SHORT

Laurie Morrison taught middle school for ten years before writing *Every Shiny Thing*, her middle-grade debut with co-author Cordelia Jensen. She is also the author of *Up for Air* and *Saint Ivy*. She received her MFA in writing for children and young adults from Vermont College of Fine Arts. She lives in Philadelphia.